PENGUIN BOOKS

H◯KITIKA T◯WN

Charlotte Randall is the award-winning author of five novels. Her first, *Dead Sea Fruit*, won the South East Asian/South Pacific section of the Commonwealth Writers' Prize for best first book and the Reed Fiction Award in 1995. Her much-praised second novel, *The Curative*, was joint runner-up for the Deutz Medal for fiction at the 2001 Montana New Zealand Book Awards. *What Happen Then, Mr Bones?* (2004) and *The Crocus Hour* (2008) were finalists for the same award.

Randall was born and raised in Dunedin, New Zealand, and now lives in Christchurch with her husband and two children.

ALSO BY CHARLOTTE RANDALL

Dead Sea Fruit
The Curative
Within the Kiss
What Happen Then, Mr Bones?
The Crocus Hour

HOKITIKA TOWN

Charlotte Randall

PENGUIN BOOKS

PENGUIN BOOKS

Published by the Penguin Group

Penguin Group (NZ), 67 Apollo Drive, Rosedale,
Auckland 0632, New Zealand (a division of Pearson New Zealand Ltd)

Penguin Group (USA) Inc., 375 Hudson Street,
New York, New York 10014, USA

Penguin Group (Canada), 90 Eglinton Avenue East, Suite 700, Toronto,
Ontario, M4P 2Y3, Canada (a division of Pearson Penguin Canada Inc.)

Penguin Books Ltd, 80 Strand, London, WC2R 0RL, England

Penguin Ireland, 25 St Stephen's Green,
Dublin 2, Ireland (a division of Penguin Books Ltd)

Penguin Group (Australia), 250 Camberwell Road, Camberwell,
Victoria 3124, Australia (a division of Pearson Australia Group Pty Ltd)

Penguin Books India Pvt Ltd, 11, Community Centre,
Panchsheel Park, New Delhi – 110 017, India

Penguin Books (South Africa) (Pty) Ltd, 24 Sturdee Avenue,
Rosebank, Johannesburg 2196, South Africa

Penguin Books Ltd, Registered Offices: 80 Strand, London, WC2R 0RL, England

First published by Penguin Group (NZ), 2011
1 3 5 7 9 10 8 6 4 2

Designed by Glen Drake
Typeset by Pindar NZ
Printed in Australia by McPherson's Printing Group

ISBN: 9780143565390

A catalogue record for this book is available
from the National Library of New Zealand.

www.penguin.co.nz

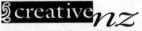

ARTS COUNCIL OF NEW ZEALAND TOI AOTEAROA

The assistance of Creative New Zealand towards the production of this book
is gratefully acknowledged by the Publisher.

For Rose

PART I

HOKITIKA 1865

ONE

I never seen nothing like this. Papa say whitey do things different from us, but he dint say how. Now I see it with my own eyes. Whitey's ships is so big they choking up the river. Them ships got poles big as kauri trees and the poles got cloaks hanging off them. Mebee no one believe that back home, but I swear — whitey's ships wear clothings. But I keep forgetting, I not live at home no more. I live in whitey town now.

Rilly I live in the bush. I not ezactly moved into the town yet. I kind of creep around. My tuakana tell me if you do what whitey say, he give you coin. That's my aim, deal in coin. I not ezactly found out what that mean yet. Most of the time I creep around worrying about my stomick. I dint realise how much learning go into eating. I always standing in the bush looking at them berries and wishing I listen to what Mama teach me. Sometimes I catch a fish down at the river. That's when I see all them whiteys coming off them dressed up ships.

My tuakana once teach me how to speak some of their words. 'Whereyerfrom?' I say to whitey. They all from different tribes, San Francisco Ballarat Melbourne. I seen the spellings on their crates otherwise I dunno what they saying. 'Whatchooherefor?' I ask. Some say gold, others say mind yer own business you little picaninny.

The gold and the coin got some kind of joinment I not unnerstand. If you find a bit of gold, whitey give you coin, but if you already got coin, whitey give you a bit of gold. They not the same but somehow equal. Not that I ever done this swapping, but I seen it. Sometimes I get tired tryna figure it all out. I go for a sleep in the sun on the river bank. When I wake up fresh, that's when I like to go to Hokitika town. I go down the street with all them hotels. All them young whitey girls stand in the doorways in their pantalons. They call out 'What yer staring at, little boy?' and pull up their long skirts to show their pantalons. If I do what they want, let my tongue hang out, act like a dog that want a big drink, the girls laugh and throw a piece of bread. I not unnerstand what's intresting about seeing them frilly pantalons around whitey girls ankles but I do pretty much anything for their bread.

'What yer doing here, little boy?' one of them pantalon girls ask me one day.

'Not little boy. I called Halfie.' Whitey not want to know about my mountain my sea my river my waka, jes me.

'Harvey?'

I nod. She jes haffta call me what she want.

'I'm Violet. I come over from Ballarat.'

Their langwich what were a fog to me is starting to lift. I dint unnerstand Ballarat were a place. Now I do.

'Bet you don't even know where Ballarat is,' Violet say. 'It's over the sea. In Victoria.'

'Why yer ships wear clothings?' I been wanting to know this a while now.

'They aint clothes, they're sails. The wind blows the sails and moves the ship along.'

'Why not paddles?'

'Paddle from Australia? Are you crazy?'

I look at the ground. Still a lot to unnerstant.

'Run away to yer Mama, little boy.'

Before I go she gimme a thing to eat that's hard and sweet. I never had nothing like it. When I suck it my mouth come full of spit.

No Mama now. I sleep out. It still warm so that's alright. But it rain a lot. Then I sleep in a cave. This bush is all chopped up. You go through a lot of big trees then chop, chop, the trees is all lying down and a whitey family have put up one of them mean huts. Not a big house like in Hokitika town, jes a small pile of wood. Sometimes there's a whitey woman sweeping the whakamahau, I dunno what whitey's word for that, but most of the time it all a big mess. Whitey's firewood his cooking pots his egg birds, they all there in the mud together.

In the bush there's some of them gold miners that's yella. Well, they called yella but they not look it. I seen a flour they say was yella and the yella miners is different from that. The yella men speak their own langwich and their crates have spellings on them what's like tattoos. When one of the yella men is sick, I bring medsin out of the bush for him and he pay me with rice that's already boiled. I dint listen to my Mama about the food but I listened to my tuahine – that's the sister of a boy and can't be said in whitey langwich – when she took me in the bush to collect medsin. My tuahine were called Moana and she gone now too. Me and the yella fella that get sick the most is learning up the alfabet and whitey langwich with each other. Some days he know a new word, some days I do. But I get the most learning from Violet.

'That's V-I-O-L-E-T,' she spell me. 'And what yer doing still hanging around here? Where's yer Mama?'

I look at the ground. I not got the words to tell.

'Do you want me to ask Mr Flewelling if there's some work you can do?'

'Who he?'

'He owns this hotel.'

'I want coin.' Haffta get everthing straight from the start.

'Money, little boy. Of course he'll give you money. It aint work without money.'

Violet drag me in the hotel by my arm. The miners is all sitting around drinking dirty water. Violet call over Mr Flewelling and he squat down – my yella fella learn me that word – to look in my eyes. His own eyes is black with yella cords through the white and the rims is red as makomako.

'Are you an honest little boy?' he ask.

Seem like a trick question.

'I need a boy to collect the dirty glasses when we have a dance. You have to wash them too. Did yer Mama teach you to wash glasses?' His breath stink like rotten ferns.

'I'll show him,' Violet say.

'How many coin?' I ask.

Mr Flewelling hold up three fingers. 'And a big hot dinner thrown in.'

I hope he mean thrown in me. But I sure hope he not doing the throwing.

Mr Flewelling stand up, he creaking and shuddering like his legs is tore, and clap his big hands together. 'Good. First dance is this Saturday night. You come over here when it gets dark, OK?'

I nod and Violet push me to the door by my shoulder.

'What did you think of Mr Flewelling?' she ask when we out on the street.

'Dint think nothing.'

'Well, don't you be annoying him when you come. He's got a lot on his plate.'

I glad he got a lot on his plate. I eat a lot.

I go back in the bush to find a place to sleep. It getting more colder all the time. I reckon Violet's skirts is so big I can sleep inside them, but whitey girls got some funny ideas I not unnerstan. If I say, here Violet, I give you coin to sleep inside yer skirt, she sure I jes wanna look at her pantalons. I not sleeping with them yella diggers neither. They packing up and going away, no one want them here.

Anyway, you rilly haffta see this bush to see how much it been slashed around. Everwhere there's broken bits of trees showing fresh wood white as a cook poaka. Nothing get cleared away, it jes pushed to the side and all lie about higgledy piggledy. That's another word I learn, but not off Violet. I learn it off my hatter.

Hatters is mad old men in funny clothes. I have a hatter friend called Ludovic and he live in a hut in the bush. I ask him, do you come from Ballarat? He laugh so crazy I ask him, how yer call laughing like that? He say fit to split. Ludovic laugh fit to split when I ask if he come from Ballarat.

I gonna ask Ludovic if I can sleep in his hut when I get coin from Mr Flewelling. I already menshin this to him in a sneaky way.

'It getting more colder all the time,' I say.

'It is, laddie,' he agree.

'It sure cold sleeping under a ponga tree.'

'Don't sleep out, laddie. It's bad for the bones. Sleep in a hut.'

'Atchilly I agree. But I not got no hut.'

'No hut?' Ludovic look shocked.

'Nope. No hut, no Mama.'

'Poor little boy.'

I dunno how many times we done this ezact conversation.

Violet not like it. 'What yer talking to that smelly old hatter for?'

'He not make hats no more. He . . .'

'Ask him where he comes from,' Violet interrupt. 'Then you'll find out something.'

Before I ask Ludovic where he come from, Saturday night come round. I wait in the bush aiming to judge when the dark come. Mr Flewelling a fool if he think it come all at the same time. It sure dark under the ponga trees but not all dark where the sun go down in the sea. Then I afraid I miss the throwing of the dinner and set off for Hokitika town running. Mr Flewelling's hotel sure look different from the day. Everwhere is lights miners and all them pantalon girls dressed up better than them ships. Their dresses is all fancy and showing off their uma. I not see Violet anywhere. I go in, and Mr Flewelling spot me. He come over and say he sure glad I come. He ask my name.

'Halfie,' I say.

'Well, Harvey, I'm Caradoc ap Dafydd ap Leuan ap Griffith ap Meredith. But you can call me Mr Flewelling. Now where's that fucken Violet? She said she'd teach you the ropes.'

Dunno what this got to do with ropes.

Mr Flewelling look around with a big scowl. Then Violet come running, her whitey face all red and wet looking like she been leaning over a big cooking pot. Mr Flewelling scowl get even bigger. Violet drag me by the arm to the washing place. She tell me to get all them dirty eating and drinking utensils off the tables and wash them up. She show me how it done whitey way. I do that all night. I so small and sneaky I clear away and when whitey look back at the table his plate gone and he not seen who took it! Some of them miners stand up and say, the drink is gone to me head, I haffta go home.

Now I see what the pantalon girls do. I were thinking they

put on a show, but no. The miners take them pantalon girls in their big hairy arms and turn them in circles. Then everone clap and look mighty pleased. I look to see what make the music. It a big wood box with yella teeth. It make a very happy sound, not lonesome like our putatara on a windy beach. But me and my brothers and sister were not rilly lonesome there. We have there our aunties and uncles and cousins and all them others. But something go out of us when Mama die. Something rilly go out of Moana. Papa say it her hinengaro – what's not ezactly the brain but what it do. Chop, I not think about that no more. Some of them miners is lonesome though. Live alone in them huts in the bush, go off getting their gold alone, then need to come in here looking for a pantalon girl to warm the front of their trouser for a hour.

At the end the dinner what gets thrown turn out pretty good. Meat and potatas and tapioca pudding. Violet do the spellings. T-A-P-I-O-C-A, she say so I know I unnerstand.

I wake up in the bush. I been dreaming. I touch the coin in my pocket – tahi rua toru, all there. Today I ask Ludovic if I can sleep in his hut. When I get to his place no smoke come out his chimney, he still asleep. I squat down to wait. Ludovic not bother about keeping no hours. Ludovic do what Ludovic want. I dint tell Violet but I already ask him where he come from. He stroke his long grey beard and say he come from Russher. I say what's Russher, and he draw me a picture in the mud with a stick. He say he come from Sevastopol – right there! – and poke his stick hard into Russher.

Ludovic say Russher have a big war of ships and guns with the Ottermens, then he escape on the biggest war waka in the world that were called *Mahmudiye* – he done the spellings – and what had a hundred and twenty eight big guns called cannons. He draw me a cannon and say what they fire out of them is cannibals. My tuahine warn me about that. She tell me, you watch out, whitey say you a cannibal. I not a cannibal, I say loudly to Ludovic, but he already drinking his dirty water.

Now Ludovic finally wake up. He stagger out in his long johns and have a mimi. When I run over, he pulling on his trouser. He do up hisself then rub my hair and smile. His teeth is yella like that music box. Ludovic light a fire and put on his old black kettle. He make his funny drink with leaves what's like medsin to me but not bitter. He give me a hard piece of bread. I tell him I got three coin off Mr Flewelling and I want to give him one for sleeping in his hut.

'What? One coin every night?' His eyebrows is now shooting up.

I dunno about that.

'You don't need to pay me. You can jes bed down by the stove when you want. It's cold these nights.'

'You dint say that before. It been cold awhile.'

'I don't recall you ever mentioning it, laddie.'

We eat our bread and drink the stuff what he call tea. After a while I say, 'Ludovic, I sure wanna know more about Sevastopol.'

'Sevastopol?'

'Where you come from.'

Ludovic laugh fit to split.

'You say you come here on the cannibal ship *Mahmudiye* . . .'

'Ee, that's right, laddie. But I come from Esstanbool. I was a friend of the Sultan and lived in the Dolmabahce Palace, where all the chandeliers and staircases are made of crystal.'

I dint make no sense of his long string of whitey words.

'Who show you how to make them hats?' I ask.

The bright look go out of his eyes. 'My father. Like father, like son. That's how it is.'

Not that Sultan fella then.

So tonight I sleeping in front of the stove. Ludovic snoring like a old dog. I creep in after Ludovic already asleep. Today I went with Violet to Rosstown, where her sister live. When we got there, there were one of them men with a machine to make pictures. He were out in the main street with his head under a cloak, and all the people that work in them rickety shops and hotels come out to gander. I dint want to go in the main street with that man and all them whiteys so I creep at the edges while Violet go to see her family. I try to count all them hotels but it too hard. Violet tell me later there's fifty three and show me the countings with her fingers. It sorta like Hokitika town except not solid in the same way. When I look out the back of all them buildings it like the dark bush gonna eat it all up.

Violet bring me something she call cake, what's like bread only soft and sweet. We go for a little walk and have a sit down under a tree. Violet seem very happy.

'I'll tell you a secret, little boy. Sometimes I give a kiss to Mr Flewelling. What yer think of that?'

'I not think nothing of it.'

'Mr Flewelling's got a wife.'

Dunno what she want me to say.

'And sometimes I give a kiss to Mr Flewelling's son too. He comes in from the diggings to sell his gold every once in a while and to have some drinks. Yer think there's lots of hotels here? Lemme tell you, there's plenty more in Hokitika. At least a hundred. He comes in and we go off to one of them other hotels and . . .' Violet stop talking and stick her tongue out of her mouth and wriggle it.

Then we haffta go back quick to Hokitika town. Violet explain me that Mr Flewelling is having dances every night now. Seem he only need me for them special ones. Anyway I still got my three coin, the stove here to sleep by, and if Ludovic jes stop his snoring everthing be perfic.

The next morning I see a man walking down Revell Street what gimme a fright. It were his light see-all eyes. He see everthing as he walk, them what's good and them what's bad, them what's full alive and them what's got the dying shadder creeping up on them. Violet tell me it Mr Sale. She tell me he the King. I say, yer a liar, I not a whitey but I know the King live in Ingland. Violet roll her eyes and say not to take everthing so literal, whatever that mean.

Violet explain me. 'King Sale walks round saying he's the govermint. He says the govermint aint gonna pay for the streets of Hokitika, it's already paid too much for the roads over to East Canterbury.'

'When the King ever talk to you?' I starting to think Violet jes making things up.

'Mr Flewelling has meetings in his hotel and I listen to what the men are saying.'

'What men?'

'The men of the Improvement Committee. They want the King to fix up the harbour, the hospital and the gaol. He tells them to do it theirselves. But they're already dealing with all the mud, the river and the fires.'

I not rilly unnerstand.

'Mr Flewelling wants to be on the Council if it ever comes about. That's what the Improvement Committee is aiming for.'

'What's a Council?'

'A Council takes money off the folks that live in the town.'

'What? Jes go up and steal their coin?'

Violet don't answer my concern. She say, 'Mr Flewelling says when the gold tails out all these hotels are gonna collapse like a house of cards. So he wants a position.'

'What's a position?'

'A position is the job where you tell folks what to do and get paid their money to tell them.'

'This what he talk about between them kisses?'

'Don't you be cheeky, little boy.' Then she say mean, 'So did you ask yer stinky hatter where he comes from?'

'He come from Russher. From Sevastopol. Then he move to Esstanbool and live in a palace.'

'Is that right? So one minute he's a good Christian, the next he's a Mahometan? Good you got the truth out of him at last, aint it?'

Ludovic not the best company when he drink his dirty water. He lie on the floor talking to it. One time he lie in the upthrowings from his stomick, sometimes he lie in his mimi. I clean everthing up. I put Ludovic upright by his cot so he not choke hisself. Ludovic wail and call out to his gods. I seen this kind of thing before. Not from drinking dirty water, there weren't none of that where I come from, but my sister Moana wail and call out and scratch her uma like she turn porangi. My Papa say she jes putting it on so she not haffta marry the fella he pick out for her. He were right. When he go away Moana take me into the bush and she happy as anyone alive. She go along collecting them plants and singing and telling stories. She think I too young to notice the change. Papa get me by the ear and say, what yer sister doing in them bushes? But I act dumb.

Anyhow, I not thinking about all that. I got a busy life now. I got them dances to clean up and Ludovic to clean up, I haffta get fish from the river to stretch my coin, and Violet show me some of the spellings outside the hotel in the afternoons. She also teach me the G-R-A-M-M-A-R. She teach me to say aint and don't. And somehow I always running about for Mr Flewelling. He call out to where me and Violet sitting, then he send me to fetch something from the store or to clean up a mess in his hotel. He call Violet too. She go off indoors and that the end of the learnings.

Violet say to me to get a broom and do some free sweepings

when the Improvement Committee is having them meetings in the Bathsheba. That's the name of Mr Flewelling's hotel. She say it a big lesson for anyone. She say I learn to talk fancy whitey talk and get more coin later. It seem a good plan to me. Last night I get the broom and sweep under the feets of them men in suits and whiskers. They all arguing and shouting. At the end, one man stay behind that seem to be a special friend with Mr Flewelling. I creep in the dark corner with my sweepings and hear them talk.

'Why yer putting up with all this?' Mr Flewelling's friend ask. 'They're a bunch of gibbering monkeys.'

Mr Flewelling pour his friend some dirty water and say, 'It's the Improvement Committee, aint it? And whose hotel is gonna get all the improving when the Committee gets above itself?'

'This place is good enough.'

'Sure it is. But it aint got no more reason to prosper than the ninety-nine other places in Hokitika. It'll be a different story when the Council meets here. Don't you think the Council will want to meet at the same hotel the Committee spent all their money on? And don't you think everyone else will come too, hoping to chew the ear of a councillor?'

'What I think is that yer too many jumps ahead of yerself.'

'No such thing as that, my friend.'

I talk to Ludovic about Mr Flewelling. I ask, what's whitey words for shadowy ways to get coin to have a life better than the next fella?

'Feathering the nest,' Ludovic say. I unnerstand the picture. Others got cloaks but Papa's cloak were the one that have the kiwi feathers. But that aint shadowy like Mr Flewelling.

'Mr Flewelling feathering the nest,' I tell Ludovic.

'We've all got to do that from time to time,' he say. Then he sigh. 'If we can.'

'He giving free food and drink to them Improvements Committee so they make better his hotel for no coin. Then it the best hotel in Hokitika town and everone come.'

Ludovic sigh louder. 'As things go, that's rather a minor immorality, laddie.'

I dunno what Ludovic saying.

'In fact, some people would admire his forward thinking.'

'Jumping too forward is what his friend say he doing.'

Ludovic don't answer. He shut his eyes and rock on his little stool. There something sad in it like he outside the life of jumping, forward or back.

'Where Mr Flewelling come from, Ludovic? He got a funny look to him.'

Ludovic open one eye. 'Now that's an interesting story. Even more interesting than mine. He comes from Barbados.'

'Is that near Russher?'

'Not at all. It's in the Caribbean. A long time ago some Irishmen were sent there as a punishment. He is descended from one of them.'

'How yer know all this?' I now thinking of the way Violet look when I tell her what Ludovic say. How she look mean like it all a lie.

'I know it from Caradoc himself. We go a long way back.'

A few days later I go to the Bathsheba for spellings and grammar with Violet and she aint nowhere to be seen. One of them dancing girls come out and say, what yer standing around for, urchin? I say where's Violet, and she explain me that Violet gone off to a grog shop with Griffith Flewelling and not to tell or she thrash me with a stick that have a nail in it. I wait under a tree and I think about Violet. I don't see nothing pretty in her stringy yella hair and them sky colour eyes. She got straight teeth and none of them gone missing yet, but they aint set off well next to her whitey skin.

Her lips is also a bit thin. Seem to me the men is like two dogs what want the same pick bone.

Mr Flewelling come out of his hotel and stand in the mud. He look up and down the street like a man what expect something. He see me and beckon me over. He squat creakily down, hands on his knees, and look me in the eye. His own eye still black as a devil.

'What yer got to tell me, sonny?' he ask.

'Aint got nothing.'

'I hear you moved in with the hatter.'

'It cold now.'

'You could sleep in the hotel kitchen.'

'No thanks. Ludovic need me.'

Mr Flewelling slowly straighten up. 'Needs you to wipe his arse and clean up his vomit, eh?'

'I aint wiping no arses.'

'People are always wiping arses. Some jes don't know it.'

'Whose arse you wiping?'

Mr Flewelling stare at me for a moment. Then he say, 'Quite a few that've disguised themselves as faces. Now be off with you, you cheeky bedwetter.'

I aint got nothing to do so I go spying out Violet. She in one of them places what aint a building, jes a tarpaulin and barrels and men and no place for a girl like her. Griffith Flewelling, I figure it him, is a real fine handsome chap, tall and strong and with the same yella hair as Violet only more thicker and shiny. And his lips is big and greedy, he suck up his dirty water like he drinking Violet's blood out. They laughing fit to split and doing their disgusting tongue thing. It make me feel sick. I watch and think about what Mr Flewelling do if he come here and see them. I dunno much about whitey world but this sure look like a secret that one day spill the blood all down them streets.

I jes about to go when I get picked up from behind by the back of my shirt.

'What yer looking at, Cocoa?' the man say in my ear as I dangling down. Then my shirt rip and I lying in the dust.

'Aint looking at nothing what concern you.' I rilly frightened. What if my looking show there's something worth seeing when before there weren't?

It a young man what drop me. Younger than Griffith Flewelling, tall and still thin, no meat on them bones yet. But he dirty and hairy and missing a eye.

'You wanna earn some money for yer looking? Instead of looking for nothing?'

'Dunno. What yer want me to look at?'

'Jes the road.'

'This road?'

'Nah, Cocoa. The road over the Pass. What the coach goes up. You stand on the road and when you see the coach, you let me know.'

'Dunno why you can't do yer own looking.'

'I've got more important things to do.'

'I'll do a think,' I say, and run off down the road before he grab me.

When I go past his hotel, Mr Flewelling still looking up and down the street like he waiting for devils to come from both ends, but I jes scurry on past and get home to Ludovic. I tell him about the one eye fella, and Ludovic say he part of a gang, don't you go getting mixed up with that lot, they all very bad.

Ludovic aint too sick today and washing his long johns. So they clean for the winter, he say. He got a old pail and some yella soap and he sitting there on his platform in his altogether. His body all withered and I say yer a man what need a big feed of poaka.

'I'm like a string bean because I'm really an Armenian. A-R-M-E-N-I-A-N,' Ludovic say.

'What's that?'

'The poor victims of the Sultan in Constantinople.'

'That Sultan what were a friend of yers?'

'He weren't any friend of mine, laddie. The Sultan was a cold-blooded murderer.'

I now thinking what Mr Flewelling say last Saturday night when I clean up after the special dance. He talking to one of his friends about the hatters, I dunno why. He say them hatters is mad as effing snakes. He say it don't help that some of them drink so much it the reason they can't rememory a fucken thing. They haffta make everthing up to fill the big hole their memory is.

Now I looking at Ludovic and thinking, something haffta be true about him. Even if all them stories is lies, he here on this earth now and someone born him someplace and he come here across the sea somehow, and that the truth about him what can't be wrong.

When I see Violet today, she all full of herself. I tell her I look for her, I seen her. She say, you keep yer trap shut or I pull out yer tongue. I say, don't worry, I used to keeping secrets. And I am. Moana used to take me in the bush collecting them special plants that do magic. It weren't allowed for a girl like her. She say she make her husband that Papa pick out for her vanish in the wind. I ask her why she don't do what Papa want and she reply that she a special person what want a special husband. I laugh and say, what's so special about you? She say, I aint dumb like the rest of yous.

Anyway, back to Violet. She smiling and humming little songs. I spit in the mud and ask, 'What yer so happy about?'

'Griffith Flewelling says he'll take me away from here.'

'Away from his father, he mean?'

'No, he don't mean that. He don't know about that, you fool.'

'Who the fool then? The girl that got fire in both hands and herself in the middle?'

'Shut up! You don't understand nothing.'

I keep quiet or mebee Violet hit me.

'Anyway, Mr Flewelling, Griffith's father I mean, he's too bothered with the Council right now to worry about me. The elections are pretty soon and it aint looking good for him. From what I hear, hardly anyone will vote for him. And how can you move the money around to yer own advantage if you can't get yer hands on it?'

'What do vote mean?'

'Voting is when everyone says who they want and they all get counted up.'

'Why they don't vote for him?'

Violet shrug. 'He don't come from England or Australia.'

'He come from Barbados. Ludovic tell me.'

'Don't tell me what Ludovic says, he's a lunatic!' Violet point her fingers at her ears and move them round and go all cross eyed.

When she finish her show, I say, 'He say he know Mr Flewelling a long time.'

Violet don't listen. 'What d'you think I'll look like in a white wedding dress? D'you think I'll look pretty?'

'Depend how much blood get spilled on it,' I reply.

TWO

It don't go good for Mr Flewelling. In the election he don't get enough votes to be in the Council. Not only that but Violet tell me the first meeting gonna be at the Gridiron. She take me to the Gridiron and we look at it.

'So this the place what's gonna get all them improvements now?'

Violet shrug.

'This the place where them drinkers come to bend the ear of them important arses?'

Violet don't reply. She tell me Mr Flewelling borrow a lot of money for his hotel and he were counting on being a Council man for when the gold run out.

'Don't look like it gonna,' I say.

'Gold always runs out, stupid. Otherwise all those diggers would still be sitting in California and Bendigo eating their tucker off them golden plates.'

'Why don't Mr Flewelling go and find some gold for hisself, then?'

'Can't. Can't bend down no more. His joints is all fucked.

Don't you know about a digger's life? Up in Collingwood they were in icy water up to their eyeballs. Some of them rivers is so cold their beards freeze up.'

'Don't see what it got to do with bending.'

'It jes freezes them up for life, doncha see? One day an old miner bends over and the freeze gets him. He can't ever stand up straight no more.'

Next time I see Mr Flewelling I look more careful at the way he walk. Violet is right. His legs aint straight and his back is a bit bent looking. He all the time making faces like he in pain. Other times he look right as rain – what's about the dumbest saying I ever hear.

'Where all them hats you been making?' I ask Ludovic when we having our supper of a fish I catch.

'Hats?'

'Yer a hatter.'

Ludovic laugh. 'That don't mean being a hatmaker here, laddie. Hatters here are miners who work alone. Miners who keep things under their hats.'

'What things?'

'Where their hopes are.'

Hopes? Sometimes a talk with Ludovic rilly slow going.

'Keeping things under yer hat means keeping secrets. The secret we hatters keep is where we hope the gold is. But our biggest secret is where we *know* it is.'

I dunno what to say.

'But it happens that I dint always work alone. I was a forty-niner with Caradoc Flewelling.'

'What's a forty niner?'

'A digger from the California rush of 1849.'

'That's a long time ago aint it?'

'Sure is.'

'How come you don't do no digging now?'

'Don't I? Are you watching me all day?'

I aint convinced. Ludovic mebee know the biggest secret, but he never leave the hut. Except when he go down a drink bottle. Mebee then his imagination fly off alone.

'Anyhow, I hit pay dirt. I don't need to work.'

'Then why aint you still in California eating yer kai off them golden plates?'

Ludovic get up and poke at the stove. 'I lived in an hotel for a little while. Laid my old body down between those starchy white sheets and looked at plaster ceiling roses instead of the stars. Listened to fights and music and breaking glasses instead of the big night silence. And one day I say to myself, Ludovic, yer a rich man, yet yer living poor. Poor in the feel of things. Yer a dead man. So I gave up the fancy life and returned to the old.'

'And where all yer coin go?'

'Down my throat, laddie.'

'Not on them dancing girls, then.'

Ludovic sigh. 'I've done my share of dancing in my time.'

I can't imagine no pantalon girl with dirty old Ludovic.

'But once I had a wife. When I was young and handsome and full of hope.'

I notice hope a popular word with Ludovic.

'She was very beautiful,' he say dreamy.

For all I know it were a dream. 'Where yer wife gone now?'

'To be with the Lord.'

'What lord?' I hear of this word already. There's some lords from Ingland that live in East Cantaberry.

Ludovic look shocked. 'Christ the Lord, of course.'

Dunno what the lord of course is.

'Is that why yer so sad?'

'Sad? I'm not sad. I'm melancholic. That's what sadness grows into. If you give it enough time.'

Melon cow lick.

'Melancholy is grown-up, filled-out sadness. Sadness that's put on a lot of weight.'

'Mebee it jes the drink. Mr Flewelling say too much of the drink make a man gloomy.'

'Well, he should know.'

'Why he should?'

'Who d'you think I turned into an old soak with? In forty-nine, Caradoc was my twin at the bar. Joined at the hip we were.'

Haffta say, half the time I still dunno what Ludovic on about. Sometimes I get tired of all this whitey talk. Sometimes I hide out in the bush to hear my own talk. I see them hunters going past and their talk reach out to me like Mama's arms. But I don't jump out in case they say, you come with us little boy, and drag me off by my ear. Then I get no coin. And no whitey life what's full of Sultans palaces Ottermens forty niners hatters and hope that gets lost.

But also in the bush I see that One Eye from the gang. He lurking and creeping and it give me the shivers. 'Hey Cocoa, a job's still waiting for yer two eyes on the Pass,' he call out to me.

I standing outside the Bathsheba looking up and down for Violet but she aint nowhere to be seen. Then Mr Flewelling run out and collar me. He all in a sweat and his eyes is wild looking.

'Where's Violet?' he shout.

Before I can say mebee at her sister's, he start dragging me into the hotel and up his stairs to where all the bedrooms is.

He say, 'My wife has fallen down and I need someone to help me lift her up.'

At the top of all them stairs he throw open a door and I see Mrs Flewelling all in a heap on the carpet what's pretty ugly with big red flours. Mr Flewelling tell me to get hold of her feets and he will hold the heavy part. Then we swing her onto the bed like we throwing a body off a cliff. Mr Flewelling reach in his pocket and get me a coin but I stubborn and keep out my hand for two. He say, two then and fetch the doc quick. I say, I know about medsin, but he look like a storm of thunder ready to break so off I go. When I bring back the doc who were drinking dirty water at the Gridiron I stay a while in the shadders to watch his doctoring. I aint very impressed.

'My legs went suddenly weak,' Mrs Flewelling tell the doc when he bring her round. 'Then I suppose I fainted.'

She a very fat lady but a pretty one with big blue eyes and heart shape lips. I seen a heart in a dead pig and it sure dint look like Mrs Flewelling's pretty mouth, but heart shape is what Violet say and I aint one to argue about the Inglish. Mrs Flewelling is one of them women what's all atremble atremble in the flesh like a jelly, and her bottom lip atremble when she look up at the doc to hear her fate. But the doc look like he got no idea, and when I stand forth saying I know everthing about medsin Mr Flewelling fly into a rage and chase me out of the bedroom.

I go back to Ludovic and he lie down drunk as a fiddler's bitch.

I tired of all that today serve up. I go down the beach, but it the way I don't like, the westerly blowing up the sand everwhere and tryna shake you out of yer clothings. And the light what come out of the sky a mean light what burn out yer eyes, and you jes don't feel right in yerself, you feel afraid yer tupuna that watch over you from the land of the dead jes packed up and left.

Jes about every evening Ludovic and me eat them fishes what I catch in the river.

I suck them fish bones and say, 'Ludovic . . .'

'Call me Ludo.'

'Ludo, aint you rilly got no pay dirt left? Not even a little bit?'

He suck his bones and say, 'Jes some pound notes hidden in my travelling trunk. I keep them for a rainy day.'

'It raining now.'

'No, laddie, it aint.'

Dunno what rain he seen in his life but it sure pissing down.

Ludo get up to cut the damper, a thick slab each.

'Look, where you rilly come from?' I ask when he take his stool again.

'What's it to you? What d'you know about the world?'

I eraserperated and make a noise that show it.

'As it happens, I come from Spain. I was captured by the Barbary pirates and sold into slavery. Me, a white boy. Well, white enough. But those Musselmen don't care about the colour of our skin. They took us because we were Christians.'

'What's a slave?'

'Someone who must work for no pay.'

No coin? That frighten me. Coin is the way I escape the sweepings, escape the grip of Caradoc. Then I begin thinking about how Papa tell me of them capture warriors that cook in the ovens and carry the burdens, that can't touch the kumara and haffta go naked into the wahi tapu. Mebee that's what a slave is.

'Do you haffta go naked into the burying grounds?'

'What?'

'Naked. Where them Barberrians bury people.'

Ludo tell me I a very strange little boy.

'Tell me about them pirates then, Ludo.'

Ludo grimace and shake hisself. 'Most evil men in the known world. They'd travel up the Spanish coast . . .'

'Is that near Russher?' Rilly hoping them pirates live a long way from here.

'No, laddie. Come out on my veranda and I'll draw it for you.'

We go out on Ludo's muddy planks with the lantern and Ludo take a stick and draw in the mud. Me and a big black rat watch with intrest. First a big Russher then some Musselmen land then the good christian lands and then Spain near the ocean.

'Where's us?' I ask.

Ludo wave his stick wide, going far and more far, then he stab it down far away from the pirates as can be. I let out a big blow of air like I been saved.

'They travel up the coast,' Ludo continue, 'and snatch the good Christian children from their mothers and fathers . . .'

'Rilly?'

'Yes.'

'How many?'

'How many? A million at least.'

It sure hard to imagine all them dressed up ships chock full of screaming tamariki sailing off with them Barberrians. Now Ludo show me a picture. The Barberrians got pointy slippers and heart shape shields and very baggy moleskins.

'Ludo got took by them Barberry pirates,' I tell Violet next time I see her.

'Don't be stupid, little boy. He was brung up by some nasty little hatmaker in Glasgow.'

'He weren't!' I tired of know it all Violet. 'He tell me he aint that sort of hatter.'

'It don't make no difference what sort he is now. When he were a kid he weren't nowhere near them Barbary pirates, whatever the hell they were.'

Violet don't know a thing about pirates.

'I sure Mr Flewelling know,' I tell her.

Violet burst out laughing, laugh till water come in her eyes. 'Caradoc knows that stinky old hatter is a drunk and that's all he needs to know.'

'No, it aint.' I sure mad with Violet. Under all the drink, real Ludo still there, and Ludo is a man what got born with more intresting parts than jes about anyone.

'Where's Glasgow?' I ask Ludo.

'Glasgow?'

'Violet say you rilly from Glasgow.'

'Is that so?'

I nod hard.

'Well, what would Violet know? She's sailed from Ballarat to Hokitika and thinks she understands the world.'

Ludo fetch a scrap of paper and stub of pencil. 'It happens my foster father was a Glaswegian. Here.' Now Ludo stab a place on a little island he quickly draw near the good christian lands.

'What's foster?'

'It means taking on the care of a child when the child has another Papa.'

Mebee Ludo is my foster Papa then.

'But my mother was Spanish. She took me as a babe in arms to see my grandparents.' Ludo lean in close to me, his eyebrows is twitching like a menace, and he say, 'Then we both got snatched! Along with many other fit young men and women. But the old people were put in a church and set on fire.'

'No!'

'Yes!'

Ludo sure get around. He go from Glasgow to Spain to California to Hokitika. But he a rilly old man, so mebee it the truth.

'So what them Barberry pirates do with yer Mama?'

Ludo look rilly sad and soon a tear come in his eye. 'They did unspeakable things and then worked her to death. Same as they did with everyone, laddie.'

'What unspeakable mean?'

Ludo look like he aint gonna speak what he call unspeakable, what make sense atchilly, but I sure like to hear it.

'So how you escape, Ludo?'

'A great many countries were troubled by the Barbary pirates. So America paid a ransom. Then there was a big commotion down at the docks and I found myself being shipped out. Nobody was more surprised than I was. Nobody was more pleased than I was to see those crumbling white hovels disappear into the distance. The sea and the sky were as blue as paradise, laddie, but that white town had a black and rotten heart.'

'What unspeakable mean?' I ask Violet.

'Means you can't say it.'

'No, what doing it mean?'

'I dunno. Depends on the circumstances.'

'Circumstances is Barberry pirates and Ludo's Mama.'

'Well, acting like I believe that stupid story, it prolly means they raped her.'

'What's that?'

Violet pinch up her mouth.

'Tell me or I hit you.'

She arrange her skirts like she the queen and she get a look on her face like she gonna tell me what King Sale do next. 'Well, you prolly won't understand most of this, but it's like me and Griffith and Mr Flewelling. I give them a kiss and all that, but I do it because I want to. But them Barbary pirates, they steal kisses, d'you see?'

I pretty disappointed. 'What's unspeakable about that?'

Violet look cross. 'You can't jes go round kissing other men's wives. What about the babies?'

'What about the babies?'

'The babies come and what then?' Violet now getting red in the face. 'A pirate for a Daddy. No thank you!'

'They get a baby on her? That's what raped mean?'

Violet nod hard.

'Then Ludo's Papa rape the Mama too?'

It Saturday night and I go to the Bathsheba to wash up them dishes at the dance. When I go in, there's Griffith Flewelling drinking with his Papa. It early and the miners still seeing to their own trouser fronts out at their diggings, so them pantalon girls jes hang around like rich ladies that got all the time in the world. Violet jes hanging around too, and humming and calling out chirpy to her pantalon friends, and jes generally tryna get some attenshun. She getting it too. Griffith's twisty greedy lips watching and gone all wet looking, and Caradoc's left eye follow her, looking like it move separate from the right. Violet poke out her uma and her arse, then into all this commotion come Mrs Flewelling in her nightgown. I get a shock because she seem a bit porangi. She stand there with the light coming through her gown and wave a hanky at them groggers like she going off to sea.

Father and son stand up. They try to take Mrs Flewelling back up the stairs, but she still waving like it something else she want, someone to save her mebee, I dunno what from.

I work rilly late but when I go home Ludo still up drinking. We have a talk about Gertie.

He say all dreamy, 'Ah, you never saw a prettier girl in all California than Gertie Flewelling. Course her name wasn't Flewelling when Caradoc met her. I've forgotten what it was. But oh she was a peach. Peaches and cream skin, and blue eyes like a china doll.'

'What Caradoc do to her?'

Ludo frown. 'Nothing. She did it to herself. When he was in the money, she'd open that pretty mouth and shovel in food like she was fattening the Christmas goose. Chocolates, blancmanges, marzipans, she gobbled them all up faster than a cook could cook them.'

Well, that don't make no sense. Do she eat the food raw?

'But I tell you something, laddie, before you get too sorry for her. That woman's got a terrible secret. Yes. Because she's got the sugar disease, and I know from a most experienced medical doctor that it's caused by lying outside all night in a state of intoxication.

It jes aint right for a lady to get so drunk she can't find her way home.'

'It alright for a man then?'

Ludo narrow his eyes. 'I don't know what yer implying, but I do all my drinking under a roof.'

Few days later I take a stroll and see Mr Flewelling standing outside his hotel looking for them devils from both ends again. He call me over. He don't squat down on them creaking joints, it one of his bad days. He talk from up in the clouds.

'Where's Violet?' he demand.

I shrug.

'She aint been home all night.' He show a thundery look.

I on the alert now. 'Mebee she sleep out.'

'What? It was pouring. Don't be ridiculous.'

Now I worry Violet were lying outside all night in a state of intoxication and get the sugar disease. Well it aint a real worry. Fact is, what I care? It sure nice to have a worry that vanish so quick.

'I think she visit with her sister in Rosstown.'

'Sister? The only sister she's got lives in Ballarat.'

The thinking come up in me that Violet tell me a big lie on the day we visit Rosstown. 'Mebee she stay with Ludo.'

'Where were you, then?'

'Oh you know me, I all over the place, in the bush, up a ponga tree . . .'

'Why would Violet spend the night with Ludovic?' Mr Flewelling interrupt.

I start thinking fast. Then I bang my head with my fist. 'Oh I were forgetting. She got some lady troubles and go to see the quacksalver. Then the rain come down and she rush in to shelter with Ludo.'

'Quacksalver?'

'Yair, the one in the bush.'

I terrified Mr Flewelling gonna pick me up with my ears and

shake the daylights out of me. I peek at him out of the corners of my eye. I see he aint sure what to think. He stand for a minute, then turn and go inside. Now I need to catch Violet before she spill some different beans. I wait for her all morning. Jes before the hotel lunch she come dreamy along the street.

I rush over to her. 'Where yer been? Mr Flewelling been waiting for you.'

'I been to Greymouth.' She still in a dream what gonna get her throat slit.

'Mawhera.' The name jes come at me like a mind ghost.

'I don't know them names, Half-pint.'

'You been with the son,' I accuse.

'His name's Griffith. Yes, I've been with him. We went to the races.'

'Races of what?'

'Horses, stupid. Why yer so ignorant? Then we had ourselves a fine dinner at a hotel, and then we slept there. But not much.'

'Not much what?'

'Not much sleep.'

'Were them beds hard?'

Violet giggle and say, 'Not the beds.'

I sick of all this. I tell her Mr Flewelling think she visit with a medsin man and stay out of the rain with Ludo.

'And he believed it all?' Violet look rilly surprised.

'Seem to. But why you act so stupid?' I flame her. 'Yer wanna be catched? Yer want a big fight in the street? Yer want one of them men dead, with poor old Gertie looking down on the one that die?'

'Gertie?' Violet look confused.

'Mrs Flewelling, what's a prisoner up in them sleep rooms.'

Violet snort. 'She aint a prisoner. She gets up real late, almost in the evening, and comes down to the bar with her giant bosoms all over the place.'

Now I see Mr Flewelling come out of the front door of his hotel. Lucky he look the wrong way.

'Oh God,' Violet groan, 'I wanted to get back in without Caradoc seeing me.'

'What's it matter now you know what them beans is?'

Violet frown. 'He might check me. He might say, show me your women's trouble, Violet Athelstan. Or he might be hankering for a kiss and I've not had my wash.'

Mystery atop of mystery, that's what Violet's talk is.

Then out of the shadders walk a lanky figure. He go over to Mr Flewelling and start chewing his ear. It that One Eye! Mr Flewelling don't take much notice, he still look like a storm brewing, arms folded across his chest like he lock his heart in, but One Eye still going gabble gabble gabble. Then Mr Flewelling turn to him, seem drawn in, then he talking too, then they trot off down the street together.

Violet let out a huge breathing.

'You were telling me about Gertie,' I remind her.

Violet look angry. Then she reach out and pull my hair. 'Run away to yer putrid hatter, little boy. You aint got no business poking yer squashy little nose into grown-up affairs.'

THREE

I been here all my life, I used to the rains, but it sure pissing down now. It been pissing down all night, all day, all night, them streets in Hokitika town is all running, only them shops what got their backs on the beach is draining the water out. There's mud everwhere, particully outside Ludo's hut what he say is become an epic swamp.

He a bit confused what swamps is, but I don't say nothing because he in a big grump about all the mud. He say he tryna keep everthing clean, and go on like a old hen about my boots and them drips what fall off on his dusty floor, plip plip plip, they turning into wet dirty slicks at once. Ludo go grumble grumble grumble, complain that he soon be growing mould in his oxters. Later on, mebee after a lunch of old bread that he fry in oil, mebee later, after a game of cards we play at his little rocking table, he start to drink then the grumble go out of him. Soon he think he sitting in the sun in Heaven.

But Ludo's hut aint no Heaven. For a whitey, he live poor. I dint notice before now.

'Ludo, why yer don't feather yer nest?'

'Well, laddie,' Ludo in his cups and slurring, a word that he explain me and then show many examples of. 'I told you, I've been busy tryna be alive.'

I don't unnerstand. Aint Ludo upright and doing his breathings right in front of me?

'Alive in the feel of things. Dint I tell you? Or someone else, maybe. I've told a lot of people. Some people sleep in satin sheets, but when yer asleep what's it matter if they satin or not? No, that feel of satin, I want it deeper than my own skin. I want it here,' Ludo clutch his chest, 'and here,' Ludo bang his forehead with his fist.

Haffta say I got a feeling this gonna be one of them nights Ludo spend lying in his upthrowings.

Now Ludo shut his eyes and rock on his little stool. 'There's satin mornings, laddie, and satin seas. There's satin skies and satin solitude.'

'What's that last thing?'

'It's in the bush when the westerly dies down and yellow warmth wraps you up like the Lord's hands reaching down.' Ludo still got his eyes shut and go rock rock rock. 'There's the smell of rain in the tree fern, in the mosses and roots . . .' Ludo sniff like he in paradise with all them flours. 'There's satin everywhere.' Now he open one eye and it pierce me. 'But we don't get much each. And how much each is it right to ask for, eh? That's the big question.'

'Oh, that the big question.'

Ludo eye me. To see if I giving him cheek. Look like he think no for he slur on. 'Some are too busy feathering their nests to get any satin. That's the real sin, laddie, turning away from satin to gold.'

'That mean coin don't it?'

'Take Caradoc, for instance. He's all the time plotting and scheming and suffering his joints, but what's he got for his consolation?'

'He got all them pantalon girls.'

'That's a bad bargain too, a devil's bargain.' Now Ludo topple over, fall sideways like a chop tree in bush, lucky for him his body near the bed that lying there like arms to catch him. Then he moaning satin satin into the pillow like a lost child calling for his Mama.

I put a blanket on him and go outside where it a satin night for sure, and mebee that's why Ludo crying in his pillow. The satin he been talking about aint nothing you can wrap yerself up in. Fact is, I rather have them stiff bed sheets and not some drunken dream what's warm and yella.

'So what do you and Ludovic talk about when yer holed up in that hutch of his?' Mr Flewelling ask next time he see me.

'Satin.'

'Ah, he's given you his satin talk, has he? Did he tell you he buys his satin with my money?'

Uh oh, now we in Caradoc world, a world that's hard and real. Aint sure what real rilly mean here, it a very tricky word, but it a word that men of his type use a lot.

'Ludo don't buy no satin,' I reply him.

'No, no, he lives it, don't he?' Mr Flewelling laugh mean with his evil eyes all aglint. 'That's what he tells you, don't he? Satin in the soul and all that rot? But the truth is, Ludovic's life is one long lack of liquidity.'

Dunno what that mean.

'And who sends the liquid over, eh? With a mutton leg and a bag of puha?'

'Dunno.'

'Yours Truly, that's who.'

Yaws Trooley? I never met him coming or going. It surely a Caradoc lie.

'Is it a girl?'

'Is what a girl?'

'Yaws Trooley.'

Caradoc frown dark at me. 'Yer a very strange little boy, did anyone ever tell you that?'

Tonight Ludo aint too drunk and he show me a picture of the Gold Escort. It a group of men that escort the gold from Hokitika town to Cantaberry. Dunno what I expect, mebee a couple of old diggers in clothings what's torn, couple of old nags past their best, some of them rusty old muskets, but the fellas in the picture is dressed up all shiny and new, look more like a army, the army of that palace what have them cristal staircases. It sure hard to imagine a entire staircase made of it. When them soldiers all run up, why don't it crack and they all fall through in a big rain of splinters?

But back to them Gold Escorters. They all got up the same, their britches is tight, they got high boots, they got jackets that have shiny buttons, they got little perky hats what look like buckets uptipped on their heads, they got new guns. They been trained over the mountains in Cantaberry, Ludo say. Then he say they don't look like men what have a dangerous job, they look like the entertainment. I say to Ludo, what is the entertainment, and he tell me it like them dancing girls at the Bathsheba, except them Gold Escorters forget to put their skirts over their pantalons and they don't have no uma. Ludo wink at me, and I sure like it when he like this and aint giving me them long lechers about the Lord.

Ludo go on to say the Gold Escorters have lodgings in Hokitika and Cantaberry, they have twenty one top hole horses, they have five stations on the way over the Pass, they have wagons and pack beasts galore, they have the best young fellas from everwhere. But he hear it said they don't know how to shoot and they all the time falling off that expensive horsemeat.

Soon after I hear about them Gold Escorters, One Eye get me by the shirt tails again. He say there a lot of coin still waiting for my eyes on the Pass.

'I don't care about that coin. The entertainment gonna kill me.'

'What yer talking about, Cocoa?' But he don't wait for a answer. 'We haffta scratch each other's back, I scratch yers, you scratch mine.'

'I aint itchy.'

I go to run but he get all mean looking and say, 'When that draggle-tail moll dint come home the other night, who was it that walked out and intercepted Mr Flewelling so he's occupied when the skirt slips back in the door?'

'How yer know to do that?' I rilly dumbfounded.

'I mebee got only one eye, but I employ it to the best advantage. So you listen to me. One good turns deserves another.'

'But it aint me you done something for.'

'Is that a fact?' He show me his yella teeth that got his dinner stuck on them. 'I know yer seen that draggle-tail with Griffith Flewelling. But do you tell yer employer? Nope. You take his coins and keep the secret. Yer think he's gonna give you coins when Yours Truly spills the beans?'

Dunno who that person is but I getting rilly sick of him.

'How I stop the beans spilling?' I ask dismal.

'Already said. You haffta keep a lookout on the Pass.'

I don't unnerstand how keeping a lookout on the Pass stop One Eye telling Yaws Trooley about Violet, but mebee they friends. I wriggle all around in my skin this way and that, tryna think of a way out, but it look like I got another job.

The morning come when I haffta leave for the Pass. Ludo still snoring off the drink when I creep out. It early, the sun aint up proper, and it very cool. I drag my feets over to Revell Street where One Eye live near the Bendigo Hotel. It one of them cottages that have a back door straight out on the beach. When I knock he open up blinking and rubbing his hair that stand up like a scrubbing brush. He grumble about what I doing there at the crack of dawn, then he make a joke about dawn's crack and laugh.

'I aint going no place till I get a feed,' I make bold to say.

One Eye open the door wide and in I go. It sure a fucken mess. Bottles and plates and clothings is everwhere. Then he call out and some flossie come out in her lady johns what aint stained and holey like Ludo's but fancy and stuck with lace. She got a pile of ginger hair and something that I hear Violet call a beauty spot but it sure look ugly. Seem she the cooker. She open the stove, shovel in some coal and bang them pots around like noise is the most important part of cooking.

One Eye get dressed in a room jes off. Flossie keep banging and sizzling for a while then put in my hands a plate that have two bits of fry damper on it. She make me sit down opposite her at a scratch table, and her uma jump out of her lady johns so much I dunno where to look.

'You his wife?' Seem like a good way to start the talking.

'Eh?'

'You,' I point at her with my fork, 'his wife?' I wave my knife where One Eye still swearing loud in the other room.

Ginger open her throat and laugh. Her throat frighten me, red and raw as meat, but her tongue even worse, it look like a animal what's been skinned. She also got teeth big as a horse.

I put my head down and eat up. What I care anyhow. I gonna look at the Pass once for One Eye, then we all square.

It a long way to the Pass. I ride on the back of One Eye's horse and I sure haffta cling on tight not to fall off. But it a rilly good view from a horse, a beast I aint ever been on before. I get to see a lot of the sea, and it go past fast, not slow like it do when you walk. Soon as we get to McIntyre's Hotel jes before the Pass, we have a stop.

'Look,' I say to One Eye, 'tell me what I gonna be looking for on this Pass.'

'Yer jes pretending to be stupid as fuck or what? Yer looking for the Gold Escort.'

'Them Gold Escorters is back in Hokitika town. I seen them.'

'Not for long they won't be.'

Slowly it come in my brain what's happening. I get angry. 'Why yer can't look yerself?'

'We haffta hide, Cocoa.'

'We?'

'You dint think I was gonna rob the Gold Escort on me own? And if I don't take a full part, I don't get no full cut. So listen here. That gold procession is gonna stop and water theirselves at the hotel. You send a signal when they leave again, alright?'

'What for?' I even more dismal. Seem it all arranged.

'So we have time to get ready. We can't see the hotel from the Pass, and we don't wanna be sitting on our horses with our guns half cocked for hours, do we? So you give a signal when they leave.'

'That's stupid. How yer see my signal?'

'You haffta run up that hill over there.' One Eye point. 'We can jes see the top from the hideout.'

Now I see why they want a boy. They want a body that aint so effing clapped out as what One Eye got.

'You haffta wave this shirt.' One Eye pull out a thing that's red as blood and checked.

'What? Everone see me.'

'Nah, there aint no window on that side of the hotel, see? And here's a penny or two for a feed. Hide the shirt and act natural. Anyone asks what yer hanging around for, say yer waiting on yer brothers. Yer all on yer way over the Pass to see yer Mama.'

One Eye gallop off in big cloud of dust.

I stand there feeling like all eyes is on me. Don't seem like no bright plan to me. No winder on that side of the hotel? What about them groggers that stumble out to throw up their stomick? What about the comings and goings? I sigh big. All I want is coin but I dint want it from no Gold Escort. And speaking about that, what about my cut? Violet were so stupid with them lips, poor little Halfie don't even get a cut.

I sit for a while where the horses is tied up and the sun beat down on my head. I get to thinking about food. Mebee they got a roasted mutton in the hotel, mebee a roasted beef. But when I go in the publican say, not enough coin for the lunch boyo, here, you can have a beer.

He stick a glass of dirty water that's throthy in front of me, and I so dry I drink it all down blink of a eye. It make me feel very happy. I got some more coin so I get another. I drink that all down blink of a eye too. Then I see a most frightening A-P-P-A-R-I-T-I-O-N. That's Ludo's word. He say when he drink his dirty water he get all happy in the head, then confused, then he see a apparition.

My apparition come in the doorway and it rilly huge. It look dark like a shadder. Then it turn into Mr Sale. He start looking around like he want to know who is loafing instead of slaving, who is drinking instead of eating them mutton chops. He look down on me from a big height, his face go all queer and working, and I scamper out like a scare dog. When I outside everthing look strange and I afraid I forget what I haffta do. I climb the hill where I give the signal from and sit down in the grass.

Next thing I know, I wake up to a big clamour. The Gold Escort is banging along below, there's a rattling carriage and a lot of entertainment on horses. Now they pulling off at the hotel for their chops. Right behind them come a man on a sweaty horse, look like he been galloping galloping galloping all his life. But he don't look like no Gold Escorter, he dressed all in rags. Don't seem like he got money for chops, he gallop right on past. I sure hope One Eye and his no counts don't jump him by a mistake.

I stand up. When were I spose to wave the shirt? Never mind. I pull it out, start waving it around like a porangi boy, dunno if them groggers or the apparition see me or not. Then I figure I done my bit. I walk down the hill, then I start running. Don't know how One Eye expect me to get back to Hokitika town but I don't care. I run all the way to the lake. Today it beautiful and satiny like Ginger's lady johns. It so beautiful my heart hurt. Or mebee it all the running. Or the beer.

I still hiding in some bushes when I see a few warriors going past. I want to jump forth and say, take me back to Papa, but one or two of them words somehow gone missing. While I run all over my brain looking, the warriors go on quickly, they out of sight when I get them words lined up. A while ago I were afraid they take me back if they see me. Now I afraid they don't.

When I feel a bit more safe I swim in the lake and climb a tree. Then the rain come. It go drip drip drip while I sit up in them branches. Then I get to thinking about poor Ludo. Who is cleaning up him? Mebee he drowning in his upthrowings, mebee the police come and say, where that no count boy of yers, we gonna get him for a most teerible crime. Mebee Ludo say he don't know. Then they get him by the ear, drag him off to the gaol for tryna hide a criminal.

I sleep up the tree. In the morning I look for a eel to tickle up but no luck. Aint nothing for it, haffta go out in the daylights and beg a ride back to Hokitika town.

When I get back to Hokitika town it looking jes the same. It a dance night at the Bathsheba, I go in there, everthing the same. Evertime I grab a plate to wash I expect to hear them diggers talking about the Gold Escorters that were shot in the Pass. But I don't hear nothing.

'Where yer been?' Violet hiss at me one time when we pass each other. 'I got something important to tell you.'

'Aint been nowhere,' I hiss back and scamper off.

When I get to the hut after the hot dinner Ludo asleep and snoring jes like I left him. Mebee he don't even know I been away.

Next day I go out early. I go down Revell Street, tryna get the courage to go to One Eye's cottage, ask Ginger or whoever answer, is this the day they gonna find them Gold Escorters dead like stuck pigs?

Next minute a hand reach out and grab me. It don't pick me up and dangle me like One Eye but it a big hand that have a vicious grip on my arm. I turn and it the worst ever. It my apparition.

'Well, I never,' say Mr Sale. 'If it isn't the boy from the hotel. Why do I keep running into you, sonny? You're like my own shadow.'

I very afraid of the King. I keep my mouth tight shut.

'Tell me, what were you doing at McIntyre's?'

'On my way over to visit my Mama.' It come out a squeak.

'Your Mama? What town does your Mama live in?'

'Cantaberry.'

Mr Sale smile. 'We're all in Canterbury here, sonny. It's Canterbury from east to west.'

'We in Hokitika,' I don't like to argue with the King but it haffta be said, he don't know where the fuck he is.

The King show his teeth again, this time not ezactly a smile. He looking at me like I a beast he gonna eat. 'Do you always stop off for beer on your way to see your Mama?' Before I can think of a answer he add, 'What does your poor Mama say when you turn up drunk?'

Well, I were so scared he gonna start talking about a boy on a hill that's been seen waving a red shirt I fall into a different trap.

'In fact, your Mama doesn't live over the Pass, does she? You're just an alcoholic getting a head start, aren't you?'

I freeze. I haffta think quick but no thinkings coming.

'Where do you really live, sonny? I'm going to visit your Mama, whom I'm sure lives right here in Hokitika. I'm going to tell her what you've been up to. What do you think she'll say? I'm expecting her to be rather surprised.'

'I work for Mr Flewelling,' I squeak. 'I take the plates at the hotel.'

'Oh, you live at the hotel,' Mr Sale nod, agreeing with hisself before I say no. Then no somehow don't come out of me. Then he bend down and look all mean. 'I hope you haven't been helping yourself to Caradoc's grog.'

I see my out, at least for now. 'No, I aint. You can ask him if you want.'

'Well, that I will, sonny, that I will. It's for your own good, mind. There are more prosecutions for intoxication in this town than for everything else put together.'

Mr Sale stride off and I let out my breathings. Gonna be trouble when the King talk to Mr Flewelling. He say, no, that little bedwetter don't live at my place. But meanwhile I get more boned up on them dead Escorters.

A few days go by. Nothing happen. The wind blow, the rain come, the sun shine. Violet take me down to Evan Prosser's Western Drug Hall what rilly thrill me with all them medsins already picked, no need to go dragging through them bushes. They already boiled down and poured in them special bottles, all set out very nice and wearing signs. Violet and me go along looking at everthing, she reading out them signs to me. They say Hopgood Hair Cream, Fowler's Solution, Keating's Cough Lozenges, and Odonto Odontalgic Essence, what turn out to be for teeths cuts and broken knees. It seem strange you haffta give coin for the medsins. What happen if yer sick and aint got none? But after that no problem. If you got coin there's plenty of them bright potions, red yella orange and green. Also if yer a lady there's Hooper's Female Pills, complexion powder and floury perfumes, and for the dirty diggers there's washings and cuttings of the hairs, teeths pulled scaled and stopped, and baths hot and cold.

Me and Violet go up to Mr Prosser and we buy four bottles of Fowler's for Gertie, and for Mr Flewelling six bottles of Perry Davis Vegetable Pain Killer. The Vegetable Pain Killer got little angels on the picture and writings that say Joy to the World. Violet say that sure is true. She say it got a O-P-I-U-M in it. She take some once when she have a bad headache and it were like she gone to Heaven. Well, Ludo talk to me about Heaven all the time, and also the Lord Of Course, and I sure wanna go there. So I take out my coin and give it to Violet who buy me a bottle. She say, don't drink it all at once Half-pint, or yer go to Heaven for good.

We go for a little walk near the wharf. Now and then I take a swig from my bottle of Perry Davis, and Violet drink something too, I dunno what. Soon them sparkles what flash on the river start flashing round my head. Violet tripping over her feets and giggling like a halfwit. Then she lying in the mud. She sure having a party for one. My own Heaven a bit less loud and dumb.

Some bit of time go missing.

I wake up on the river bank with the sky turning orange. Violet sitting beside me rubbing her head and moaning. She point out some upthrowings she done. I look and a brown river rat look. Prolly look like dinner to him.

We get up and start to walk back to the Bathsheba.

'What yer call it when yer glad some time go by that you dint haffta live?' I ask.

'Refreshing,' Violet reply me.

'Yair, it fucken refreshing, that Vegetable Pain Killer.'

Ludo sleep and drink. Halfie sweep and sweat. Then the next dance come. Early on Mr Flewelling come down them stairs. He wave me over.

'I had George Sale button-hole me at lunch yesterday. Said he caught you drinking up at McIntyre's.'

'I dint have enough coin for no mutton chops.'

'Forget the fucken mutton chops. What were you doing up there?'

'Drinking.'

Mr Flewelling look at me long. Then he bend down creaking creaking, he move so slow and stiff I expect his knees to snap. He look me in the eye. I try to look straight back but his eyes is like black pits going down to Hell.

'I don't want visits from Sale.' He look rilly menacing. 'I got balls in the air, irons in the fire. I don't want the Chief Regulator sniffing around, see?'

'Yep I see.'

Mr Flewelling slowly rise again with a grimace on his face. But he looking less angry. He say, 'I reckon that hatter is having a bad influence on you. I don't think you would of started drinking of yer own accord.'

That sure true. But it aint Ludo's fault.

Mr Flewelling stay looking long at me. This leading somewhere I don't wanna go.

'I'm thinking I should pay Ludovic a visit,' he say.

'What for?' I get a alarm now. What Ludo gonna say if Mr Flewelling tell him I been drinking?

'Sort out a few things about yer upbringing. Expectations and the like.'

'Ludo aint upbringing me. I jes sleep by the stove now it cold. When the summer come in I everwhere again, out in the bush, up a ponga tree . . .'

'Listen, Bedwetter, you can't be running wild around here.

This is a decent town, haven't you noticed? It's already got six churches and a synagogue.'

'I aint wild. Violet learn me how to spell and Ludo give me them reading exercises.'

Before I convince him, one of them Piccadilly Whiskers come down from the bedrooms of the hotel. Mr Flewelling say, 'I've got business to attend to now. But you come here tomorrow morning, seven-thirty sharp.'

'What for? Why yer need me?'

'D'you think a man like me knows his way around the bush? Knows exactly where Ludovic threw up his pile of sticks? Look at the shine on these boots. Am I shod like a mud dweller?'

I aint got no answer to that. I scuttle off down to the beach. Them waves is loud crashing, but the wind is wild and warm jes how I like it. I sit on a big drown log and think about the trouble coming my way, the trouble what come from Ludo when Mr Flewelling visit, the trouble what come from the law when they find them maggoty Gold Escorters.

I toss and turn all night long. Sometime in the night when them rats start scurrying all round tryna find their daily bread I think of waking up Ludo, warn him that Mr Flewelling gonna pay him a surprise visit. I light a candle and the rats flee in the shadders. I peer over at Ludo, he snoring loud.

I prod him and he make a little jump and a big snore, then he roll over away from me, settle to his heavy breathings.

'Ludo, wake up.'

Big snore.

'Wake up Ludo!' I shake him with his shoulder. Waking Ludo like waking the dead. But finally he sit up blinking. 'Holy mother of God, where's the fire, laddie?'

'Caradoc Flewelling want me to fetch him here tomorra morning,' I blurt out.

'What?'

I blurt again.

Ludo aint hearing me. He still in a dream with his eyes wide awake. Dunno what he do if I wet him with cold water or coax a rat up on him. Prolly run screaming out in the night, gone forever.

'Never mind,' I say as he sink back on his pillow. 'Get yer beauty sleep.'

But no more sleep come to me. I rilly worry. I dunno what the time is but I run off to Hokitika town soon as the sun get up. Nobody stir in the street except them desperate rats that lap up the upthrowings. Nobody stir at the hotel and the big front doors is still locked, so I squat down to wait. After a while the fatso cook open the doors and throw out bone tucker for some skinny dogs what's hanging around. They all whining and snarling and licking and chomping, I haffta push through them to get in the door. I follow the fatso cook who's called Prosper. He waddle to the scullery, put on a big apron that once were white but is now rilly stained. He aint a pretty sight. Bald except for a tuft of black hair on the top, face hanging down with fat folds, mouth like a slash throat.

Mr Flewelling come down them stairs looking like he fall off a horse. He all bent up, his hair everwhere, his shirt hanging out of his trouser. He doing so much coughing and spluttering he don't look much better'n Ludo when he first wake up.

He say he must have his coffee. He tell Prosper to give me some too. It sure look nice but it bitter. I make a face and Mr Flewelling call up the sugar from Prosper.

'Yer like the sugar do you, Bedwetter?'

I eye him. The way he ask seem like trouble coming.

'Lot of folks die for that taste,' he say.

'Gertie you mean?'

'No, I don't mean Gertie,' he snap back.

Mr Flewelling aint agreeable early.

We set off after three coffees each and a big struggle with them shiny boots. I go along the street at a trot, then I notice Mr Flewelling coming very slow behind. Seem his legs is all bent today, his back is all bent, it one of them bad days for him for sure. We go up behind Hokitika town where all the bush is, straight away we get in a mud bog. Mr Flewelling start slipping and sliding and cursing like a sailor. You jes haffta laugh. But not out loud, up yer sleeve as Ludo say, case he give you a quick thick behind the ear.

'Under normal circumstances I don't think I could be fucked going all the way to Ludo's hut,' he say when he stop to wipe his drippy forehead.

'You don't haffta be fucked now.'

'I do, Bedwetter, I do. It's my duty.'

We get to Ludo's poor little hut. It muddy and dripping as a pigsty, it sure shame me for Ludo's sake. Before we get on the whakamahau, Ludo come out the door in his long johns. I happy to see it one of his satin days, he got that strange light in his eyes like this the day he gonna sober up forever.

'Get the chairs, laddie,' Ludo say, 'and set them on the veranda.'

I do as Ludo say. Soon we all sitting on there like stupid kings. Mr Flewelling light his pipe and Ludo go off to make the tea. Ludo don't have no cake but he find a bit of damper, put it out nice on a old plate. I rilly proud of him even if he still in his dirty long johns. That's because Ludo always forget some things when he too much in a haste to seem proper.

'That all he gets to eat here?' Mr Flewelling ask when I reach out and take a piece of damper.

'Do the diggers get much more?' Ludo aint looking at the man what spoke. He all serene, that his own word for not a ripple on a lake.

'That aint the point.'

'Well, what is the point, Caradoc?'

'Point is, Sale's been coming by the hotel complaining about yer little house guest.'

'Is that so? And why would George Sale be bothering about the likes of him?'

'Because he's been seen grogging up at McIntyre's.'

Ludo turn sudden and stare. This the teerible moment when Ludo lose all his hopes of me.

'That's right,' Mr Flewelling carry on cruel. 'Knocking back the liquor like there's no tomorra. Now, don't get me wrong, I aint a hypocrite. I run a hotel and I aint got no objections to the drink. How would we of survived without it ourselves, eh? This place aint the palmy land of California. But that aint no excuse for a brat to be a boozer.'

'No, it aint,' Ludo agree.

Mr Flewelling seem very pleased Ludo take his view of things. Now I rilly afraid I lose my sleeping place at the stove. I no longer a boy that like a cave or a tree to sleep up. Mr Flewelling sit there opening and closing his big hands like they need a oiling, Ludo stroke his long beard and stare into the bush.

'There's plenty kids that live more bad than me,' I make bold to say. 'There's two that live in a pigsty near Greymouth, and one girl, she say she only nine, that live all alone in a tent.'

'You don't lessen the blame by spreading it more thin,' Mr Flewelling say.

Ludo now shift around in his chair like he got fleas down them long johns. Then he make us a speech. He say, 'There's a laddie that comes to me complaining of the cold and I tell him he can sleep by the stove. Did I put my signature to a paper with the King's stamp on it? No, I did not. Did I agree to churchings and thrashings? Again no. Bed and board? Not even that. Did I vow to stay sober so he won't pick up the drinking habit? Not on yer life. I only make promises to the Lord, and even He aint got that one out of me.'

Oh no, the Lord is stepping in.

Ludo carry on, 'Even were I to have the intention, which I haven't, I aint got the will. Even if I got the will, I aint got the . . .'

'The what?' Mr Flewelling ask when Ludo jes stop.

Ludo shrug. 'The life doesn't go all the way.'

Eh? All the way where?

Mr Flewelling sigh and move his big feets around. Seem he got a inkling about where Ludo's life don't go.

Ludo say, 'Don't think I regret anything . . .'

'Yer life's fucked and you don't regret anything?' Mr Flewelling look astonished.

Now Ludo rilly get started. 'I don't regret giving up the fancy hotels, the stiff sheets and the big dinners, if that's what yer think. And don't imagine I was gonna sober up jes from sitting down at a starched tablecloth with the parson. By the time I got my gold, the life was already thin . . .'

Mr Flewelling do more shuffles. 'The life, the life! You talk like it aint yer own.'

'Well, is it? If it were my own, couldn't I have fashioned it a wee bit better?'

A silence fall. It like everone chewing on if Ludo were able to make his life better'n what he did make it. Then gradual them chewings stop, them teeths go quiet, everone seem not to care no more.

'Well,' Ludo say, 'now that we've sorted that out, do you fancy a wee drop yerself?'

'Don't mind if I do,' Mr Flewelling reply, even if nothing been sorted.

Ludo go in to fetch them glasses and bottle. He come out and pour the drinks. Down go one two three. They talk of this and that, nothing rilly serious, then Mr Flewelling say with a dark kind of cackle, 'Stuck out here in the bush, I suppose you aint heard about the Gold Escort?'

My blood freeze up in a instant.

Ludo shake his head.

'Funniest thing,' he say.

Funny they all dead in the Pass? He sure a man that aint got no heart.

'You know there was such a fuss about it in East Canterbury. How are we gonna get the gold from west to east without a dray road? How are we gonna get all the gold along a dray road without an escort?'

'No, Caradoc, I dint know,' Ludo say.

He have too many drinks. Or mebee the morning ones is meeting them ones from the night before. 'You do know, Ludo,' I say. 'They what you call the entertainment.'

'Oh yes.' It like he bring up something from a dream.

'Well, they got the dray road and they got the Escort sorted out,' Mr Flewelling say. 'Then the banks couldn't make up their minds whether to use it or not. In the end the whole dang thing arrived in Christchurch with only a few nuggets and a couple of rocks rattling round in the lockbox.' Mr Flewelling find this hilarious, he laugh and slap his thigh.

It arrive in Christchurch?

'They aint all dead then?' I make bold to ask.

Mr Flewelling turn one black eye on me. 'Now, why should they all be dead? I think you've been reading too many rubbish novels with that Violet.'

Mr Flewelling stand up, he all bow legs, he do some funny stretching, up down up down, then say he haffta get back to town. 'It's been nice seeing you again, Ludovic. Why don't yer come and visit me at the Bathsheba sometime? Why not come for Christmas dinner?'

'Or you could come here again,' Ludo say.

Mr Flewelling set off and Ludo grasp the bottle like it a baby he don't ever wanna lose. Look like this aint the day he gonna get sober forever.

Now I dunno what to think. I sit up a tree from where I can see everthing, the bush what's before the sea, the sea what's glinting and roaring, the wind what bend the trees over jes about sideways and then thrash em. It sure relaxing up a tree. Might not wanna sleep there no more but it sure beat the earth in the daylights. In the daylights there more beasts out roaming than what roam under the moon. These is beasts what go on two legs not four, beasts what make all kind of trouble for poor little Halfie, a boy that jes wanna have coin and a easy life.

I scratch my head, dunno what that haffta do with thinking, but Ludo say that's what you do so I do it. I scratch and scratch and what come out is my own little picture story of what One Eye and his gang do in the Pass.

One Eye and his gang jump out on them Gold Escorters. The Gold Escorters is so surprised and useless they jes fall off their top hole horsemeat. Then One Eye stick his gun in the head of the smallest, shout open up that lockbox, and smallest done it otherwise he get his head blown off. One Eye and his devils fill their pockets, then make smallest lock up again. Even if them other Gold Escorters find their wits and fire their guns they so useless the bullets jes go bouncing off them rocks. Then One Eye and the gang go off galloping and firing their guns and the Gold Escorters haffta spend hours cleaning up their fancy britches before arriving in East Cantaberry with jes a speck of gold and a few rocks in their lockbox.

'What yer doing up that tree, Cocoa?'

I look down and Godsaveus it One Eye! I nearly fall outta the tree.

'Get down here,' he order.

'What for?' I figure he too clapped out to climb up and make me.

'Don't question yer betters, Cocoa.'

'I weren't.'

One Eye jump up and down tryna swipe my leg. I go up quick to a more higher branch. Then I lean out and dangle down a string of spit.

'Er, you filthy little fuck,' One Eye cry.

'Least I aint a fucken murderer. Or a robber,' I add, seeing it turn out there weren't no dead Escorters.

'Who's a robber? Yer got everthing all wrong. Come down here and I'll tell you.'

I sure wanna hear so I get down. Don't feel so safe on the earth but I reckon I get up the tree faster than One Eye can grab me.

'You dint think we'd risk our necks for no sure gain, did you, Cocoa?' Now One Eye begin his big show off story. 'We dint have no idea how much would get put in that lockbox. Some of the banks in Christchurch were in, some were out, they were chopping and changing their minds like whores choosing their drawers. So we put a man to spying. He got a fine suit on, stayed near the Escort before they left Hokitika, chewed everyone's ear, chewed the ear of the Editor from the newspaper who come to get a fancy story. Soon our man hears the gold aint much to write home about. Soon he sees the lockbox being carried out, and is it like carrying the King's coffin, heavy as a bleeding elephant? No, it fucken aint. Even a dainty English virgin could of loaded that box onto the wagon. So he gets on his horse to warn us, rides up the Pass and . . .'

'That man dint have no expensive suit on!'

'What?' One Eye squint at me.

'I seen that man what gallop past. He were all rag and bone.'

'You dint think he owned that fancy suit, did yer, Cocoa? Before he left, he had to get it back to the man he borrowed it from.'

'Who were that?'

'Yer friend, Mr Flewelling.'

'Mr Flewelling give him his suit? That a lie!'

'Well, he dint exactly give it. Prosper borrowed it for a little while.'

'Yer got Prosper in on this?' Now I rilly furious. Prosper is too close to the Bathsheba, the Bathsheba too close to everone I tryna stay tight with.

'Calm down. Prosper aint the sort to go blabbing.'

'How yer know? You dint do no robbing so he dint get no cut. Yet still the suit got wore by yer filthy friend. Still Fatso got to sneak up them stairs and steal it from under the eyes of old Gertie.'

'Lend.'

'I don't care what the word. What happen when Mr Flewelling put on his suit for a funeral or a wedding? It stink to high Heaven.'

One Eye stare at me for a while and then he fish in his pocket.

'I nearly forgot,' he say. 'Here's yer cut, Cocoa. Yep, we dint rob no Gold Escort, but we're an organised outfit, aint no bunch of pants-pissing amateurs. We got us a kitty. That's where I get yer cut from.'

He put in my hand a paper coin, and when I look at it, it turn out to be a whole pound note. I jes about to shout for joy when he say mean, 'But don't go thinking I looked all over for you jes for the fun of it. I've got plans for you, Cocoa. Big plans.'

Later on I sit with Violet in the afternoon sun what run over us like warm milk.

'What's a kitty?' I ask.

'It's a baby cat. Short for kitten.'

I confused. 'How you get coin from a cat?'

'What?'

'I got a pound note.'

'You never! Where'd an urchin like you get a pound note?'

'From a kitty.'

Violet narrow her eyes. 'If you don't stop talking shit I'm gonna slap you.'

'It the truth!'

'Show me, then.'

I take my pound note out of my pocket and unfold it. Violet stare at it. 'Yer sure you aint met with them counterfeiters?'

'What's a counter fitter?'

'Someone that makes fake money.'

'No I told you, I got it from a kitty.' Violet is rilly annoying when she dumb like this.

Then suddenly she get a look of unnerstanding. It like the sun rise. 'Oh my God, you mean pussy. You turned pimp!'

Now I rilly foxed.

'Who put you up to that?' Violet demand in a loud and angry voice. 'I've a good mind to . . .'

'What's pussy?'

'Aw, come on. You don't haffta pretend to be all innocent with me, little boy. I know Caradoc don't pay you much, but you dint haffta take on no pavement nymph.'

Seem I going more and more deep in water that's clear as mud.

'I jes don't know how you talked anyone into it. They're mainly paying for protection. What did you do? Threaten to set upon the cheating customers with that chief that's in the circus? The one that tomahawked twenty men?'

Seem it time to go. More I ask Violet what everthing mean, more I mix up. I stand up but Violet catch my arm. She pull me down beside her. Now she no more look like a angry bitch. Fact is she look rilly worried.

'Been meaning to tell you something, Harvey,' she say. Then there's a long wait while her face work like a slave. Then jes when I about to give up she blurt out, 'Harvey, I'm gonna have a baby.'

FOUR

Seem to me it a nice idea to buy Ludo a present with my pound. I go looking for a store that sell food. I find one pretty nice. It painted up, it got kai out the front what's piled up neat. I take a long time looking. I bring home four big eggs.

'Ee laddie,' Ludo say with a frown. 'Eggs are rare as hen's teeth. Where'd you get em?'

'It a surprise.'

'It sure is.' But Ludo don't look happy. He roll a egg round on his big spade hand and we look at it.

'Listen laddie, I don't want to be hearing any more bad stories about you.'

'Find a chicken, find a egg,' I say chirpy.

'Yair, that's the problem. Number of free chickens around here I could count on the fingers of one hand.'

I take the egg from his hand. 'Let's eat up, Ludo.'

'Yair,' he agree a bit grim. 'Let's eat the evidence.'

Soon we eating damper and scramble evidence on the whakamahau.

'What's a circus, Ludo?' This the question I put when everthing all cleaned up.

'What yer want to know that for? It's a place of great cruelty.'

'Why a chief in one? Violet say a chief in the circus in Hokitika town.'

Ludo stroke his long grey beard.

'I wanna see the chief. And I want you to come with me.'

'What for?'

'Pertection.'

'Protection from what?'

'If they got a real chief he gonna be rilly mad.'

'They aint prisoners. If there's a chief showing himself, it's because he wants to. He's probably doing it for the money.'

'Coin? Yer get coin for showing yerself?'

Ludo nod.

'Then mebee I can . . .'

'No, you need to be special in some way. Got to have fins or buttocks as big as wedding cakes. You've got to be a hunger artist or . . .'

'What's that?'

'A man who starves himself for money.'

'Who wanna see that? Lotsa diggers round here starving theirselves for free.'

Ludo sigh.

'How that chief special?'

'Lots of men are new here. They've never seen the likes of it, a savage that's got tattoos all over his face and buttocks, and bones in his hair.'

'That aint a real chief, for sure.'

'Well, I don't know. The tribes are searching for gold along with everyone else. But sitting in a booth getting shillings for who you are is a lot easier than panning out there in the soaking bush.'

'Please Ludo. We go to Hokitika town and I see the chief, then you can have yer kai at the Bathsheba.'

Ludo mumble and grumble but I see something of it sounding good to him. Dunno what. Mebee them drinks and crissmiss dinner.

'What ezactly is a crissmiss, Ludo?'

'Ee, that's the Lord's birthday, that's what. Sometimes I wonder where you've been all yer life.'

Where I been sure starting to fade a bit. Mebee because I always going chop when the rememorying come up in me. Can still rememory Moana and what it feel like to hold her hand, can still hear her singing as we go along. But also as my unnerstandings grow up with me it seem there were something wrong. Seem like I were borned already walking. I appear like magic then I stand up and walk. I walk over to Moana who gimme cuddles, but some others are always grabbing my ear and shouting. It like they dint know talkings can fly through the air, no need to bring the ear up to yer mouth. Mebee that's why I need to see the chief. See if he angry at me. See if he even know me.

Next time I at the Bathsheba washing them dirty glasses Prosper bang around his kitchen making dinners for them diggers what come to the dances and I jes know he looking at me. Not straight but kind of sideways. Out the corner of his eye he circling me. I sure like to get everthing out in the open, jes walk up to him and say, look Fatty, I only wave a old shirt, geddit? That's all I do and all I ever gonna do. If you tell Mr Flewelling, I tell him you put yer poxy friend inside his best suit. But of course I can't do it. So I get a bit depressed. Then at the end of the evening Mr Flewelling aint there. Prosper say, sit down, Thumbsucker, I give you yer dinner. He slap down a full plate spilling with meats and gravies, and he sit down too, but he aint got no dinner jes a bottle.

'Well, now,' he say in a voice that make them meats and gravies taste like they been cooked in the dishwater, 'Violet tells me you've taken up pimping.'

'I aint taken up nothing.' Fact is I dunno what he mean.

'She says you've been waving around a pound note. Fortunatus says you've been buying eggs. Eggs that sell for a small fortune.'

'Who Fortunatus?'

'He's the storekeeper near the Gridiron. He owns the store you've been doing yer buying from.'

'It were my cut,' I object in a angry voice. Prosper already know, but he tryna pin something else on me.

'It were yer cut,' Fatty repeat, and then he take a few glugs.

I dunno where this going.

'Doncha think yer cut is something that oughta be kept private?' he ask when he put down his bottle. 'There's a lotta money washing around this town, but mainly it fetches up at the bars or the brothels. Aint much is expected to fall into the hands of little pants-pissers like yerself. You go on a big spending spree and everone starts to talk, geddit?'

'What they say?'

'They say, don't tell me that brat got a lead. Don't tell me that brat found some gold we don't know of. How about we jump him, put him in a sack and take him off for torturing till he spill the beans?'

I get a big fright. I put down my fork and can't eat no more.

'So yer friend Prosper has to sort them out. Has to say, nah, you got it all wrong. I give him the pound note for all the fishes he brings me. But then what? Then one of the men I sort out comes in here and says, right in front of Mr Flewelling, I sure am tired of all this mutton, I want one of them special fishes you've been hiding, Prosper. Now Caradoc dint come down in no last rainfall, and he say, I hope you aint been abusing my trust, Mr Dirago. I sure aint, I reply, I been sending all them fancy fish dinners up to yer wife.'

I let out a big breath.

'So this is where you come in, Thumbsucker. Yer got to make

this right, see? Now Caradoc Flewelling aint the kind of man that spends a lotta time attending to his Mrs, but we can't take no risks. You gonna get me a big fish, and I'm gonna cook it and dress it with a cream sauce, and then you gonna take it up to Gert and tell her you been bringing her poisson de la crème for weeks.'

'But I aint!'

'No, you aint. But she's sick and confused, so you haffta convince her.'

'Why yer can't do it yerself?'

Prosper look mean. 'You rilly think I'm gonna improve my prospects with the proprietor if I start going into the bedroom of his wife? His wife that's wearing her nightdress and lying in the bed?'

Seem like the black cloud come down even harder on the bright day that my life once were. Everthing sure a lot of trouble, and when I follow it back again I see it all go back to Violet. But what I can do? Don't matter what trouble go back to, it come forward the same way. I tell Prosper I catch him a big fish soon as I can. He say better be for Gertie's next lunch or he put me in a sack hisself.

Next day I going up them stairs to Gertie's bedroom all atremble. It aint jes the heavy tray what's loaded with everthing that might spill, including a little red flour in a glass of water, it also being scared of the job that Prosper gimme. Catching the fish were easy compare to this, even with the rotten old fishing stick Prosper give me what turn out worse than the one I made for myself.

When I give the fish to Prosper, Mr Flewelling were leaning on the bar drinking coffee. He nod like he unnerstand everthing. Prosper say loud, now you come back and take the lunch up to Mrs Flewelling, one of them scrubbers have the clap and dint come in today. So I go out and hang about in the shadders of Revell Street. There's rilly a lot of folks I don't want to see, it start with King Sale and go all the way down to them evil kidnappers with sacks.

Now I kick open the door and Gertie Flewelling what were still asleep nearly jump out of her skin. She start blushing and fluttering but I aint intrested if the crack in her uma breaking free of her nightgown buttons.

'Here yer lunch, Maam,' I say, putting the tray on the bed where her squirm can't spill the flour. 'It poison de la crem.'

'Poison?'

'That's what Prosper say.' I take the silver lid off so she can get a look.

'Oh no, Halfie, I can't eat that. It's too rich. All that cream.' She shudder like it a dead dog.

I take a big breath and say, jes like I have a surprise, 'But you been eating it all week.'

Big blue eyes fix on me. 'Is that what Prosper told you? It's a lie. He just wants to make Caradoc think I'm not following my diet. But I am. Less rich food, the doctor said to me. Less rich food, Gertrude Flewelling, and you'll be right as rain in no time.'

'He giving you medsin, aint he? His medsin making you forget everthing. I been here with fishes about ten times. Sure sometimes they jes fried plain, sometimes even boiled. I haffta agree that's when you like them the most.'

Big blue eyes now full of a struggle. Is it sweet little Halfie what's lying to me, or is them drugs fucking with my memory?

'Can you fetch me a drink from the decanter, please?'

I fetch her drink and she gulp it down.

'Mebee it all them spirits,' I suggest.

'No, this is only water, Halfie.'

Silence come on the room while Gertie think it out.

'Please have a little fish jes for me,' I plead. 'I catch it special.'

'You caught it?'

'Jes like all them others I brung.'

Gertie sigh. My heart ache. I happy to lie to everone except Gertie and Ludo, but thems the ones what get all the lies because thems the ones I haffta look good to.

'Well, you feed me a little.' She reach over for the napkin.

I sit up close and give her a bit of fish. She sure seem to like it. I give her a bit more. Soon we going pretty fast. Soon the fish all gone and she lick the last drips of cream off the spoon.

'Oh, Halfie,' she lament, 'we've eaten it all.'

I sit a bit while she stroke my hair.

Seem like the time to ask a question that's been bothering me. 'If a girl kiss two men, who the Papa?'

Gertie, who closed her eyes while stroking me, now open them up. 'The Papa of what?'

'The baby.'

'Oh, I see. The husband is the Papa. That's what marriage is for. And don't you forget it.'

That mean Caradoc the father of Violet's bubba. But I haffta make sure. 'What if she take off her clothes and wriggle with two men?'

Gertie do a big frown. 'Good grief, Halfie, only a prostitute does that.'

Well I sure aint gonna do no more big spending in Hokitika town. But what's the use of coin if you can't get no kai with it? So I walk past the store where I buyed them eggs tryna get a look at this merchant called Fortunatus. Way I figure it, if I see what he look like, then I always make sure he aint watching me when I buy a little bit here, a little bit there, but nothing in his shop ever again.

When I go past, Fortunatus standing out the front of his store like he gonna collar the customers. He wear a big calico apron and big black whiskers down his jaws, meeting in a tuft on his chin. He wear his top lip naked in that way what look ugly. He aint got no corporation, what's a big surprise when he own all that food. Seem I aint as invisible as I think. He call out to me in the shadders, come here Harvey. I surprised he know what I called. I stand in front of him and look at his feets.

'Not buying any eggs today, young 'un?'

I shake my head.

'Run out of money, have we?'

I nod.

'Jes wait there a minute.' He turn and go in his shop, minute later he come out with a tin cup that he give me. Inside is a egg what's broke.

'I dropped it this morning,' Fortunatus explain me. 'You might as well have it. Eggs don't agree with me.'

I go on one foot then the other. How to say, nah, eggs don't agree with me no more neither?

'What I do with the cup?'

'Jes drop it off when yer going past. It's only an old thing.'

Fortunatus aint a monster. He don't seem the kind of man to be a friend of greasy Prosper.

'Why yer tell Fatso about my shopping?' I make bold to ask.

'Prosper comes here for supplies. I told him you'd been buying eggs in case he thought you'd been thieving from his kitchen.'

I all bristles. 'You do this for all yer customers? Tell their bosses what they buy with their own coin?'

Fortunatus laugh. It what Ludo call good natured.

'It sure get me in a lot of trouble,' I say in a angry voice.

Fortunatus put his hand on my shoulder and invite me in his store for a C-O-M-P-E-N-S-A-T-I-O-N. It turn out to be a sweet thing that he say come on a ship from Fee Jee. It yella on the outside but inside it look like a potata only more squidgy. It sure nice. While I eat, Fortunatus lift me up and sit me on his counter. This a bit embarrassing for me. I small but not *that* small. Then he stare at me with a smile.

'Do you know where Fiji is, young 'un?'

'Nope.'

'It aint far away at all. And d'you know what? They eat people there. That's what long pig is. What d'you think of that?'

'Long as they don't eat me I don't care.'

Fortunatus laugh big. 'Nothing more selfish than a child.' He say it like he think that rilly good.

'No one eat me. They all my aunties and uncles out there.'

'Out there where?'

I hesitate. Seem like out there is everwhere around Hokitika town.

'Maybe yer aunties and uncles will eat half the men in this town when they discover we've been harbouring you instead of tanning yer backside and sending you home.'

'Mebee. Prolly they got better things to do.'

Now the compensation all gone. I sit on the counter wondering what to do. Sure I can jump down easy but mebee it aint the correct manners.

'It aint right all you young 'uns running around alone,' Fortunatus say. 'And don't think yer the only one. There's that little girl all alone in the tent in Greymouth and those two in the pigsty. Countless others, no doubt.'

'Yair, I seen them.' I told Ludo and Mr Flewelling I visit them but that aint strickly true. Strickly true is I creep nearby. I seen that dirty little girl boiling her billy out the front of her tent, gimme a feeling what's a big ache. Yair, I all alone it seem, but not rilly. Mama and Moana still looking down on me, and I haffta hide if ever I went to Maori Gully, there's so many what take too much of a intrest in me. But that little girl, her family prolly in Russher. She haffta get on one of them ships and sail uphill for more'n a year to get back to them.

'I go and visit her now and then,' Fortunatus tell me. 'Take her a bit of food. You should accompany me sometime.'

'What for?'

Jes then some customers come in the store. Fortunatus wink and lift me down. I scuttle out. Seem when I tryna get out of things I jes going in more deeper all the time. When I say to Ludo about this, he say that's what all folks is like, if you go near them, they always find a way to pull you into their muddy little puddle they all like crocodiles.

Ludo promise he take me to the circus after crissmiss. He say that's when all the shows is on for them diggers what come into town for New Year. It aint no good to go before crissmiss, he say, half the booths is empty, all them freaks is out doing their crissmiss shopping.

Soon enough me and Ludo fling open the big front doors of the Bathsheba and step inside for the crissmiss dinner. It sure been hard getting there. Ludo spend two whole days in his long johns so he can fuss over his moleskins and pea jacket with a cloth that he dip in water then kerosene then spirit. He tryna fuss over me the same way but I always jump away. Then jes before we leaving Ludo open his old trunk that he keep his candle on and haul out a old suit from California, one that have a fish tail cut in it. He put it on and ask, what d'you think? I say, yer sure a string bean, yer sure a Armenian, because he so shrunk inside that suit it look like it were made for two of him. Ludo now happy and hum while he trim his nostrils in the bit of glass he got hung on the wall. Then he smear down his hair with a old comb he dip in a tin can. He light the lantern and we all set to go. Course it all slippy and slidey so by the time we get there Ludo's fish tail is rilly muddy.

I swear I never seen such a grand sight as a crissmiss dinner. There chandeliers candles and big white clothings on them tables. Also lots of people done up in silk and jools and pile up hair and Sunday best. Mr Flewelling come over to shake Ludo's hand. He got on the borrow suit. I take a big sniff to see if it stink of low downs.

'What's the fucken matter with you, Bedwetter?' he hiss at me.

I take Ludo's hand and lead him to the bar where all them bottles is lined up for the guests. Tonight scowling Violet doing the pouring. She wave away Ludo's coin saying jes for us it Caradoc's shout. I don't care how much Ludo drink, all I want is Ludo happy. Ludo allow me a small beer seeing no one paying much notice. Then we turn and lean against the bar and look at the room.

Everone come. Griffith Flewelling laugh with One Eye's Ginger, what must account for the scowls from Violet, and One Eye play a fiddle in the band. That sure a shock. Means mebee he weren't brung up to be a robber, he jes fell in and dint climb out. Gertie Flewelling lie back on one of them long chairs, she sip what Ludo call champagne, she sure look beautiful for a fat old lady. Her hair is gold and shiny, her lips is a red heart, her dress a mile of expensive stuff same colour as pounamu. Beside her sit a little girl all dressed in a big puff of pink, and Fortunatus feed them turn about from a big plate.

Ludo go over to speak to the doctor. Big plates is everwhere about, they got bits of meat and fish and bread cut up small, and bits of plant and yella stuff what's rilly sour. I eat a whole plate, then ask Violet for more beer. She so angry she fill it up, it splash all over the counter when she shove it at me.

'Don't see why I haffta do all the work,' she say. 'Aint it my Christmas also?'

'It crissmiss for Prosper too and he doing the cooking.'

'He's the fucken cook, aint he?'

'What's he cooking anyway?'

'What yer think? Whole lot of Canterbury lambs and Christmas puddings.'

I follow Violet's eyes. They all the time darting to Griffith and Ginger.

'How Griffith know Ginger?' I ask.

'How do *you* know Ginger?' she come at me.

'She the girlfriend of that One Eye playing the fiddle. I seen them in Revell Street.'

'She aint his girlfriend, she's his sister. And seeing aint introducing. How yer know her name?'

'It her name? I thought it were jes like when One Eye call me Koko.'

Violet stare at me with mean eyes. 'Yer starting to sound pretty intimate with them two. Maybe Ginger's the pussy that's been earning yer pound notes?'

'Mebee, mebee not.' Seem it better to be a bit mysterious with Violet.

She reach out and grab my collars. She tryna pull me up close. My feets leave the ground and I afraid my clothings get tore. 'Don't get funny with me, little boy. You'll get yerself into a lot of trouble hanging around with prostitutes.' Then she drop me like a brick.

So Ginger a prostitute? Now it make sense. A prostitute want to wriggle with two men, dint Gertie tell me? So Ginger now got her eyes on Junior Flewelling. And why not, he sure a lot better looking than her ugly brother.

Then Mr Flewelling go up the front near the big doors, clap his hands, the band stop, and he do some throat clearing for quite a while, then he go into a fine speech that I don't make nothing of because the beer now swilling around inside my ears.

Now everone sitting theirselves at the tables. I scurry over to Ludo jes in time to get the last seat where he sit down. I very happy because I don't get no enjoyment without him. I see Violet come out from behind the bar and sit down with some of them other dancing girls and a few diggers. Griffith Flewelling sit at the table with his Mama and Papa and a few important arses from the old Improvement Committee. At my table there's more diggers and Fortunatus and the little girl in the pink frock. I look at her.

Mebee we have some fun after, mebee go round drinking up the brandy dregs when the adults all dancing, mebee we hide under the table clothings, pretend to be rats tryna go up them expensive trouser and crinolins.

Out come Prosper and some scrubbers carrying big plates full of cut up lambs, and other plates with vegetables, and jugs of gravies. A man stand up, Ludo whisper it the pastor, he start thanking the Lord for the kai. Then we all passing them plates about, all perlite, do you want this, do you want that, I gonna be wore out before I get any food in my mouth.

'So, Fortunatus,' Ludo say, 'be so kind as to introduce us to yer niece.'

'Clementine aint my niece,' Fortunatus reply. 'She's my ward.'

'Yer ward? Is that so? And who awarded her to you?'

'Who awarded the young 'un to you?'

'That would be Lady Luck.'

'What a coincidence – the very same,' Fortunatus declare.

Ludo chew a mouthful very slow like he considering something. That when I realise Clementine the dirty little girl that live all alone in the tent. Fortunatus grab her and scrub her up and put a frill on her, he must of been fussing with her for hours. But she aint eating like no starving animal, mebee Fortunatus feed her a compensation while he wash her in the bathtub. Ludo don't say very much after that, jes eat and drink. Then them plates is cleared away and the band start up again for a quick dance before the puddings. Ludo go to the bar and I go too, hoping for more beer.

Someone grab my arm.

'Here, take this over to my wife.' Mr Flewelling gimme me another of them glasses of champagne.

I a bit dizzy yet haffta steer that glass across the room and give it to Gertie. Quite a bit fizz over my hand. Gertie put her arm around me, give me a big kiss. She smell of flours and everthing nice. Then I see a big problem. Violet now sitting beside Griffith in a seat that were given up by a dancer. She flopping about drunk. Gertie and Griffith is both making faces like they smell a cow shit under the table. And that when I see from right across that big bar room the black eye of Mr Flewelling flying at our table like a bullet. Now the thinking come to me he sent me as a interruption, not jes a hand what can carry a glass.

'Are you going to the New Year's ball, Miss Athelstan?' Gertie ask the flopping Violet.

'I am if someone invites me to,' Violet say.

'Do you have a young gentleman?' You can tell Gertie jes being extra perlite. She don't rilly think Violet have anything what fit that description.

'Well, let me see. Oh, that's right, I got two men interested in marrying me. But one aint young and the other aint a gentleman.'

Griffith push back his chair to stand up but Violet lay hold of his arm. 'What about you, Mr Flewelling? Are you going to the ball?'

Everone's eye fly to Violet's hand on Griffith's arm.

He suddenly laugh and pat her hand like that the most natural thing in the world. 'Yes, I'm going to the ball.'

'Who yer taking?' Violet don't ask this playful. It like she brung out a knife.

'I'm taking my young lady, of course.'

Violet sure that's her and take off her hand. Then she smiling to herself, but she so drunk it all look twisted. While she do her show of twitchy eyebrows and smirky lips I see Gertie staring at her handsome son. She about to ask a question but her husband now striding over like he had enough of waiting for the table to explode. He sweep her up in a dance while she twittering about her poor feets. Griffith take the chance to vanish, and me and Violet sit staring at each other again. Only for a moment, soon she sag down and fall asleep in a plate of gravies. Caradoc quite a good dancer, swirl Gertie around like a rag doll, she don't even need her poor feets, and she got her head flung back like she a young girl in a perfic dream.

Then in come the King.

The band stop, the dancing stop, Caradoc drop Gertie in a chair and go over for the handshaking, soon all them important arses is surrounding King Sale like a pack of licky dogs. Prosper wheel out a crissmiss cake, everone fill up their glasses, and King Sale make a speech to a oil painting of a fat old dame in jools and a long veil. Everone drink, then the King cut the first slice of cake to a lot of clapping. The cake disappear again, the band strike up and out march a whole line of scrubbers carrying them flaming puddings. There's a lot of confusion while everone find their tables again, so I drink two half glasses of wine quick as what a wink is before going back to Ludo.

Ludo now so drunk he sit still as a headstone in his chair. He look like anyone knock him he jes gonna tip right over, gonna topple straight onto them floorboards and crack. Fortunatus help everone to pudding and brandy sauce like he the Proper Papa. While I eat my pudding what's so sweet and rich I feel a bit sick I look over at King Sale sitting with Mr and Mrs Flewelling. I sure glad to see Violet gone.

Pretty soon out come the crissmiss cake again, now all cut up in small squares, a plate for each table. I don't even want to look at it. Then I see the dirty little girl what Fortunatus call Clementine piling pieces up in a cloth napkin what she sure aim to steal from Mr Flewelling. When I think about tea and damper, damper and tea, it seem like a very good idea.

Ludo in no state to walk home so Mr Flewelling give us a room up the stairs that have a big soft bed in it. Ludo so drunk he don't know where he is. He sit on the bed moaning and I haffta take off his fish tail, his boots, his trouser. After a big struggle I put him under the blankets. I climb in beside him and everthing wobble. It like sleeping on a tapioca pudding. Before I put out the light I look around them walls what sure is creepy, long shadders running up this picture of leafs and flours that go all over the room.

Next thing I know it morning, it raining and Ludo groaning. Everthing gloomy. Ludo put on his clothings and then he start cursing while he get on his boots.

'What're we doing here, tell me that,' he say when the job done.

'Yer too fucked to walk home.'

'Watch it, laddie, I'll have to clean out yer dirty mouth with carbolic.'

But Ludo too clapped out to catch me.

'What did you think of yer first night in an hotel?' he ask, looking around the room with a frown.

'I get a backache in that pudding bed. And that picture gimme the creeps.'

'That aint a picture. That's wallpaper.'

'What's it for?'

'To cover up the naked walls.'

'That green make me feel sick like a dog.'

'Bilious, aint it?' Ludo agree with a laugh. 'But it's the musty air in here that makes you feel sick. This room's been fancied up with imported wallpaper but you can still smell the mould. That's the trouble with hotels. Every nook and cranny has been plugged up and the room can't breathe.'

Downstairs is nothing but a big mess and Prosper at the bar drinking tea. He eyeball me when I walk past with Ludo.

'Hey sonny,' he call out. 'You get back here with a fish for Gertie's lunch, yer hear me?'

'When did yer get that job?' Ludo ask as we go out the door.

'Only very recent.'

Then very slow we make our way home to our hut. Ludo now very happy. His hut have very many holes to do its breathings from.

Soon as I get Ludo home I haffta go off fishing in the rain. It pissing down. By the time I standing on the slippery river bank them waters is lapping at my feets. But I scared not to take Prosper his fish, his big sausage fingers snuff me out like a candle. The fish I catch aint very big but what I care, it getting late. I run to the hotel and slap it down in front of Prosper. Forget the cream sauce, I say, Gertie like it plain. Then it aint very long till I carrying a fry fish up them stairs again.

Gertie struggle to sit up in her pudding bed on them cloud of pillows. She smile but it crooked because the red stuff on her lips gone all over the place in the night. The black stuff on her eyes gone awandering too. She look a real mess. And her room is fresh done out in them green bilious wallpapers. This the first time I notice.

'Put the tray on the sofa please, Halfie, and fetch me a drink of water from the decanter. I'm so thirsty.'

She gulp it down like she a camel in the desert.

'There a fry fish that I catch,' I say, pointing to the tray.

'Oh no, Halfie, I ate far too much last night. I feel ill.'

'Ludo say it them wallpapers.'

'What?'

'Ludo say they stop the breathings of the room.'

Gertie laugh. 'Now there's a man looking for any excuse to get away from society.'

I nod. 'Ludo say society is ruin.'

She make me fetch her more water and she say, 'What about you, Halfie? Don't you like my new wallpaper? I ordered it from Melbourne. It's called Trellis by William Morris.'

'That stuff got a name?'

Gertie nod.

How I say I don't like her trellisbywilliammorris? Gertie look so pleased with it, I say it lovely.

'Now pass me my medicine, Halfie. Yes, that's right, the bottle with Fowler's written on it. Thank you, dear.'

She gulp down half the bottle and I ask again about the fish. She say I can eat it if I want. She pat the bed where I haffta sit with the plate. It one of them fishes that taste of mud, and the fry job Fatso done aint very good.

'Tell me, Halfie,' Gertie now say in a tone what alert me, 'have you seen Griffith out walking with a young lady?'

Violet aint a lady so I tell the truth when I say no.

'It's just that last night he said he was taking his young lady to the New Year's ball.'

'I heared him,' I agree.

'I wonder who he means.'

'Mebee that Ginger.'

'Oh no.' Gertie look shocked. 'She's a pavement nymph.'

Violet tell me that's a perlite name for a scrubber.

'Come here, honey, I want to ask you a favour.'

I sit closer to Gertie and she look in my eyes and ask me to follow Griffith about the town. She say he in Hokitika till after the ball. She take a ten shilling note out of her uma and say it for my expenses. I ask what them things are, and she say a decent young lady don't often agree to meet on a street corner, mebee I haffta pay to follow her in somewhere, mebee the opera house, or mebee I haffta eat some cakes at the tea shop. I take Gertie's note thinking how this the easiest coin I ever earn, one of them feets-up jobs like her husband got down at the bar. Can't say, no, it only Violet yer son snogging in a grog shanty, it only greedy stringy Violet what's also snogging yer husband.

FIVE

Next day it pouring and the river spill over them banks and come visiting the town. All them diggers what come for the crissmiss the street sports and the New Year ball now being rowed about in little boats. They so drunk they smile like stupid kings. It wipe the smiles off their faces if only they knowed how much Hokitika town tryna part them from their gold.

Griffith Flewelling come out of the Bathsheba all done up. His boots squeak when he walk. He going to the street races for sure, but why he bother with his clothings so much? Mebee this the day he gonna ask Violet to marry with him. I hope he aint gonna do it in the main street. Not only do he get mud and rat shit on the knee of his trouser, his father shoot him. I think mebee I better follow him and earn some of them expenses. Gertie get so upset if she see her poor son dying in the street.

Griffith don't go to Revell Street, he go into one of them more fancier hotels. I settle down outside, not sure how long I haffta wait, but soon enough out come Griffith with a lady and a old man. The lady is all done up in yella, colour of a kowhai flour, and she look more prettier than gold. I follow them when they go down the street. They don't notice, they in a world of their own. Then at a mud puddle the lady lay hold of Griffith's arm and I see trouble with a capital T. That pretty lady laying hold of Violet's Griffith don't plan to let go, and he don't want her to neither.

Now I don't know what to do. Jes know I can't tell Gertie. For sure she like to hear how her big boy find hisself a pretty lady, but who know how far that news travel? Perhaps all the way down them stairs to where Violet is scrubbing in the kitchen. Then she fly ranting and crying at Griffith when he come in. Flewelling senior get me by the ear and say, why that little bitch care what happen between my son and that girl? It make me shudder jes to imagine it.

But anyway I rilly curious about them two, Griffith and Goldie, and following them is like following a sun beam when the day is miserable. Mebee they think they can step away from Trouble, but that's more like leaving the earth. They go to Revell Street where the crowd is piling up. I push into the front. Already the half drown diggers is doing the egg and spoon. Goldie and Griffith laugh and paw, but not like Violet in the grog shanty, none of them wriggly tongues come out. Dunno if Griffith see me but he act like he don't. I jes happy I don't see no one else that might be trouble. Jes see One Eye, Ginger and the Gang of Rags but they aint part of this particular problem.

After all the doings Griffith take Goldie and the old man back to the hotel and don't come out again. I figure they all eating a fancy meal, one of them that have sherries and soups and go on for hours. I go back to the Bathsheba and find Violet alone in the big room the dancing girls live in. She trying on a dress for the ball in front of a big mirror.

'What yer think, Harvey?' she ask me, showing herself off. The dress is red and shiny and her uma don't even want to be in there, they everwhere like the things what hang off a cow.

'Nice.' I feel guilty now. It were Violet what got me a job with coin, it were Violet what teach me the spellings and the grammar.

'Nice?' She seem cross.

'More'n nice,' I say like she want me to. 'It rilly pretty.'

Violet look in the mirror and hold up her yella hair. She tell me she gonna stick it up with a fancy comb and a flour.

'Who all going to this ball?'

'How should I know? Anyone can go. You jes haffta buy a ticket.'

'Can I go?'

'Yer got any money, Cinderella?'

'Got ten shillings.'

Violet look all mean and squinty. 'Where yer get that? More earnings from Ginger's pussy?'

'No it aint. Who this Cinderella?'

'Never mind, I aint got time to explain that now. But if you turn up, stay away from me, d'you hear? I have to tell Griffith about the baby and I don't want you hanging around messing up my chances.'

I creep out the door. I wanna sit on the beach or up a tree but it pissing cats and dogs. So I haffta do my thinkings in a little cave in the bush. It go drip drip drip while my brain whirl. All sorts of imaginings play in my head. The worst is Violet telling Griffith about the baby in front of Goldie. Griffith go throthing crazy. Then Papa Flewelling hasten to the commotion, soon it everwhere bleedings and stabbings. After that Gertie a widder, the Bathsheba get sold and poor little Halfie aint got no more coin. Seem I haffta do something, but what?

It come to me I need help. But who I get help from? Then a light come on in my head. The man I think of aint no good but he smart and know how to get things done. I run back to Hokitika town and soon I knocking on One Eye's door.

'Well, if it aint the little fuck. What yer want?'

'Haffta talk.'

'Talk? What you got to say to me?' One Eye scratch his balls through the holes in his long johns and look ugly.

'It a job I want you to do.'

One Eye burst out laughing.

'I got ten shillings.'

'Ten shillings, eh? I don't get out of bed for that.'

Seem we going the way of them bleedings and stabbings. I done what I can. But then Ginger come along the street. When she arrive at the door she crush me to her uma. She jes ignore One Eye, and soon I inside eating a old bit of crissmiss cake. Then Ginger go out the room to take off her wet clothings.

I blurt out, 'Yer gotta stop Violet telling Griffith Flewelling she having a baby. She gonna tell him at the ball.'

'She's expecting to him?' One Eye seem like he got a real intrest.

'And his Papa.'

The air feel like yer can slice it with a knife.

Then Ginger bustle back in, bustle around with the coal scuttle, she all the time chattering, aint even noticing the loaf of air.

'Ten shillings?' One Eye say, coming out of his deep thinkings.

I nod.

'Ten shillings for what?' Ginger ask.

'For nothing. You can keep yer money, Cocoa. I'll do yer little asking for free.'

I rilly pleased when he say this. One Eye do a job for me and I keep my coin.

'What little asking?' Ginger seem suspicious.

'Cocoa here wants a ticket to the ball. Course he aint old enough, so he ask me to . . .'

'I have tickets,' Ginger cut him off. 'I've been selling them at that freezing booth all afternoon.' She take some out of her uma and wave them at us.

One Eye snatch one and hand it to me.

'You better come to the door I'm on,' Ginger say. 'Don't know if the others will let a half-pint in, even if he does have a ticket.'

'Jes clear a few glasses if anyone starts looking at you funny,' One Eye instruct.

Then he go and open the door. When I again standing in the rain, out of earshot from Ginger, I ask if we got a deal. Sure, he say, but you keep yer little pie hole shut or we all eating shotgun.

There's a few more nights till the ball so I go home to Ludo. I tryna avoid any more trouble. Sure there what Ludo call loose threads flying around Hokitika town, Gertie wondering what happen to them expenses, mebee Prosper thinking where is a fish, Fortunatus asking what happen to his tin cup – but what I care? On the way home I buy Ludo some mutton at a different store to Fortunatus, and I make sure I use my own coin not a ten shilling note so talk don't go round. Ludo aint too drunk when I get back to the hut and he sure look pleased when I open up my meat parcel. He send me out in the bush to collect wood. It hard to find dry wood these days, but we get our little stove going and soon we roasting up the meat with some old potatas. While we eat I get to thinking how hard it is to spend all my coin, everone always watching me and counting.

'Ludo, I been thinking of getting a new job.'

'Dint know you had a job, laddie.'

'I been doing the plate clearings and sweepings at the Bathsheba. How yer forgetting?'

'That aint a real job, laddie. Caradoc's jes doing you a favour.'

'Mebee it aint a real job but it real work.'

Ludo take a swig of his bottle then a big bite of mutton.

'I wanna earn more coin. I never get enough to . . .'

'To what?' Ludo look at me careful, still going chew chew chew.

I shrug.

'To get out of here?'

'You can come too.'

Ludo put down his old plate and start poking at the fire in the stove.

'I can earn us a lot of coin and we can live in a hotel.'

'I told you I don't want to live in an hotel. Those wallpapers would be the death of me.'

'Well, mebee we get a cottage in Revell Street.'

'And maybe we get washed out to sea when a storm tide comes in.'

Ludo sure stubborn.

'Yer jes gonna sit here in the bush till you die?'

'I went to Caradoc's Christmas dinner, dint I?'

'One trip to Hokitika town a year? That all?'

'I'm an old man, laddie. Too old for adventures.'

'A cottage aint a adventure.'

Ludo don't want to talk about it no more. He say he had more adventures in his life than all them diggers in West Cantaberry put end to end.

Ludo light his pipe, take another swig and I do a bit of cleaning up. The rain come hard on the roof. I haffta place a few old pots for the leaks, but still everthing seem cozy and safe. I haffta agree with Ludo that safe feeling aint much to do with wallpapers and beds like clouds.

'Violet having a tamaiti,' I say when I finish the cleaning. The word jes come to me.

'A what?'

'Little baby. She having a little baby.'

'Surely not. She aint married.'

'No she aint,' I agree.

'But she should be married,' Ludo start spluttering. 'She should be married in the eyes of the Lord.'

'This Lord, what he care what Violet do?'

Ludo look shocked. 'Dint yer Papa teach you anything?'

'My Papa not that sort.'

'I'm talking about the Son of God. The God who made Heaven and Earth. Who commanded that men and women be married before bearing children.'

'If he organising everthing, why he don't stop the babies coming till after the wedding? Seem like poor planning to me.'

Ludo shake his head mournful. 'You can't speak like that, laddie, it's blasphemous.'

I heared this blasfemus word a lot of times. It mean when you act the way yer made, even though God do the making.

Ludo suck on his pipe.

'Well, spill the beans,' he finally say. 'Who's the father?'

'I dunno.'

'Come now, you spend enough time with her. Even if she aint telling, you must see her out and about with someone.'

'Never.' It make me a bit squirmy telling more lies to Ludo. Why I start this fucken conversation?

'Well, maybe I'll have a word to Caradoc. He sees fit to come here and point out the shortcomings of Yours Truly. But what about that poor girl? Aint she meant to be under his protection? Do you think her poor Mama would have let her come to such a wild outpost without someone to look after her?'

Here a tumble of words that set my heart going hard. First, Yaws Trooley is in there causing trouble again, second, what Caradoc do when he hear from Ludo that Violet having a baby? He think, that little Bedwetter find out something he oughtn't to know, then he go blabbing it!

'I think the Papa is One Eye,' I say quick.

'That lad from the gang?'

I nod hard.

'Did Violet tell you this?'

I shake my head. 'I seen them wriggling.'

Now Ludo look shocked again.

'I means their tongues,' I say even more quicker.

Ludo sigh.

Then he have a long suck on the bottle.

Night of the ball come round. I tell Ludo I haffta do the plates. I ask if he can clean me up. He get out his kerosene his shoe polish his clothings brush. He at me for what seem like hours. Then I shining like a new pin.

'Dunno if I make it back tonight,' I say.

'Ee that's alright, laddie, I know how you love the wallpaper.'

I say no to the lantern he offer. I a boy what can go in the dark across all them roots and tangles. I pretend to be a tiger in the jungly. Ludo always say, no it J-U-N-G-L-E, but jungly sound more dark and twisty.

When I get to Hokitika town I walk down Revell Street and get to the Corinthian Hall pretty soon. It on the sea side of the street and made of iron that Ludo call corrugate. Ludo also say it a bit of a dump, but tonight they done it up. I find the door where Ginger take the tickets. Inside it sure is beautiful, all them chandeliers, and the music is lovely, not jes one or two playing but a whole pile of different sound boxes that I aint ever seen before.

First person I see is Violet, second is Griffith, third is Goldie with the old man, fourth is Mr Flewelling with One Eye chewing his ear. All of them in different corners. Mebee I imagine it but they all flicking around their eyes, looking for what their hearts set on. Mr Flewelling flicking at Violet, Violet flicking at Griffith, Griffith flicking at Goldie, and that where the circle stop and turn back to Griffith. And only One Eye to stop the stabbings.

Then the band begin a dance tune. One Eye walk right up to Goldie, take her in his arms and press her to his trouser like he been dancing the ladies all his life. She too perlite to say eff off. Her Papa frown hard. Then, before Violet can do anything, Ginger sweep across the floors and do a extravagant curtsy to

Griffith. Violet look like a big storm but too bad, Griffith do the decent thing and dance Ginger off.

They dance past Violet. Ginger laugh with her head back, big mouth open like a mine shaft. At jes the right moment she grab his nono and Violet look like she gonna explode with rage. But Goldie don't see it, she been danced into a dark corner by One Eye. It all so fun I take a big throthy glass off a table and drink it down jes to celebrate.

For the next dance everthing change. One Eye take Violet, Ginger take Mr Flewelling, now Griffith free to take Goldie and he do. Course Violet aint perlite, she find it easy to tell One Eye to eff himself, but it seem she all mixed up. She think it better for Griffith to dance with Goldie, jes as long as it aint Ginger, that slut what makes free with men's arses. Then there's a break and some drinks, more drinks for Halfie, but when the dances start again Griffith and Goldie gone. Violet don't know nothing about Goldie, she jes see Ginger still in the place, so she laugh and carry on with Papa Flewelling. He tryna slap her down like she a bitch what want a dog.

I been creeping in the shadders all this time, anybody that see me jes think I working. Now I creeping out the door. There's a big moon, but horses drunks and loose animals is filling up the street, I can't see them lovebirds anywhere. Then I get a idea and run off to the fancy hotel that Goldie stay at. I get a box, look in them winders all hung up with lace, sure enough there Griffith and Goldie sitting in them velvet chairs, he holding her hand. They staring right into each other's eyes like they wanna climb in there. It clutch my heart. I seen that look before. It the look Moana get when she see the man she pick out for herself. She go in them bushes with me, the man come, they look inside each other but something wrong. A tear come out of Moana, it slide down her cheek, it go drip drip drip. There aint no drips from Goldie. She think everthing fine. She aint got to the crying part yet.

I tired and dizzy and I seen enough of the stupid ball. Look like One Eye and Ginger have everthing worked out, they stopped Violet from making her announcement that explode the town. But I dint get no supper, so I look for a store that's open. I expected Fortunatus were at the ball or I don't even walk past, but he still standing outside looking to hook in them late customers. Course he shout out to me. I go over to him, ask how much is a compensation.

'A what, Sonny Jim?'

I point to them yella things that are on show outside.

'They're called bananas. All the way from Fiji, they are. But they're far too much for you.'

'What else yer got?'

'Tell yer what, if you come for a little walk with me I'll give you a banana for free.'

'Little walk where?'

'To the tent Clementine lives in.'

'But that's miles away.'

'Well, yes. We'd haffta get the coach along the beach.'

I aint been long at the ball, it still early, but one binarna seem a bit mean for a long trip. 'Some of them binarnas is in a joinment. Mebee you give me one of them ones.'

Fortunatus look at me hard. 'Yer a shrewd little bugger, I'll give you that.'

'Spose yer gonna tell Prosper I buy a joinment of binarnas.'

'I won't tell if you don't.'

'What I got to tell?' I surprised. Why I tell Prosper I buyed binarnas? He have me fishing for him for years.

'I mean, if you don't tell about us visiting Clementine.'

'Why I can't tell about that?'

'Look, Harvey, I want to look after her. Jes like Ludovic looks after you. But folks have some funny ideas. So I got to do it in secret, you understand? But jes in case anyone sees me . . .'

'It dark. Everone at the ball,' I interrupt.

'We're not going tonight, you silly boy! We haffta go when the coach goes.'

'When that?'

'Day after tomorrow.'

I sigh big. I getting a bit sick of all my days being used up with other people's plans.

'So if you come with me,' Fortunatus carry on, 'well, that'll make it alright then, won't it?'

I don't rilly see how, but I getting more hungrier all the time. I say to him it a deal, jes gimme something to eat. Fortunatus give me a joinment, then he go locking up his store and I sit down on a bench in front for a feed. Them binarnas sure is lovely but Fortunatus aint happy when he see all them yella undressings lying in the street.

'How do we keep our secret if you scatter the skins about?' he grumble. He walk all around and pick them up, then take them out the back where the rubbish pile up.

I go home to Ludo. I were wanting to take him a binarna but I dint want no trouble like with them eggs. Ludo reading his Bible. Once I tell him a different story about the makings of the world, it were one that Papa told me. But Ludo say my story aint true. I say, how you know yer own story true? He say the Lord tell him. I ask, when the Lord talk to you? Ludo say the Lord talk all the time into his heart. What, jes go whisper whisper whisper? Ludo nod. I dint say nothing but I reckon it Jimmy Bottle what's whispering all the time inside Ludo.

Ludo ask me about the ball and I give him a good thrilling telling. He say I home pretty early for so much fun and who they got collecting them plates and glasses? I think of something that make sense, then I get busy making us some tea. It seem if I keep talking Ludo soon have me on them ropes. We drink our tea and Ludo light his pipe, start telling me a story from his Bible.

He say once there were a man that got sick and lie down on the road. That seem pretty stupid to me. I imagine him lying in the Pass where One Eye and the Gang of Rags pick out his pockets. Ludo say no, another man come along and help him, a man called Good Simaritan. I too perlite to say it aint rilly much of a story. Ludo look stern and say, so you see, you haffta help them people what lie down on the road.

'Even if they drunk?' I ask.

Ludo nod.

'What – go around all night picking up them drunks off Revell Street?'

Ludo nod but a little bit of doubt go across his eyeballs.

'What I do with them?'

Ludo wait a bit then say, 'You jes prop 'em up against a wall so they don't drown in their own spew.'

'Why you don't do it?'

'Ee laddie, I aint got the strength to pick up drunks. But a man does what he can.'

'What you do?'

'I've got you.'

'But I don't need no picking up.'

Ludo pat me on the head. We give a big smile to each other. But I don't unnerstand his stupid story. I a boy who got coin. I a boy that can look after hisself.

Next morning I go to the river in Hokitika town. I gonna catch a fish for me and Ludo. But first I go past the Bathsheba to see what's going on. One Eye is jes then coming out the front door and see me.

'Hey, Cocoa, come over here.'

I go over dragging my feets.

He collar me and pull me round the back of the hotel.

'I done yer little job,' he say, seeming very pleased with hisself.

I get out my ten shillings.

'No, I told you I don't want yer money. Caradoc Flewelling jes paid me.'

Not sure what he mean but this a nasty surprise.

'Yair, I told him I know his dirty little secret. And if he dint want his wife to find out, he better cough up.'

My stomick suddenly feel funny.

'That solved one problem. Caradoc left the ball straight off. Then I looked around for the other trouble, but he was gone too. Ginger and me had a nice time for a while, then Junior came back.'

I all atremble.

'I fixed Junior the same way. Told him if he dint want Goldie to find out he's the kind of man who goes about making bastards . . . well, I'm jes off to collect from him now. He goes back to his claim today.'

One Eye hook his thumbs in his braces and stick out his chest. 'I'm sure glad you did me this favour, Cocoa. Blackmailing is a whole lot easier than robbing.'

I watch him go down the street, off to milk Griffith.

I still standing there when Violet come out. She see me and make a face. She go flouncing off down the street, opposite way to One Eye. I run and catch up. She stop and tell me to go away, she got important business down at Evan Prosser's Drug Hall. I follow her anyway. She all the time tryna swipe me but I faster than a sandfly. We get to the drug hall but she tryna stop me coming in.

'What yer getting you don't want me to see?'

'If I don't want you to see, I aint gonna tell you, am I? Are you fucken stupid or something?'

I try to soften her up. 'Dint you have fun at the ball last night?'

'I did for a while.'

'Then what go wrong?'

'Don't get funny with me, little boy. I saw you in the shadows.'

Seem she don't know what to do now. Moment come for her to flounce in the shop but she know I come in after. Then she grab my arm, pull me away from the doors and say Caradoc found out she having a baby.

'It weren't me what tell,' I say quick.

'I know it weren't you, stupid. If it were you, you'd be effing dead.'

'Who were it then?'

'He says one of the other girls seen me chucking up. He says he put two and two together.'

Two and two what?

'So now everthing is messed up. How can I marry Griffith if I'm expecting to his father?'

'You were before.'

'Before what?'

'Before the father find out.'

Violet stare at me mean. 'Are you tryna be clever?'

I shake my head.

After thinking for a moment she sure I too stupid to be clever. 'Well, it's all different once he knows, aint it? So the baby has to go.'

'Go where?'

'Heaven.'

'Yer gonna kill a poor little baby?'

'Ssh,' she hiss at me. 'It's jes like taking a shit.'

Then she give me a big shove, tell me to go home to the stinky hatter. I so shocked I let the shove turn into a run. I run because I haffta tell Ludo that Violet gonna murder a poor helpless bubba. Jes because it a whitey one don't mean it none of my concern. But when I get back to the hut Ludo is more drunker than I ever seen him.

SIX

The day come when I haffta go to Greymouth. That's the trouble with taking the payment first, when it come time to do the job yer gone off the whole idea. I meet Fortunatus at the store. He done up in a black suit like a bridegroom. He shaved and oiled and carrying a open sack what have joinments of binarnas poking out.

'Let's go down to the highway,' Fortunatus say. This a good joke. The beach is the only highway. The beach full of fancy horses and packhorses, men with swags, bullock wagons and Rowley's Express Line, that's the coach to Greymouth.

'It takes only six hours,' Fortunatus say pleased. What, one joinment of binarnas give me six hours of Fortunatus? Godsaveus! He already sweating in the heat, his suit so hot and tight. Then when I see him pay the coin I nearly fall down on the sand. It thirty shillings each. And what about them rivers, the Arahura and the Taramakau? What if they running too full for the ferries and six hours turn into six days? Fortunatus melt inside his wedding suit and jes his stink pour out all over me.

Lucky for us the rivers aint up and the ferries have a easy time.

But the tide on the beach is a whole other thing. It all the way gobbling up the sand, and sometimes a wave throw itself at us, drench us to the bones. Fortunatus is angry his bridegroom suit get wet. He say the coach driver a madman that drive too close to the ocean. But another man what ride with us say that the way it haffta be, that where the hard sand is, and it the hard sand what make the good time. I don't say nothing. I sure aint having a good time stuck between the sweat and the salt water.

At least Fortunatus feed me. He aint giving me binarnas, but he brung plenty of bread and cold mutton. And when I aint being sprayed by them waves I can sleep. Ever time I wake up Fortunatus grumble how anyone can sleep in such a commotion. When we been going for hours and nearly there, he start pulling at his collar like it gonna hang him and he start talking of wards again. He rilly annoy me when he talk. He say it a teerible thing for a little girl to live alone in a tent because her father in gaol and her mother gone off to the goldfields with her skirts over her head.

'I'll be glad when the tramway is laid along the beach,' Fortunatus declare to the driver as he gets down at the stopping place. 'Then you won't be able to select yer own course along the sand.'

'It will be an excellent day to be sure,' the driver agree. 'One can only hope that the tram track will always be higher than the reach of the breakers.'

We hasten to the tent where Clementine live. I ask Fortunatus how he first know her and he give me a mumble story hard to unnerstan. It seem to involve the *West Coast Times* and tracking them poor children what gaol and gold turn into orphans.

We get to the tent and Fortunatus tell me to say hello. When I go in the flap, Clementine asleep on a pile of old clothings. I poke my head out and tell Fortunatus. He look impatient and say to wake her up, he got a binarna he want to give her right away.

I put in my head again and shake her foot. She spring up like a animal in a cave. That's when Fortunatus come crashing in and she give a squeal like a sticked poaka.

'Shut up,' he growl. 'Someone might hear you.'

But she don't shut up. Her squeal turn into a scream that wake up all the ngingongingo in Mawhera. Fortunatus panic, try to put his hand over her mouth. But she bite him like the little beast she is.

'Clementine, it me,' I shout. Surely she rememory me from the crissmiss dinner?

Nope, or she don't want to, or she think I also in the pay of Fortunatus and come to do her evil. But now Fortunatus put down the bag of food and make some noises to calm her, then he back out of the tent, and when I look at him tears start pouring down his face like his heart is broke.

So that were the end of our adventure in Greymouth. That were the end of Clementine becoming a ward. We walk to a hotel for the night. It rilly seedy but what I care when Fortunatus pay for our bed and dinner? It turn out to be a big bowl of nice shellfishes. It been a long day and I soon asleep. Even if the bed aint a cloud but a big sagger that swallow me up like a whalefish.

The rivers aint so agreeable on the way back to Hokitika town. They throth and rear up like lunatic horses. On the way there I were thinking six hours with Fortunatus a hellish burden, now it seem like Heaven. On the return he talk and talk and talk, half melon cow lick, half angry, he talk like talking wipe away everything what jes happen with Clementine. I don't listen to what he say. I jes stare at the river or the ocean or the bent trees or whatever go swishing past.

Fortunatus elbow me in the ribs. 'Hey, Sonny Jim, aint yer gonna answer my question?'

'What question were that?'

'Why yer run away from yer own people?'

I say it because Moana die and I were too sad to stay.

Fortunatus nod and don't ask no more.

But now he brung up the rememorying. Now I haffta think about it all again. It do seem a long time ago, but the thinking come up in me that the little boy who look down on them dressed up ships dint rilly know why he were doing anything. It only the bigger boy he grow into that know. It sure a funny thing growing up is like that. Like yer hinengaro haffta get bigger than yer life. Dunno what happen at the end though, how yer hinengaro grow big enough to unnerstand the last day?

Mebee I don't think about that, it make my head go dizzy.

When I get back to Ludo he muss my hair and tell me not to sleep out nights, it aint good for me. I sure happy to be back in the hut. More'n more I see why Ludo prefer a hut to what he call society. In a hut you can sit in yer long johns by a fire and drink. You can shout and sing and swear and laugh. You aint all the time B-E-S-E-T by yer fellow men. And what I jes been on but a most horrid besetting? I eat my fry damper and bit of cold mutton, then I lie down by the stove feeling happy as a old dog.

The morning come. I haffta go off to the Bathsheba and see Violet. I haffta argue with her, argue so much she give in and say, alright, I keep the little blighter, I don't strangle it in the cradle. But then I rememory again that Caradoc know about the baby. Mebee he pin it on me for telling One Eye. I start thinking, where is a place no one find me for a while?

'Ludo,' I say. 'I got a job I haffta do.'

'Eh?' He been cleaning the wax outta his ears, mebee it aint done yet.

'A job. I gotta do some deliveries. For Caradoc.'

'Deliveries? Where's he sending you?'

'Rosstown.'

'Then make sure he gives you the money for the ferry boat. I hear it costs two shillings.'

I sigh. Haffta go out and be beset again.

I pay my two shillings and take my place on the ferry boat. As it go along the river I get more and more glum. I get to thinking about that Mr Simaritan. If he say you haffta save them drunks, do you haffta save a baby from being murdered? How I do that? Snatch it from out of the cradle and run off into the bush? Mebee I take it to Papa, but I pretty sure he say, that aint one of ours, take it back, are you tryna get all our heads blowed off? That only leave Ludo. He go crazy about eggs, what do he say when I turn up with a bubba?

I get off the ferry and soon arrive in Rosstown. It a curious thing for me to be there. It have different stores where no one know me. I can look in and no one collar me. No one say, where you get yer coin, Bedwetter? It sure intresting to me. Everwhere is diggers and everwhere is stores with big signs saying they sell everthing that's needed for gold getting, everthing that's needed for living on yer claim, calico tents, lantern, camp oven, blankets. Everone shouting and buying, them that already buyed everthing stand smoking and drinking in the grog shanties.

Then I see a most awful sight. Down the main street go Griffith, Goldie and the old man. The first two is clutching arms. It come to me the old man is her Papa and Rosstown is the place they live in. I also now sure it the town that Griffith's claim is near. That's how they meet, that's how Goldie and her Papa come to Hokitika town. Here were me thinking Griffith go back to them diggings and Goldie go over to East Cantaberry and Violet's problem go away. But no. Here her problem walking down the street in a dress that look like it come off a princess. Now I certain that little baby haffta be saved. If Griffith think it stop him from marrying with his Goldie, he gonna be the one that butcher it in its cradle.

I still have enough coin for a good feed. I find a hotel with a dining room. I have a mutton stew and bread that aint damper. The waitress look at me like a criminal and take my money before the food come, that aint right I know, but then she give me a sweet smile when it turn out I aint a gobbler that run. I sit in my chair by the winder feeling good and then again I see Goldie coming down the street. Now she alone, except for a girl that look like a scrubber. They go into a clothings store.

Haffta say Goldie is a beautiful apparition in Rosstown. For a start, there aint that many ladies around, even less than in Hokitika town. Them important arses is all the time saying we gotta bring girls in on ships, if we bring in five hundred they all go off civilising them wild diggers inside a week. For another thing, most what's here aint Goldie's type, they all what Prosper call sluts. Truth is Griffith aint Goldie's type neither. His father come up in the world and Gertie come down, that's what Ludo say. Gertie come down to the gold that were coming up. Ludo say the money and the manners meet in Griffith but the handsomeness trump all. He say if you put Griffith Flewelling in a bonnet and crinolin he married with King Sale by lunch time.

By the time I done eating and looking at them stores it start to rain. I stand under a awning and see Griffith Flewelling going off to his claim. He all done up in his digger clothings and he walk like a happy man, not creeping through the storm. Then I put the ferryman's coin for going back in my pocket and look for a bed for the night. It sure a dive, it got a dirty sleeping room that look like a rat hotel and it full of all kind of scum belching and farting theirselves to sleep. The rain come hard on the roof. It a noise I rilly love, something I never say to whitey. They all the time praising Otago Victoria California, all them places they say is dry and hot like Heaven.

Yair, I love the rain on a tin roof, but woe, in the morning a flood come! At the dock the ferryman say no ferryings today. He look at the river and go all gloomy, it his coin what's going downstream, not ourselves. Soon there's a big group of angry diggers waiting in the rain.

One of the diggers look rilly disreputable. D-I-S-R-E-P-U-T-A-B-L-E is a word that Gertie spell me. It mean seedy, and that mean born low and getting lower. She say half of Hokitika town is that. This man waiting for the ferry boat wear a suit what's tore and that have a greenish black look to it. It look like a rock the slimy weed grow on. His hair is all wild, not short like them important arses, not long like the dancing girls, more like a halo but dirty brown.

The rain piss down so much we soon all trickling inside our clothings. Someone say we orta go to a hotel for shelter. The hotel he choose also disreputable. It aint sweeped clean like the Bathsheba, it aint got a Prosper cooking up them meats and gravies, only a skinny rag selling the drink, and insects everwhere. Soon we strangers sitting altogether at a table. I don't like seeing Mr Disreputable sitting next to me.

He smile at me. He aint old but his teeth is yella and all apart, they look like a old whitey graveyard. Then a digger ask him where he come from.

'Berlin. But before coming here, I am in Paris.'

'Don't sound like good places to find gold to me,' the digger say.

'They are not,' he agree.

'John Wicks,' the digger say holding out his hand for a shake.

Mr Disreputable say something I don't catch.

Wicks seem to lose intrest after that. He only talk to the diggers that sound like him.

Mr Disreputable turn to me and say, 'Where is your Papa, liebling?'

Dunno what kind of a insect that is, but I sick of everone asking where is my Papa. I say my Papa a fierce chief in Hokitika town what once show hisself for a shilling. I say Ludo were gonna take me to see him but he leave the circus before we go. And before Mr Disreputable can ask where is my Mama, I say she dead. And Moana too.

'Who is Moana?'

'She my tuahine. That's a sister.'

'And where are the others of your people?'

'They all down getting gold in Maori Gully.'

'Hmm,' he say like he aint believing something. Then he say, 'I am being on my way to the diggings on German Hill.'

'Where yer claim ezactly?'

'Nowhere.'

'What yer here for then?

'Adventure!' He say it like he leering. That's what Violet say the men do when they see her uma or pantalons. But there aint none of them things here so I don't unnerstand why he look like that.

'Why yer look so wicked and sly?' I ask.

'Wicked and sly? How are you seeing under my mask?'

'What's that?'

'Something that covers the face.'

'You aint wearing a mask.'

'Yes I am.'

I don't talk no more. This a madman that I sit beside.

Mr Disreputable take a half broke old book from out of his jacket pocket. Then he place it on the table while he fetch more beer. I steal a quick look inside, see his name written there, Kaspar Schmidt, and see a bunch of strange writings like I never seen before.

'Ah, you are liking my book, liebling,' Kaspar Schmidt say in my ear. He come back more quicker than I expect and make me jump.

'Don't even know what it say.'

Kaspar Schmidt put his beer on the table and sit down. He

grasp his book and say, 'I am translating some for you.'

Before I can say, no thanks, it aint intresting to hear what madmen read, he begin, 'Now it is clear, God cares only for what is his, busies himself only with himself, thinks only of himself, and has only himself before his eyes; woe to all that is not well pleasing to him. He serves no higher person, and satisfies only himself. His cause is a purely egoistic cause.'

Fuck, jes as well Ludo aint here to hear that.

'Look at the rest for yourselves,' Kaspar Schmidt carry on. 'Do truth, freedom, humanity, justice desire anything else than that you grow enthusiastic and serve them?'

Now I see some of them diggers shrinking away from him and throwing him evil looks out the corner of their eyes.

'Look at that Sultan who cares so lovingly for his people. Is he not pure unselfishness itself, and does he not hourly sacrifice himself for his people? Just try it; show yourself not as his, but as your own; for breaking away from his egoism you will take a trip to gaol. The Sultan has set his cause on nothing but himself; he is to himself all in all, he is to himself the only one, and tolerates nobody who would dare not to be one of "his people".'

That Sultan again? This lunatic know him too?

When Kaspar Schmidt finish his ravings and mysteries someone come running in saying a ferry boat going. Half them diggers run out into the rain and I follow. On the bank where the river flooded up to there's a drunk ferryman that say he take all of them that want to take the risk. Some men get in, then he say he can take one more, haffta be small. When I stand forth he nod and take my coin. The men is all nervous, chattering about drowning but also saying how they very busy and got to get back, can't wait for no river to calm down.

Then we go whooshing off. It sure a lot of fun for me, but them men in suits is turning green. I aint worried if we spill out, I get to the bank and pull up a tree branch that's hanging down. One thing

I happy about as we go along and that is Kaspar Schmidt put my bad worries out of my head, my worries about Goldie and Griffith and the poor baby. Seem every problem can be sorted out long as I aint like him. But I also hear down inside me a little voice saying, he sure a apparition, Halfie, not one like King Sale or the ghouls that flit around Ludo but something that's fascinating like gold.

When we come opposite the wharves but aint yet crossed the river, we see all them ships crowding the landing, we see a whole lot of men with boat hooks watching to see if we get swept out to sea and drown. The ferryman suddenly push out in the flow, the river rear up, and we whoosh along like we on the back of a bucking horse. Somehow he get us over to the wharf where them men with hooks reach out and grab us before we fly on to death. The men all happy and clap, but mebee Kaspar make me nasty because I love to see them suits and whiskers going in the drink.

I rilly happy to go home to Ludo. I feel like I been drowned inside my clothings, not by a angry river but the rain. When I take my clothings off, mebee only water there, mebee it pour out on Ludo's floor and he say, oh my, where poor little laddie go?

But when I get home, Ludo gone.

I do the sweepings, tidy Ludo's cot. I light the stove and boil the kettle. I make the damper same way Ludo show me. I put on a old big shirt of Ludo's so I can dry my clothings. I stuff balls of the *West Coast Times* in my wet boots the way Ludo show me. I eat a bit of damper and drink a mug of tea. Waiting for Ludo sure is nasty. It come to me he go on one of them satin walks and now he lying in the bush somewhere. Or he think he still a hatter, go looking for them hopes up a river that have a flood in it. I imagine Ludo floating out to sea, going round and round in them breakers. I hope he rilly drunk when the taniwha pull him down, mebee he don't notice he getting et.

I asleep on Ludo's cot when he come in. He throw the door

• 103 •

open loud, come in crashing and cursing. I expect he rilly drunk but he aint. Now it Ludo that's needing all them dryings and stuffings. He wrap hisself in his old blanket while he dry his clothings and long johns. I make tea for him, fry him up a piece of damper. But he don't fall on it like a hungry beast. He say he aint hungry, he already eat in Hokitika town. I ask him what he were doing there, and he say he go to see One Eye about Violet's baby.

This a big shock. I don't say nothing, jes try to imagine One Eye's face when he see Ludo at his door. I ask Ludo how he know where One Eye live, and he say he ask Caradoc. Caradoc say he aint sure ezactly, so Caradoc ask Prosper. Proper say, what yer wanna know for? Ludo say to me he think Prosper is very rude.

Now I all atremble waiting to hear what Ludo's reply were.

'So I said to Mr Dirago, well, if it's any business of yours, which it aint, I'm going to pay him a call to ask his intentions about Miss Athelstan.'

'And what Prosper say?'

'He say, what d'you mean intentions? So I tell him I heard she's expecting and Paddy O'Irish is the father.'

Oh, Godsaveus!

'Well, Caradoc was furious. He dint say a word, but I've known him such a long time, I could tell. His face went white as a sheet and he made fists with his hands. You know that aint easy for him to do with all his rheumatism. No doubt he gave his word to Miss Athelstan's Mama that he'd look after her, not let her give herself up to ruin.'

Now I afraid to hear the end of the story.

'Of course, being the man he is, Caradoc said he'd see to it. But I said no, in this instance I am taking it upon myself to be the Good Samaritan.'

Oh no, not him again, that Mr Simaritan causing a lot of trouble, I getting rilly sick of him.

'So I went to visit Mr O'Irish, and d'you know what, laddie? He laughed at me! Straight in my face. I said, listen son, this aint a laughing matter. He said, Mister, I wouldn't touch that slut with a boat hook. Then he slammed the door.'

I say One Eye a liar for sure.

Ludo nod.

Ludo sigh.

'What's the problem now?'

'Well, who's going to marry the poor girl?'

'Why yer don't let Mr Flewelling do the sorting? He more mean than you. He get a gun and make One Eye marry her.'

'That's what I'm afraid of,' Ludo say reaching for his bottle. He drink down two big glasses quick as what a wink is, and before you know it he start talking about the dinner that Prosper give him. He say enough meat to feed a army, enough spotty dick to keep Gertie happy for a whole year.

I soon lying in the dark listening to Ludo snoring. But I can't get no sleep. I worry and worry about seeing Mr Flewelling. He think a dancing girl tell One Eye about Violet but who do he think tell Ludo? Ludo aint the type that get the front of his trouser warmed. Mr Flewelling think, the person what told were that little Bedwetter! Now poor Halfie can't go to the Bathsheba ever again, he haffta get all his coin another way.

Seem I do get some sleep because one minute it dark of night, then it light of morning. I wake up and rememory my problem. I drag my feets at all my tasks. When I get water from the stream I very depressed. It come to me when I soak my feets in the sweet water that it aint any good jes to leave the Bathsheba, I haffta get a job out of Hokitika town. If I were at the Gridiron or the Bendigo or anywhere, Mr Flewelling still find me easy enough. So that mean I haffta leave Ludo. That give me two very big worries – one, what happen to Ludo when I go, and two, what happen to me?

'Chin up, laddie,' Ludo say when I come back with the bucket. 'The sky's already fallen.'

I put down the bucket. 'Ludo, I got a problem.'

'Oh? Yer jes a boy. What problem could you have?'

'Aint got no more job at the hotel.'

Ludo raise his eyebrows.

'It were my own doing,' I say quick. 'I say I need more coin, haffta do more than jes glasses and sweepings. Mr Flewelling say sorry, that's all he got.'

'So you quit, did yer?'

I nod.

'Well, how is that a problem? All around you there's gold for the taking. I was starting to wonder why you were still fetching gristle and crumbs out from under Caradoc's tables.'

'I dint think a boy were allowed to buy a claim.'

'Forget about a claim. Jes go along the beach and start digging. Haven't you seen the beach tailings?'

'Yair, I seen them.'

'Well then.'

'But where I live?'

'Under calico. Like the rest of them.'

'I aint got no calico.'

'You'll have to buy some.'

'Aint got enough coin.'

'Well, you should of saved up. Instead of buying eggs and what not.'

It aint strickly true I got no coin. But I tryna get around to them sad talkings about how we no longer be together.

'If I find some gold, what happen?' I ask. 'Them rough men jes come and push me out of the way.'

'Not if I'm there, they won't.'

I look at Ludo. 'But you aint there. Yer here drinking and seeing them apparitions.'

Ludo get a look on his face that seem to say he been planning a change. I sigh big. It all a lie to hisself. Ludo unnerstand my sigh. It seem I offend him.

'Listen, laddie,' he say, leaning in. 'I don't need to be sober to help you. I jes have to sit there on a log. Then the rough men say, there's that hatter who knows Caradoc Flewelling. And aint Caradoc the one who owns the Bathsheba, that fine hotel that's visited by Commissioner Sale? See? Suddenly you've got a circle around you.'

That sure is funny. King Sale go in the Bathsheba complaining about me drinking, next minute he somehow on the beach pertecting me. It don't rilly make no sense. But I aint got nothing to lose. Mebee I find a lot of gold, get inside them stiff sheets what Ludo hate, sit down with them parsons eating pork and cake.

'Sure, we'd have to give up this hut for a while.' Now Ludo look round like it the first time he think about it for real.

The hut is rilly a sorry sight so I don't see no problem. It sound like fun to camp out with Ludo, even if he drink a bottle every night. We get a campfire and a fish, mebee when the gold come even them mutton chops. We can have stars and the moon, prolly hear the happy piana music from the Bendigo. We hear them little waves lapping, then them birds, and the sun wake us up every morning. But then I look at Ludo and something very afraid come in his eyes.

'Why yer afraid?' I make bold to ask.

Now a look of shame come over him.

'I look after yer,' I say. 'You put a circle round me, I put a circle round yer.'

Ludo rub his big hands and laugh sort of nervous.

'Yer don't think I got a circle? Lemme tell you, I go to Papa and say, this the man that gimme a place by the stove, this the man that gimme a feed. Then he send them warriors, they gonna cook anyone what disagree.'

'When you did yer drinking, how did you feel?' Ludo suddenly ask.

'Tired.'

'Anything else?'

'All mixed up.'

'And?'

What's he waiting for? I have a hard think. Then I say, 'When Mr Sale first come in the doorway, he were a big shadder that look like a devil.'

Ludo nod. He shut his eyes. He tell me all around him is flying shadders. It like huge bats attacking him. Then he sober up and the Lord's light burn a hole in him. That's how it always go – dark light dark light, it all a hellish fantagasmoria.

'The beach fix you up,' I say pleading. 'Come to the beach and leave them fantagasmorias behind. I get us a lot of fish. You haffta help me Ludo, you haffta help me escape them washings and sweepings.'

Ludo keep shut his eyes and rock hisself.

I dunno what go on in his head but his face sure a sight. It go grimace smile grimace smile. No yes no yes no.

Yes? No! Yes? Yes!

Yes yes yes yes yes!

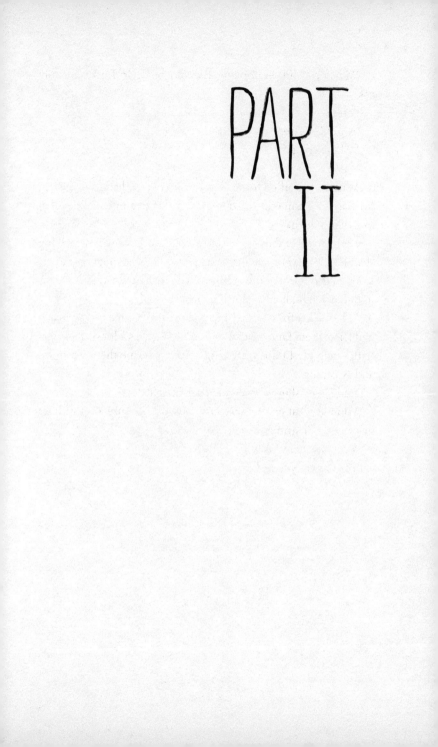

PART

II

SEVEN

Me and Ludo go down Revell Street and step onto the beach. Here a miner found gold right outside his front door what happen to be the flap of a tent pitched beside the Duke of York Hotel. Prolly we aint gonna be that lucky, so we haffta go along the beach. Ludo is more sprightly than what I expect. As we walk he go on and on about it being the black sand what have the gold in it, but prolly it aint rilly black, jes not blinding white like Ludo say them Barberry pirates have.

It a good day for Ludo. He smiling and chattering, he got his long grey hair in a little knot, he got on his fancy top coat that he say were made for him by tailors in California when he were rich as Croesus. C-R-O-E-S-U-S he spell me, dunno who he were, but mebee the digger that got the biggest nugget. And it a good day for me too, the sun is out, the waves is all blue and white even if a bit crashing and the wind strong. I hold Ludo's hand while we walk. It sure feel bony and dry like a old fish bone that's been lying on the beach. But it give me a good feeling as if I the one leading him out of P-E-R-D-I-T-I-O-N.

Back in the hut Ludo once give me lessons about perdition. He spell it out a lot of times for me because it have a T creeping in where a S orta be. Inglish aint a langwich that behave itself. Perdition is a place of fire, of weeping and nashing of teeth, where Ludo's Lord put them that done evil. It give me the shudders to imagine poor Ludo weeping and nashing in the fires, better he come along the beach, be some use to hisself and to me.

We look for a place to build our tent, but it only T-H-E-O-R-E-T-I-C-A-L at the moment because we haffta go to the store and buy some calico. I ask what theoretical mean, and Ludo say that's when something is still only a idea. I say, c'mon, it more than that. Soon we come to a big sand working. It got a ladder going down. Ludo look in and exclaim the hole is twenty five feets. When I look down them twenty five feets I can see a lot of streaks of black sand. I get rilly excited. Ludo tell me to go down the ladder and have a look.

I go down and at the bottom is men with long shovels, also water in wooden tubs. One of the diggers gets a shovel of sand, then he shake it in the tub of water till all the sand fall off and leave behind a pretty pile of gold dust. The men all stand around admiring until they see a little picaninny behind them and Ludo's old wrinkles looking down on them, then they say, scoot or we give you a good whack. When I back up the ladder Ludo shiver and say he don't go down that ladder for all the tea in china, who know when a big wave crash in and drown everone or when the sides cave in and plug up their breathings with sand.

We go along for quite a while and come to beach workings that look like a town. Everwhere is tents shovels tubs and strange beasts that Ludo say is cradles and sluice boxes. Everwhere is shouting and measuring out the beach, it sure look like the exact place to get rich. Ludo and me plop down in the sand. He take out the lunch, damper for me, and damper and bottle for him. I happy because I know when we live on the beach I find mussels and kina every day, we don't jes eat this tough old damper what's like eating cloth.

'Yer think this far enough?' I ask Ludo when we finish eating.

'Far enough for what?'

'Far enough away from Hokitika town.'

'Why would we care about that?'

'Aint a adventure if we jes camping near the town.'

Ludo sigh. 'It's already too far for me to go back and buy calico. You'll have to go.'

'Me?'

'Don't worry, I'll give you the money.'

I can't think of no objection to what Ludo say. It the thing to do. Aint I the one that's young and fit, the one that can run?

'When I go?' I ask a bit depressed.

'Now, if you don't want to sleep out tonight.' Ludo start getting out his fat purse from a hiding place deep in his clothings. He give me a lot of paper money, tell me to get a whole kit. Then he tell me how to wear it but I already seen how that done. Everwhere is diggers going about with their roll of blankets tied up with flax and tied the long way, not the side way, on the back so it don't get in no fights with them bushes that's everwhere hanging down. Then on the roll you hang yer shovel pick tin dish and billy, pretty soon you like a crissmiss tree. Ludo peel off another bit of paper money, say we haffta look the part, so get us each a wide-awake hat a sheath knife and a axe.

As I run along the beach I worry about the shopping, not jes about the choosing when I don't know a hat that's awake from a hat that's asleep but also about being seen by all them townfolk what's out to get me. I sure wish we done more thinking before we go for our theoretical. But it were hard enough jes to get Ludo out of his hut. I haffta try everthing. In the end I haffta say, Ludo, come for a walk on the beach, we jes take a look. He say, that's a good idea, jes theoretical, and off we go without nothing except our lunch and our blanket capes in case a cold wind come up. But as Ludo go down the track over them roots and tangles I hang back, make sure the fire is out proper, make sure the door is shut tight. Then I think a bit, go in again and get his Bible, stuff it inside my blanket cape, otherwise when Ludo get drunk and see them apparitions the Lord start crying out to him, oh, come on back to the whare Ludovic, it yer Lord calling.

I all out of breath when I get to Hokitika town. I look for a store that's on the edge. I hide in the shadders to see who is about. Everthing a bustle but I don't see no one I know. I worry about who gonna be inside the store but I jes gonna haffta take one of them risks. I run in. In the gloom I can't see if anyone there that collar me. Soon I ordering everthing from the storekeeper and it turning into a rilly big pile.

I hear a voice behind me. It saying in funny Inglish, 'I am seeing you have survived your ferry trip, liebling.'

I turn around. It Kaspar Schmidt looking as disreputable as what he ever done.

'What yer doing here?' I ask grumpy.

'Ha, why you are not being pleased to see me?' He throw open his arms like he in a astonishment.

'I busy.' I turn back to the storekeeper that's finishing the pile. But Kaspar Schmidt don't go away, he start looking at what I buy. He look rilly intrested.

'Ah, you are to be a gold miner,' he say.

'It aint for me.' Dunno why I say this, mebee to throw him off me. But it don't work. When I all loaded up there's Kaspar Schmidt loaded up too, he carrying all the things I dropped. He say he gonna help me, where I am going? Now this a conan drum, that's a word Violet learn me, it mean having two men at a time, but can mean also two problems. So conan drum apply to me. One of them problems is I can't carry the whole pile on my own, the other problem is Kaspar Schmidt. I stagger out of the store and

Kaspar Schmidt follow me laughing. Then he tell me to put it all down, we share the load out more fair. I aint gonna do that in the daylights so I jump back in the shadders and dump the pile on the earth. Kaspar Schmidt then busy hisself making two fair piles.

Soon we both got our piles loaded up and tied correct on our backs. Kaspar Schmidt want to go through town but I say no. Then all the way along the beach he wanna know everthing about Ludo.

I stop and put down my pile. 'Why yer coming with me? Aint yer got anything to do?'

'It is not possible for one small boy to be carrying all these things.'

'Why you care?'

Kaspar Schmidt shrug. Then he say, 'I am from a wealthy family. I do not need to be digging the gold.'

'So yer jes gonna hitch yerself to my life?'

Kaspar Schmidt look taken aback.

'Are you from Russher?' I ask before he think what to say.

'No, from Berlin. I told you in Rosstown.'

'That's in Russher for all I know.'

I pick up my pile and walk on. Now Kaspar Schmidt go on and on about where Berlin is, how it near Russher but not Russher, and near some black sea and a black forest and all of it rilly boring. Then he say Sevastopol.

'So Sevastopol rilly true?'

'But of course. I have been there.'

I astounded.

'What's it like?'

Kaspar Schmidt say we must walk on or it be morning before we get back to Ludo. He say he tell me about Sevastopol as we walk. So off we go and it sure a intresting story. He say there were a war there because Russher take some land off the Ottermens and blow up some of their ships. Then the Inglish and the French and some Turks go in and B-E-S-I-E-G-E the city of Sevastopol where the Zar's Fleet were parked. Kaspar explain me a Zar is a King from Russher. So the Russhans haffta sink their own ships – how about that! Then there were a big cannon fight, but the city weren't taken for nearly a whole year after the battle first begun.

It a bit confusing. 'Why the Inglish care if the King of Russher take some land off the Ottermens?

'It is being because of the threat of potential Russian penetration into the Mediterranean.'

Whoa! Now we gone so far inside the langwich cave we never come out alive.

Kaspar say when he were rilly young he crave adventure so he go to Balaclava. He do the spellings so I know I got it right. Balaclava is near Sevastopol.

'There I am making the Grand Crimean Central Railway. I am that which you English people call a navvie.'

'I aint a Inglish people.'

'I beg your pardon. Are you only borrowing that nose and mouth? Are you speaking their language only for a time?'

'I want coin,' I say, hoping to end talk that turn sly.

'What are you desiring coin for, liebling?'

'Binarnas.'

Kaspar reply me, 'Plato is saying that there is only one thing for which all coin should become exchanged, and that is wisdom.'

Prolly Playtoe never et a binarna.

When we get back to Ludo he frown at the disreputable man what's with me. Haffta say now I see them two together, Ludo aint looking a whole lot better'n Kaspar Schmidt, even with his hair knot and his Croesus coat. Kaspar Schmidt hold out his hand and say his name, and Ludo say his name and take Kaspar's hand like it all warty. Then he snatch his hand back. I see a look in Kaspar's eye what's first amused, then turn hungry. But it sure aint food

Kaspar hungry for. He a big strapping man that look like he et a ox every day from the time he were born.

When Ludo unnerstand what happen, he try to give Kaspar a coin for helping, but Kaspar say no, he don't need no coin. Kaspar sit down on the sand and Ludo scowl. He aint big on guests. He been drinking his bottle all the time I were at the store and I can see he aint feeling perlite. He also no use at all when it come to making the tent. But Kaspar turn out to be a big help. He soon get everthing sorted out, get the calico unrolled, get a big knife out, get the poles ready in the correct place so our tent don't fall down or sag or let in the rain. He make a floor for us too, so the cold in the sand don't come up in the night and give us R-H-E-U-M-A-T-I-S-M-S.

At the end of all this work Ludo already fallen asleep on the sand and snoring like a pig. Kaspar light a fire and send me off to fetch wood, a easy job because it lying all over the beach. Now the sun start going down in the sea and the sky all bright yella and orange. Kaspar say it a wonder, like a sea that's on fire. But it look ordinary to me. I seen it every night of my life except when there were a storm. Now everwhere them diggers lighting fires and cooking and drinking and shouting, it a lot more exciting than Ludo's hut.

Kaspar turn out to have some mutton in his swag, also some stuff that's hard and yella that I never et before. He call it cheese. He give me a bit on the knife. It salty and pretty good. Kaspar put on a billy for tea and soon the smell of frying mutton wake up Ludo. He don't look pleased to see Kaspar cooking at his fire. I take him a cup of tea and whisper, c'mon Ludo, he a big help to a boy what's tryna be a gold miner. Ludo go muttery, he say he know everthing about gold hisself, what's that krowt floating around like God's angel for, aint he got a home to go to?

Dunno what a krowt is but I aint gonna ask Ludo in front of Kaspar jes in case I don't get no fry mutton. But then Ludo drink the tea and eat up the fry mutton that Kaspar give him, and soon he and Kaspar are sitting by the fire smoking their pipes.

'I am born and educated in Berlin,' Kaspar say even though Ludo don't ask.

'Prussia,' Ludo nod.

'No, it aint Russher,' I tell Ludo, 'but it pretty near. And pretty near Sevastopol too. Ludo been to Sevastopol, Kaspar.'

'No, I aint,' Ludo say.

'Ludo got taken by them Barberry pirates,' I tell Kaspar. Then I wait for Ludo to say, no I dint. But he don't.

Kaspar now looking sideways at him.

'Thasright,' Ludo slur. He been slurring all evening because of his afternoon with the bottle but now he suddenly talk like he had a bucket of cold water throwed over him. 'I was born in a small village on the Catalan coast. The pirates took me when I was scarcely five, and they took my mother too. They took many from the village. We were shipped to Algiers and sold into slavery. Of course, my mother, being young and beautiful, was sent into a harem.'

'I am not believing you,' Kaspar say.

'Not believing me? Those Muslim corsairs took millions of European Christians. Somebody has to be one of them!'

Kaspar wink at me like he still don't believe Ludo. I dunno what to think. Mebee Kaspar go back to Berlin one day and say, I once sit on a beach with a boy what have a father that's a chief all covered in tattoos on his face and arse and show hisself for a shilling. And his guests say, I am not believing you, them savages is all cannibals, they would of et you for their dinner.

'Who buy you, Ludo?' I a bit jealous. It seem his adventure bigger than mine ever be.

Ludo look at me and say, 'Who bought me? Luckily a rich man who jes wanted some young boys to tend his animals. He took a whole group. He jes waved his hand and said, all that lot.

Otherwise, if I'd been forced to parade myself in the slave market, I surely would of been considered too small and weak. Then who knows what would of happened to me?'

Ludo stand up, he looking to end the evening. Kaspar get the picture, scramble to his feets. They shake hands and Kaspar go off. Me and Ludo start getting our blankets out.

'What that black lump over there?' I catch it out the corner of my eye and it give me a fright.

Ludo peer in the dark where I point.

'It a man, Ludo.'

'It is, laddie. What's he doing?'

'He look like he sleeping. Wait . . . it Kaspar! He curling up on the sand over there.'

Ludo sigh big. Now he haffta be like Mr Simaritan. He call out, 'Mr Schmidt, where is your tent? Come over and sleep in ours.'

So that's how my first night end. Squashed up between Ludo that snore like a pig and Kaspar that gurgle like a drowner. Then I hear them waves crashing crashing, and a big rain start on the calico. But I happy. It aint jes getting away from all them troubles in Hokitika town. It also because I feel like we rilly having a adventure.

In the morning my gold digging life begin. It all wet, mists and waters coming off the crashing sea, rains coming from the black sky. Kaspar make us coverings from the calico that were left over after the tent. Ludo laugh and say we look like ghosts. Us three ghosts got to find a orspishuss place to start, Ludo say. That aint very hard, yer only allowed to dig around yer living quarters. Ludo take charge. He say he the one that know everthing. Kaspar there like a walking flagpole in the middle of our lookings, he always in the way, we keep on bumping into him. Finally Ludo shove in the spade and say, right here, laddie, here the place you want to start.

I start to dig. It aint long before I feel a bit discouraged. Plenty of sand but no gold. Too much water. It coming from everwhere. Ludo tell me the wicked don't get no rest so keep on digging. I keep on.

After our lunch that Kaspar provide, Ludo in a grump. Mebee because he finish all them bottles yesterday. But the big trouble don't start till after our dinner. We resting in the tent and Ludo say, where's my Bible laddie, and I say, Ludo, you aint been drinking today, you don't need no Bible. Ludo get in a rage so I haffta give it to him. But I don't wanna hear no boring stories, whether Good Simaritan or his other favourite, the one about some rule that's gold. Not real gold, Ludo once explain me, yer haffta imagine this rule is good as gold. I dint say, nothing is good as that. But Godsaveus, that's the exact bit Ludo now going on and on about.

Kaspar let out a teerible laugh.

Ludo eye him. 'What d'you find so amusing, Mr Schmidt?'

'Why are you filling the poor boy with such nonsense?'

'Nonsense?' The way Ludo say it make me freeze, he gonna go crazy for sure.

Then Kaspar take out his own book, the one I seen in Rosstown that's full of strange writings. He read out loud for us. 'Now it is clear. God cares only for what is his, busies himself only with himself, thinks only of himself, and has only himself before his eyes, woe to all that is not well pleasing to him. He serves no higher person and satisfies only himself. His cause is' – here Kaspar pause, then say like a mad preacher, 'a purely egoistic cause!'

Well again I don't rilly unnerstand a word of it, but Ludo go more whiter than a calico ghost. His words is all lost. He open his mouth and no sound come. Then he stand up, he tryna push Kaspar out of the tent. But Kaspar laugh his teerible laugh and cry, 'Recall the golden rule, Mr Ludovic. I have no home, nowhere for lying down my head. You are sending me into the dark night, into the wilderness.'

But Ludo don't care. He shout he aint having a effing blasfemer in his tent, a effing atheist, and that's rilly strange because Ludo explain me once a atheist don't believe in God and here Kaspar menshin him more 'n ten times. But Kaspar leave in the end and me and Ludo settle down in our blankets. I a bit sad thinking of poor Kaspar out in the dark night, out in the wilderness. I know he got coin, can sleep in a hotel, but jes like Ludo it don't seem a cloud bed what he want.

'Yer think Kaspar sleeping on the sand?' I whisper.

There come a silence.

'Ludo?'

'How many strays am I expected to take in, laddie?'

'Dunno. What Mr Simaritan say?'

Another silence. 'Did you understand what Kaspar meant?'

'No.'

'He said God is selfish. He uses that as an excuse for Man to be selfish too.'

'No, that aint his story, Ludo. He take it all from a book.'

'He agrees with that book. That's why he carries it around with him. That's why he reads from it. That's his bible. A bible that pulls God down from Heaven and puts him on trial. To see if He's really any better than the rest of us.'

Well, I haffta say I dunno who right and who wrong but I feel very tired.

'Are you still awake, laddie?' I hear after a while.

'Not ezactly.'

'I have to go to Hokitika in the morning. Fetch supplies.'

This give me an alarm. If Ludo go wandering off, who knows what happen? Mebee he end up back in his hut where it warm and dry, or mebee he end up going gabble gabble gabble all over Hokitika town.

'I go for you. I run along the beach, get them bottles. That's what you want, aint it Ludo?'

Ludo protest, say we need meats and flours and tobacca too.

I say to him, it alright, I get them all.

Next day dawn fine. I want to dig for gold but I know Ludo gimme no peace till he sucking his dirty water again. So I set off and arrive in Hokitika town early. But I aint so lucky this time. I jes sneaking along Revell Street when One Eye come out of his cottage with Prosper. I jes about run smack into them.

'Well, if it aint Cocoa!' One Eye exclaim, grabbing me. 'Where yer been the last few days? I been looking all over for you.'

'Gertie's been asking for you too,' Prosper say. 'And Mr Flewelling's been wanting to know why you dint turn up at the dance Saturday.'

'Let go of me.' I try to wriggle out of his clutches. 'I a gold miner now.'

Them two both start laughing big.

'Where's yer claim, Thumbsucker?' Prosper ask when he manage to stop hisself.

'On the beach. If it any business of yers.'

Prosper fix me in the eye. 'Happen it is a business of mine, Thumbsucker. Gertie's all the time wanting a fried fish. Says she feels better. But I aint got the time to go fishing.'

'Well, yer can buy . . .'

'Atchilly, no you can't. All the boats around here are taken up with moving the miners about. And the fishermen that stand on the river bank aint selling.'

'That aint my problem now. I a digger on the beach and . . .'

'Hang on a minute, Cocoa,' One Eye say. 'I seem to recall doing you a big favour on the night of the ball.'

Prosper nod like he in on it.

'So now the time has come to pay me,' One Eye say mean.

'You say you dint want no pay!'

'I said I dint want no *money*,' One Eye correct me. 'It aint the same thing.'

Then they take me in the cottage, sit me down, feed me some thing they call a lolly. They say all brats love them so I spit it out on the floor.

'Right, here's the plan,' One Eye say. 'We gonna do another job like we done last year.'

'What were that?' Prosper ask and wink at me.

Now they do a little play. Prosper is the idiot and One Eye the know it all.

'Surely you know. Why, there were posters all over town about it.'

'Must of missed them.'

'Mr Walmsley, of the Bank of New South Wales, were ambushed between No Town and Twelve Mile.'

'Oh no!' Fatso slap his cheeks with his palms.

'He were robbed of eight hundred ounces of gold dust and a thousand pounds in bank notes.'

'Really? But who done it? Who were so clever?'

One Eye drop down to a false whisper. 'Now don't tell no one. It were Yours Truly.'

Fatso slap One Eye on the back like he a hero. Then they both laughing fit to split.

I rilly horrified.

Then One Eye stop laughing and say, 'Nah. All we want is for you to give some medicines to yer good friend Violet.'

That's all? This seem too good to be true. I let off a big hook. 'Why Violet need medsin? She aint sick, is she?'

'No. Griffith Flewelling wants her to have it.'

'Well, why don't he give it hisself?'

'Because he paid me to do it.'

'What for?'

'He wants her to have a big, fat, healthy baby. Aint that right, Prosper?'

'Sure is,' Fatso agree.

It don't make much sense but I expect Griffith don't want nobody to see that he taken a intrest in Violet's belly. It aint something he orta have a intrest in. I say to them, alright, but I aint going to the Bathsheba. They haffta fetch Violet here or somewhere Caradoc don't see me because I aint gonna go back and do them sweepings again, it nothing but a slavery.

'Not here,' One Eye say quick as what a wink is.

'Nowhere near the Bathsheba neither,' Prosper say with a shudder.

'We'll get her over to Fortunatus's store. We got something on him.'

This sound bad. 'What yer got on him?'

'Never you mind, Half-pint,' Prosper say. 'It aint for a boy to hear.'

So that's the way it go. Prosper go back to the hotel to fetch Violet. He gonna tell her Harvey is back and wanna see her. One Eye take me to the store. When we get there Fortunatus beaming in his work apron, sit me up on the counter, look rilly pleased to see me. But then One Eye talk to him out on the street while I eat a binarna and Fortunatus come back in looking like a ship wreck. And he look very black at me, like I were the rocks. But I aint got no time to think about it. Soon Violet flounce in the door with Prosper and she aint looking like I her most favourite person. All them men push us out the back and then leave us alone.

'I'm busy,' she say mean, 'so what yer wanna see me about?'

'Don't yer wanna know where I gone?'

'I get you a job at the hotel and then one night you jes don't show up. Now I have to work twice as hard. Why do I care what yer pathetic excuse is?'

'Aw, come on Violet. Aint we friends? And I got good news for you. I seen Griffith and he gimme a present for you.'

Now her face change in a instant. Now she looking like I something special. 'Yer seen Griffith? I aint seen him since he went back to Rosstown. Is that where you went? Here, can you give him a note for me?' She put her hand in one of them big pockets of her cleaning pinny and pull out a stub of pencil. Then she look around like she think paper jes float in the air.

'No, me and Ludo down the beach. But I seen Griffith. He gimme this medsin for yer baby.'

Why it only at that exact moment I rememory Violet don't know that Griffith know she having a baby? Why I forget in all my talkings and tellings that Violet don't get no chance to talk about the baby at the ball? Were it the sea air that cleared out my mind or were there jes too many folds in the truth and stupid little Halfie lose hisself? But now it too late. It out of my mouth and Violet aint even angry, she jes looking like the sky fall in.

'You aint seen him, yer little liar,' she say bitter. 'What yer doing? What yer cooking up with Prosper? And what's in that effing bottle?'

'It jes a tonic. For the baby.'

'My baby don't need no tonic. It's getting another kind of treatment.'

This make my blood go cold. And I angry. 'Yer still gonna murder that poor baby in the cradle?'

'What?'

'You gonna be a murderer?' Why Violet pretend she don't unnerstand me?

Then something seem to dawn on her. She get down to my size and look rilly mean into my eyes. 'Is that what yer done, you stupid brat? Yer told Prosper I gonna murder my baby? And he a Catholic?' She snatch the medsin out of my hand. 'Tell that dago mackerel-snapper to mind his own business, alright?'

Then she go off while I scratch my head tryna think what jes happen.

I come out of the back room. Fortunatus serving a customer, Prosper gone and One Eye take a big intrest in some potatas. I go on out. Fortunatus glare at me as I go past, then One Eye come out after and pull me into the shadders.

'I see she had the medicine in her hand,' he say. 'Why dint you make her drink it?'

'She gonna drink it at the hotel.'

One Eye aint happy but what he can do?

Then I get annoyed. 'Look, I got my own problems. Ludo send me here to get flours meats and tobacca. He also expect me to go to the Bathsheba for his bottles, but I aint going *there* and I too young to get bottles anywhere else and . . .'

'Calm down,' One Eye say holding up his hands. 'I'll get yer bottles, Cocoa. How many d'you want?'

'Many as what a boy can carry. I aint coming back here in a hurry.'

I expect One Eye to go to the Gridiron what's nearby but he go back in Fortunatus's store. I wait and a while later he come out with a big pile of flours bottles tobacca, all them things I been sent for. But no meats. He say I haffta go to the butcher. I hold out the paper money that Ludo give me but One Eye jes laugh and push it away. Then I rilly afraid he done something bad to Fortunatus.

'What yer do?' I ask furious. 'Do you tie him up and rob him?'

'No, I dint. Dint I tell you blackmail is more lucrative than robbing? Aint you been listening to me? You a slow learner or what?'

One Eye go off and I creep through the shadders to the butcher, one that's on the edge of town and aint fancied by them hotel cooks. As I wait for him to chop and wrap, some thinkings come up in me, thinkings I dint want, but that's the way with thinkings, they jes come, you gotta have them like it or not. What these thinkings about is Violet's baby, how soon as it born it gonna be murdered in the cradle. And it come to me I gotta do something that's more'n wishing. Wishing aint no good. Wishing jes a way for little Halfie to feel happy about hisself. What I say to Ludo's Lord, even if he a bit theoretical, when he boom at me, well, you do a lot of wishing, Koko, but what yer atchilly done? Sweet fuck all, that's what.

So I haffta stop that poor baby being murdered jes cos no one want it. That's the golden rule, aint it, do unto others what yer want done unto you? And I sure don't want no murder done unto me. But Ludo aint no good to get help from, he aint a stealer, he go throthing crazy if I say we haffta steal a baby. What I need is a man that don't care about the Lord, only hisself. Then the butcher slap a big packet of meats in front of me and it thump me out of any of my thinkings.

When I get back to Ludo he in a grump. He all shaky and sweaty, he snatch a bottle and gurgle it down like he dying. I put all them provisions in the tent, then I keen to get doing the gold mining. Soon I working and Ludo singing, it pretty good singing too, it make me very happy somehow, take away all them worries that I come back from Hokitika town with. Sure I gotta steal a baby, but now that it a plan and not a wish I can put it in the back room of my mind for a while. Violet only got a little bump, even Halfie know it haffta be big to get born.

Late in the afternoon it start to pour again. I worn out and Ludo jes woke up from a drunken sleep. We sit in the tent looking out the flaps at the rain. For a while Ludo give me a grammar lesson, teach me to say I'm, but it a bit tricky. It all about finite verbs and participles and adjectives and complements, all them things that Ludo spell out and explain me, but still it don't make no sense. So I aint gonna say it.

'How was Caradoc?' Ludo ask when we finish.

Poor Ludo – another lie coming. 'Dint see him. Prosper get me the bottles.'

'That's unusual. He doesn't often leave the bar untended.'

I wanna say, how yer know what he do or don't do? Instead I say, 'Mebee he upstairs visiting with Gertie.'

'Maybe.'

Unfortunately Ludo in one of them moods that make him soft. 'That's what we should do,' he say dreamy. 'One Sunday we should go to church in the morning, then visit Gertie in the afternoon. Have a big hot dinner at the hotel in between.'

'That's a good idea.' A good idea that I aint ever gonna do.

In the food that One Eye get me from Fortunatus there's a big sausage thing what's good to slice bits off and eat off a knife. We do that and stare out at the rain. Ludo say we like two orphans that aint got no home. We still sitting there when a calico ghost go drifting past.

'Hey that's Kaspar,' I say to Ludo.

Ludo pretend he hard of seeing.

'Aint but one man got a calico hood like we got, Ludo.'

Ludo pretend he hard of hearing.

'Hey Kaspar,' I shout. 'Come for some sausage with us.'

Ludo dig me in the ribs but now I got my own reasons for knowing Kaspar. Of course Kaspar come over. He prolly been wandering in the rain for days, crying in the wilderness.

It all a bit awkward. Ludo don't budge so Kaspar haffta squeeze into a tiny space next to me, when next to Ludo there's a big airy space going begging. But Ludo put down his stuff there. Then I haffta yank the knife and sausage off him to give them to Kaspar. Then Ludo aint speaking. Then he singing a hymn. He getting louder and louder the more I speaking to Kaspar. Then Kasper get erasperated. He take out his book and wave it about. Mebee he think that make Ludo stop his singings, but no. So Kaspar preach the bit about God is selfish, then suddenly shout out, 'What about Mankind? Mankind promotes the interests of Mankind only. It causes both nations and individuals to wear themselves out in its service and when they accomplish what Mankind needs, in gratitude it throws them on the dung-heap of history. Is not Mankind a purely egoistic cause?'

Ludo put his fingers in his ears. 'Be thou my vision, oh Lord of my heart ...'

Kaspar wave his book and shout, 'God and Mankind have concerned themselves with nothing but themselves! Let me then likewise concern myself with myself. I am the creative nothing, the nothing out of which I myself as creator create everything . . .'

'Naught be all else to me save that thou art . . .'

It sure a racket.

I bellow, 'You two is being fucken ridiclious!'

They both stop and look ashamed.

I give a little speech. I say how a boy need the help of a man that's strong. He need him to dig the gold with, to fetch and carry with. Otherwise a boy jes playing in the sand. Both them ashamed men nod hard. And it all true what I say – jes as it true I want Kaspar for more'n that.

In the morning, that for a change dawn pale and clear, a horse come clopping along the shingle and hard sand. It pull a cart and on the cart sit a man of E-N-T-E-R-P-R-I-S-E. The enterprise he selling is all the kai a stomick can dream of, and all them soothings like Jimmy Bottle and tobacca. It turn out he also got Perry Davis Vegetable Pain Killer. I buy six bottles and I say to Kaspar it for Ludo when he start sweating and going out of his hinengaro. But the truth is I like my own sips of Heaven. I aint got a plan of wasting it on no drunk.

EIGHT

Next few weeks fly by. Lot of digging, lot of rain. It summer so it warm rain but it still wet yer all through. Jes as well I got some help. Kaspar help me with the gold mining – we don't find no gold – and he help me with the tent that's starting to sag and let in drops. Ludo work at keeping a good fire going, a billy boiling and keeping up the correct level of drink in hisself so he don't go all shaky and abusing us. He also keeping up the singing, but for all our happiness he don't sing no hymns.

Every second day along come Cloppy and Mr Enterprise. I sure glad I don't haffta go to Hokitika town. Mebee blood run down them streets like rainwater, but it aint mine so what I care? Ludo give me a lecher if ever he hear such thinkings, but that's why you got a big bone around yer hinengaro, so yer thinkings don't go out to everbody. When I explain to Kaspar what I think, how I don't miss the town and don't care if they all dead, he one minute laughing and saying good, yer the master of yer own cause, and the next minute wagging his finger and saying don't you grow into no evil hoodlum. That's the trouble with adults. They carry around them books that make them feel strong, Ludo got his Bible, Kaspar got his Einziger, but when them books get shut away they always backsliding. Ludo slide back to his bottle and Kaspar slide back to being a strick Papa from Prussher.

There's a lot of drinking that go on at the beach diggings. Mr Enterprise go home rich even if no one else do. He don't do no fussing about my Vegetable Pain Killer neither. I hand over my coin, he hand over them bottles. He always know the moment when Kaspar aint looking, usually it when he fondle them sausages. So when we et our kai and sit round the fire in the dark, Ludo and Kaspar drink from their bottles and I take little sips from Perry Davis that I hide in my moleskins. Everone is very happy. But I happy in a different way from them other two. They all the time slurring their talkings and stumbling when they get up for a mimi. They sing and speechify and rave and don't listen to each other. But I go into a peace that seem very still and huge. It aint got no talkings there, or thinkings. Then we all go out cold on the sand and don't know nothing till the sea or the morning come. Ludo say we lucky we have our Matildas. Ludo argue that's his swag, but Kaspar say it were once a Prusshan word and mean yer greatcoat. Never mind, we out cold in the sand, and if we lucky and not too fucked our heads is on our swags and our not-so-great coats is over us.

One morning I wake up and Ludo don't want no fry sausage for his breakfast. He say his throat sore, been sore for days. He say it feel like he swallow a burning coal. Kaspar feel his forehead and say it seem the burning coal make his whole body hot. I tell Ludo to drink Jimmy Bottle quick, mebee last night he dint take enough before he go facedown. But he don't want none. He now complain he got a bad headache. A headache aint a new thing for Ludo but usually he say he fix it with them hairs of a dog. Now he don't want no hairs and no fry sausage neither. Kaspar and me worry.

Before we can think what to do Ludo begin some upthrowings on our calico floor.

'Ah, das ist schrecklich,' Kaspar cry, and he jump away from them little pieces of carrot and potata that last night he cook in the mutton stew and that now come swimming at us in a pool of stomick juices. Then Kaspar pull Ludo out of the tent by his feets. Outside it one of them mornings that make you wanna be dead, the wind a drizzly gale that freeze the cannibals off a brass monkey. Now Kaspar pull up Ludo's clothings and make strange noises from Prussher. He show me some red spots that come out on Ludo's skinny body.

'We must take him to the hospital,' Kaspar say. 'I am thinking it is the typhoid.'

Kaspar get two sticks long as a man, and sling a blanket between them with some fancy tyings. Then we begin a long walk along the beach with Kaspar dragging Ludo. It lucky that Kaspar, even if he disreputable, is strong enough to drag a dying shadder, for that's what Ludo soon become. All the way he doing P-R-O-J-E-C-T-I-L-E V-O-M-I-T-I-N-G, what's something rilly disgusting, and we get sprayed by the drizzle wind and the mad sea and sometimes by potata and carrot.

At the last bit, some diggers with a horse come out to help us. They sling Ludo over the horse like he already dead, his head hang down one side, his feets the other, then one of them pick me up and put me on too. Kaspar walk along behind. First I enjoy the ride, it a rilly big beast that go clop clop roll roll in a regular way that nearly send you to sleep, but then the thinkings come up in me that Ludo die. My heart go cold as them cannibals, even if I don't rilly unnerstand what brass monkeys got them for. What I gonna do without Ludo? Mebee I haffta be the son of a Papa from Prussher, but what Ludo in Heaven think when he hear Kaspar teaching me his Einziger? He rage and swear and spew. Then the Lord kick him down to Hell for sure.

Lucky for everone that Ludo don't haffta go to the old hostipal. It were jes a mildew box with a canvas roof, and all the waters come into it as they please, the rain the sea spray the drizzle wind, it worse even than the old gaol that someone in the newspaper say were more teerible than the dungeons of Naples. Now there's a new hostipal that Commissioner Sale command to be builded. He were a man I once hate, but now I love him. His hostipal a wonder compare to Ludo's hut and the beach calico, even if it builded on the swampy south bank of the river and it got two boatmen on the staff. Ludo get put in a bed that have very clean clothings and then everone cluster round him with cold sponges and medsins.

Aint nothing for me and Kaspar to do but leave. We start walking along the street and I tryna keep my head down low so no one jump me.

'What are you doing now?' Kaspar ask. 'Where are you to be living?'

'I haffta stay here to visit Ludo. Mebee I go to Ludo's hut till he get well again. It in the bush.'

'Perhaps I am seeking my old labour at the Quay.'

'What were that?'

'I am helping the stranded ships make the overland trip.'

'That sound a fine job. If only I know what yer talking about.'

'A gang is going out to ships pushed up on the spits and using screw-jacks to be raising them up,' Kaspar explain me. 'Then with wooden rollers and windlasses we are dragging the ships over the spits and into the river.'

'Mebee I do it too.'

'They are not taking boys. It is only for strong men.'

We walk on. I dunno where we going.

'Where yer gonna live?' I ask Kaspar.

'At a hotel, I am thinking.'

'Don't go to the Bathsheba. Ludo say their rooms got them wallpapers that kill you.'

'True? I am hearing about those papers. When they are damp, a creature is being grown in the glue and producing a gas.'

This sure a surprise. Jes when I think everthing that Ludo say is ravings of a lunatic, up come Kaspar saying they true facts. That make me dwell a bit on poor old Gertie. Is she still locked in her room, a prisoner of wallpaper?

'What are you sighing at, liebling?'

'Seem there a lot of people what need rescuing in this town.'

'There are a lot of people who are needing rescuing in the world,' Kaspar reply me.

I glad then that sea is everwhere all around. Mr Simaritan can't expect no boy to go rescuing people if he need a twelve warrior waka. I still feeling good about that when suddenly a teerible apparition appear. It come out of a bank and it aint Mr Sale. It walking bent up and have a black cloud atop its head.

'Mr Flewelling,' Kaspar say and walk towards him with his hand out for a shake.

I want to run but I freeze up.

'Bedwetter!' Mr Flewelling say when he see me.

Now I cowering. A blow coming to me for sure.

'Why'd yer run out on me?' Mr Flewelling ask, turning his black eye on me.

Well, here again is one of them conan drums. Mebee he know already but it a trick.

'I down the beach now. Me and Ludo is gold diggers.'

'Oh really?' It seem he holding in a big laugh. 'Come to sell yer nuggets at the bank, have you?'

'No, Ludo sick with a tyfoid. We brung him to the hostipal.'

At that moment there come a big thundercrack, it nearly jump us out of our skins. I give the facts of Ludo's sickness to Mr Flewelling, then down come a pour. It one of them that soak you in a instant, one of them that nearly blind you. I dunno if he now setting a rat trap, but Mr Flewelling say come back to the Bathsheba and I far too wet to argue.

When we get there the bar full to bursting with men come in from the rain and there's a new barmaid done up like a dog's dinner. Mr Flewelling introduce us. She called Blanche. Through the serving hatch I can see Prosper cooking in a cloud of steam. I rilly lucky he got so many to cook for, he aint got no time to twist my ear.

Kaspar pay for a room up the stairs. He ask me if I want to doss down on the floor for free, but I say I gonna go to the hut till Ludo get better. Mr Flewelling take Kaspar's coin, tell him all meals included, and he say Bedwetter can have some too. He glare hard at me and say it don't include no drinks, then he say he going to pay a visit to Ludo in the hostipal.

Kaspar and me go for a hot dinner. Blanche, not Prosper, bang it down. Kaspar look pleased. She one of them woman that have big uma pushed up, and a lot of pile high hair black as them coals that go on the fire. Blanche say recently there's been a pig hunt and sure enough it turn out to be roasted poaka on the plates. It got some cook apples to go with it, that sure is strange, but whitey have his own way with kai. Kaspar look surprised. He ask where them apples grow? Blanche laugh charming and say on a ship from Victoria.

After the dinner I set off for the hut. It still raining big, not jes cats and dogs as Ludo say, but bigger, tigers and wolfs. The track run with water and mud, and I start slipping and sliding like Caradoc of the fucked legs. But when I get to the clearing I can't believe my eyes. The hut jes a burn ruin. It jes all burned down, jes some black planks left in a heap of ashes and a chimney. I sit in the rain and feel some crying come up inside, for now Ludo and me aint got no home, got nothing but a calico what aint rilly a home jes a poor shelter for them folks that think richness jes waiting around the corner. But a beach aint got no corners.

I sit a while, then I get a stick and poke it in them ashes. I think, how a stove burn right away? It don't, so for sure it get stole by some bastard. But now I getting rilly cold. I slide off down the muddy track thinking that if I aint gonna be a homeless urchin in them cold nights then on the floor with Kaspar is my only choice.

I get back to the Bathsheba and go up to Kaspar's room. He lie on a cloud bed that look big enough for a whole tribe. He say, get them wet clothings off, there's a big shirt to wear in my swag. When I have the shirt on that go down nearly to my feets, he say now that I dry I can lie on the bed beside him but he don't want no wriggling. What do he think I am? One of them pantalon girls?

After I have a little sleep I haffta face the music, as Ludo always say. The music is Prosper, and Violet if she aint run off with Flewelling junior, and if I aint careful the music also Fortunatus. But when I creak down them stairs, full of dread, the first I see is Blanche.

'Oh Lordy,' she say, 'an ektoplasm! No Harvey, yer can't be in the bar dressed like that. You look a real fright.'

'My moleskins too wet.'

'Run and fetch them, then. I'll dry them by the fire.'

I do what she say. In a short time me and my clothings both roasting before the flames. There aint many in the bar now. Blanche say they all gone down to watch some new sinkings and drownings at the wharf. I jes getting happy when in come Violet. She go past without seeing me.

'Hey Violet, come over here. It me!'

She turn and look. Her face aint pleased but she come over. Straight away I see the tonic worked, her stomick now pretty big.

'I see yer drink that tonic,' I say.

'No, I dint. I told yer, this baby aint getting tonic.'

'What it getting then?'

'What d'you care? Should be obvious even to a cretin like you it dint work.'

Now this a big mystery but I annoyed anyway. It weren't me that got her in this mess, so why she talk so nasty?

'Is it getting a Papa then?' I ask mean as can be.

'Griffith is in Rosstown,' she say and her face drop. 'I aint seen him. But he's sure to be coming in for Easter.' She cheer up when she add this last bit.

'What's Eester?'

'It's some holidays like Christmas.'

'With balls and races?' I sure hope not. They were rilly fun, but if there gonna be that much trouble again I haffta scarper far away as Okarita.

'Of course not,' she snap. 'Easter is when the Lord were killed. It's all eggs and prayers and sad dinners.'

The Lord were killed? Like murdered? No wonder Ludo so upset about him.

'Tomorrow is Good Friday,' Violet say. 'So Griffith will arrive tonight at the latest. I only hope the river aint too high for ferrying.'

Now Violet pull a chair to the fire and sit down. We roast together with them clothings, and the thinkings is again coming up in me. What's the worst thing that can happen? Seem to me it Violet seeing Griffith coming on the ferry with Goldie, seeing Goldie looking like she own him. Violet spring at her like a tiger, claw her face to bits. Then Goldie stand in the rain with her bleeding face and Griffith get his tomahawk out to split Violet in half like a cabbage tree. But too late! Violet now stick out her belly like a fat sow and so even if Griffith split her, Goldie no longer marry with him.

'I seen Griffith in Rosstown,' I say.

'No, you dint, yer little liar.'

'I go up there for a look around after crissmiss. I seen him in the shopping street.'

Violet fix me with a stare, seem like she tryna see what I up to.

'He were going down the street with a lady.'

'What lady?'

'One that was at the ball.'

'That slut Ginger, yer mean?' Violet getting ready them tiger claws.

I shake my head hard.

Violet relax. Now she don't care. Now I gotta make her care. 'No, a other one that were there. In a gold dress, with yella hair and a lot of jools.'

'Well, if she likes jewels, and what lady don't, maybe he was tryna sell her some gold.'

Now I get a faint heart, that's what Ludo always saying. It mean the courage go out of you. For Ludo that mean another bottle, for me it mean I go quiet, and mebee everthing stay the same forever if not at that ezact moment Griffith dint come in the hotel with his Papa. They stamp their wet boots and slap each other for joy and there a lot of drops coming off their wet clothings and flying everwhere. Violet make me afraid. First her mouth drop open, then she go all red, then her eyes go slitty, then wide and round, then she close her mouth and tremble, then she grab the poker and start poking the fire like a mad woman.

But I see Griffith don't take no notice. In fact, when his eyes flit across her, jes once, they get a teerible look in them what get snuffed out quick – but too late, I already seen it. And when Papa flit across her the same way, he also give her a teerible look, not ezactly the same, it a bit less angry and more sad, but Violet sure making a mistake paying all her attenshun to that fire.

Now Caradoc and Griffith get their coats taken off of them by Blanche and they sit down at a table. Blanche bring them beer. Then Prosper come out and I tryna shrink into the shadders, but I know he seen me. He pretend he don't, start talking to the boss about what he want brung out to eat.

While the men eat, Violet lose intrest in them flames and she start tryna catch Griffith's eye. I dunno why she do this in front of Griffith's Papa, mebee because she turn desperate. But no one look at her at all, not junior not senior, and soon a little tear come squeezing out. I feel sorry for her, so I grab her hand, say come with me to see Ludo, we work something out. She agree and follow me out like a sheep.

We start walking to the hostipal and lucky the rain now jes a few spits.

'What do Mr Flewelling say when he find out yer having a baby?' I been wanting to know this a while now.

'Caradoc? He was angry at first, then he come round. He says he always wanted another baby.' Then Violet giggle. 'Bet he dint want his own grandchild.'

'Yer find out junior the Papa?'

'No, stupid. No one can find that out.'

We walk along a bit and she say, 'Caradoc says Gertie mustn't find out. Not ever. But Gertie aint the problem. She aint the one that's gonna try and kill me when I run off with Griffith.'

We go the rest of the way without no talking.

At the hostipal the nurse say visiting hours nearly closed, we can jes pop in for a minute. In the high bed, all clean and white, Ludo look a lot better. He say hello to Violet but it pretty funny how he look everwhere but her stomick. He ramble on about his medsins and his dinners, then he ask me where I been sleeping.

'Kaspar buy a room at the Bathsheba. I sleep with him.'

Violet burst out laughing but she stop when she see Ludo's big frown.

'Ee laddie,' he say in a voice full of them forebodings. 'Don't yer be listening to any readings from that Satan's book of his. He'll try to turn you away from the Lord. You have to sleep somewhere, but get some wax for yer ears.'

'What book?' Violet ask intrested.

'It all about being selfish,' I explain her.

Ludo nod. 'A long and immoral justification of selfishness. As if that particular vice weren't already popular enough.'

Then a bell get rung and out we shoved. Violet say she haffta get back to them dishes at the hotel, Caradoc taken her off the dancing list.

'What yer Mama in Ballarat say when you told her yer having a baby?' I ask before she go.

'I aint telling her till Griffith and me are married,' she reply.

In the night I can't get no sleep. I sleep good on the beach – them waves is like Perry Davis Vegetable Pain Killer. But here I warm and dry, and Kaspar don't even snore, and I awake. I aint intrested in no Eester, it sound effing miserable. Crissmiss were fun, or it might of been if I dint stand in so many piles of tutae all at the same time.

It come to me I free for a few days. I aint been free for a while. First I have them sweepings, then them diggings, now everone gonna be at the churchings. What I do with my freeness? Kaspar say the Jews still running the ferries on Good Friday, dunno what a Jew is, mebee a hard worker that got bored of all them Lord stories. But anyway, if they still running the ferries mebee I go somewhere. Mebee I go up to Rosstown and pay a visit to Goldie, try and find out if her heart is true. If it aint, Halfie's off the hook. If it is, there aint no doubt Griffith take her with the white veil. Then that baby of Violet's sure in big trouble.

I creep off before the sun up proper, and a old man take me across the river, don't know if he a Jew or not. It a perfic day, bright and cold with some snow on them biggest mountains, it rilly beautiful. It come to me Goldie prolly in one of them churches too, but if I miss her coming out I can ask someone where she live. It aint like there's more'n one of her.

When I get to Rosstown them churchings have all been done

and everone gone home for a Eester dinner. I find a boy playing in the main street all done up in his Eester clothings and looking a fright, and he point me the right way. It a big house that he point me to, one of them houses that gold build, or mebee the handling of gold. I knock on the door and a scrubber open it up. But she a rilly clean scrubber that have a white apron on. I give my name. She make a face when I say Griffith Flewelling ask me to bring a message to Goldie.

'Who?' she ask. 'Yer mean Miss Moncrieff?'

'That her name? Yair, I mean her.'

The scrubber go away to check, then come back and let me in. She take me up some fancy stairs to a room what's better'n the hotel, it all hanged and draped with wallpapers and velvet curtains, all that stuff that Ludo say make him suffocate. Goldie sit by a hot fire. She aint wearing yella or gold or white, she done up to the eyebrows in dark colours that make her skin seem even more whitey, and her hair seem bright like flames. Now I see her lips aint thin. They very large and curvy. They make me feel a bit funny in my stomick, it a kind of lost feeling that's hard to explain. She make me feel like touching her and crying all at the same time, then the touching haffta go on and on or the crying never end.

'Where is the message?' Goldie ask. She have a lovely voice that don't expect bad answers like Violet always do.

'It aint one that he write,' I say.

'Oh?' Her eyebrows go up, but her eyes what's the colour of the sea still calm.

'I jes gotta say it.'

'I see.'

I take a big breath and say, 'He ask do yer want to marry with him?'

There's a rilly long silence. Then Goldie stand up and pace about the room. Then she ask me if I like a hot drink and call in the scrubber.

'Sit down, Harvey,' she say pointing to a big chair.

I sit where she point.

Goldie stare at me with them eyes that make my stomick feel like her lips do.

'Who wants to know if I would like to marry Griffith Flewelling?' she ask me.

'He do.'

She laugh and shake her head. Her laugh is like a little bell.

'How yer know? You jes don't know.'

She hold out her left hand. It have a ring on it with bits of flashing glass. I dunno if she want me to take her hand or what.

'Look at my ring, Harvey,' she say. 'I've already accepted Griffith. So again, tell me who wants to know?'

'Gertie do,' I blurt out. All I can think of to say.

'His mother? He hasn't told his mother?' Now a cloud pass across her lovely face and it make me feel like crying out, please forgive me, it all a lie.

'He tell his Papa,' I say, hoping this do the trick.

Now she smile. 'Probably he wants to surprise his mother at the party.'

'What party?'

'The engagement party, of course. We're having it at the hotel.'

'The Bathsheba?'

She nod. Then another silence come and wild thinkings chase inside my head. They don't stop even when the scrubber come in with a tray. On it there a hot drink for me that Goldie call koko. It look ugly like mud or tutae but it turn out to be rilly sweet and make me think of the cloud bed Goldie prolly sleep in.

'What kind of party is that?' I make bold to ask.

'An engagement party? It's where we announce to everyone that we are going to be married.'

'Yer announce to everbody?'

Goldie nod. Then she say, 'Now Harvey, if Griffith wants it to be a surprise for his Mama, don't you let the cat out of the bag.'

'I aint got no cat.'

Goldie let out her little bell laugh and say, 'I mean, you must keep the secret. Tell Mrs Flewelling that I haven't made up my mind.'

'I sure will keep the secret.' She don't even imagine how hard I try.

Then we watch the flame for a while.

'Mebee you don't have yer fancy party at the Bathsheba,' I say. 'Sure it got Blanche now and it got Trellisbywilliammorris, and yer don't get no skinny pantalon girl slopping yer drink. But it still the same old dump full of drunks and rats. All them important arses now gone to the Gridiron.'

'But Harvey, it's Griffith's father's hotel. How would it look if I didn't have my party there?'

'Why yer don't have it here? It a rilly nice house.'

Goldie sigh. 'That would be much easier. And more conventional. But Father says that if the river rises, or there's a flood, most of Griffith's family and friends wouldn't make it to the do.'

'Why anyone care about that?'

Again the little bell laugh. 'I care about that! And of course Griffith would be very upset. He's one of those men who . . .' She stop and go red like she jes realise she telling her secrets to a picaninny.

'Why yer don't say?'

'Who likes everything to be done the correct way,' she finish off.

'That what yer think?'

'Don't you?'

'Mebee I jes know him a different way.'

'Yes, you're only a child,' Goldie say, and it rilly amaze me how grown ups always doing ezactly this, agreeing with you when yer dint say what they agreeing with.

Now my koko all gone and I put down the fancy cup.

Goldie stand up and go to a little cabinet. She take out some coin and give it to me. 'Here, Harvey. For the ferry back. And a little extra for something you like.'

'I like binarnas. But that aint enough.'

'Then for the difference you can use the money Mrs Flewelling gave you. I'm sure she didn't send you here without the ferry fare – both ways.'

Seem she dint come down in the last rainfall. Look like I don't get no more coin outta Miss Goldie Moncrieff.

She take me to the door. Before she open it, she ask looking curious, 'How does Mrs Flewelling know you?'

'I her fisher boy.'

'Oh, I see.'

Then I get a bit worried. 'Yer won't tell Griffith I come here, will yer? Gertie won't like it.'

'Our secret,' she say and smile at me.

'Our other secret. There the one about the ingagemint too.'

Goldie nod and open the door. When I outside, I be reft. I be reft of them lips and eyes and koko and jes . . . jes being by her, what give a feeling no one give up. Now I see Griffith don't take Violet even if Goldie said no. He go away and hang hisself up from a tree or shoot off his head with one of them muskets. He don't come down low to no pantalon girl from Ballarat. He don't wanna look at no ugly baby that come out of her. He want them beautiful babies that come out of his Princess Goldie.

I walk back to the ferry and the thinking come up in me how Griffith is jes like my own Papa. My Papa want beautiful babies out of his Princess Moana. But he want her to have a strong and handsome husband that he pick out for her, dint want her lickered up and dressed in satin, going around Mawhera with no whiteys.

My thinking bring up another rememory. It of Moana holding me close and calling me Tiwakawaka. She say, that yer real name what I give you, never mind what them others call you.

Tiwakawaka is everwhere in the bush around here. I see a lot of them on my way back to Hokitika town. They real cute little birds that flit about fast as a insect. I seen some that have yella stomicks but lots around here got stomicks that's cream, then they got perky tails that's black and white. Ludo say they have tails like fans, but I dint know what a fan was till I see Gertie go at herself with one. She tryna wave away them sweats that she call heat panics, but she don't use no plain thing plaited from flax. The one she got is bright green and it come at yer eyes like trellisbywilliammorris.

I sure hungry when I back in Hokitika town. I don't fancy no dinner with Prosper, so I look for a little dining hall next to one of them disreputable hotels in Revell Street. One of them easy enough to find. It dark inside, sawdust on the floor, everone eating also drunk and shouting. There aint a lot on the list of kai and the coin they want jes plain thieving, but when I get my mutton soup it a bowl big enough to drown in.

Next morning Prosper not Blanche slam down the breakfasts to all us sleepers at the hotel. But he don't say nothing to me because of Kaspar. His eyes do a lot of talking, jes I aint sure what they saying.

When Prosper gone I say, 'Kaspar, I got a big problem what I need help for.'

Kaspar keep on eating and don't say nothing.

'It aint one of them problems Ludo can help with. I need someone that's rilly selfish.'

Kaspar stop his fork and look at me out of one eye. 'You are not understanding me. I am having my own cause but . . .'

'Yair yair, I know. It jes that I know a baby in teerible trouble.'

'A baby?'

'A baby that aint borned yet.'

Kaspar laugh and say, 'There is nothing possible to be doing for a baby who is not yet born.'

'That aint right. Yer can give tonic.'

'Or poison.'

'What?'

Kaspar put his head down and start eating again. How you can give poison when the mouth of the baby aint in the world? I finish my kai and say, 'Anyway, I mean we haffta wait till it borned.'

'Born,' Kaspar correct me.

'No Kaspar, Ludo been learning me. You say born when it happening now. This baby is a way off yet.' I aint gonna take no corrections from a man that say, You are not understanding me.

'Tell me of this help I am to be giving.' He sound a bit erasperated.

'This baby gonna get murdered in its cradle. Prolly by one of the Papas . . .'

'A baby is having only one father,' Kaspar interrupt.

'Well this one don't. This one got two.'

Kaspar sigh big.

'But if it aint the Papa, it prolly the Mama.'

'Mothers are not often murdering their own children.'

'This aint yer regular mother.'

The talking stop now Flewellings senior and junior come down them stairs for breakfast. They both happy, aint no Fat Belly Violet sitting by the fire to remind them of their troubles. Kaspar stand up and say he haffta get down to the wharf. I gonna creep off when sudden as a kahu Prosper swerve from tugging his forelock at his boss to grabbing my clothings. He drag me off into the little room where he keep all them sacks and barrels. Dunno if he get fatter while me and Ludo down on the beach, but he sure fill the room up, aint no way I can dart past him.

'Me and One Eye got a problem with Griffith,' he say mean.

'What I care about that?'

'Yer oughta fucken care. It were you that caused it.'

'What I do?'

'It's what you dint do, Thumbsucker. You dint make that scrubber drink the tonic.'

'It alright. Her baby fine.'

'It aint alright, Fuckhead. We take pay off Griffith to get her to drink it. Now he wants his money back. But it's already gone, comprenez?'

'Where it gone?'

'That aint no concern of yours, yer cheeky brat. What is yer concern is helping to pay the money back.'

'What?'

'Thasright. Me and One Eye decided it's you that haffta come up with the cash.'

This sure a teerible shock.

'So, yer got a week. We're prepared to be reasonable.'

'How much I haffta get?'

He say a amount that's a lot of coin.

'What happen if I don't?'

'Don't?' Now he begin roaring. 'You get cooked, that's what. Boiled in fucken oil!'

Now Fatso let me go and I run out of the Bathsheba gasping for air. I go down the river bank. Where I get coin like that? Haffta do a robbery. But how a boy do that? All them bankers or joolers or gold escorters jes laugh. And it sure a big shame to poor Ludo if them constables catch me and bang me up in their gaol.

Mebee I jes run away. But who gonna save that baby when it borned? And how I leave Ludo lying in the hostipal, jes lying there day after day asking hisself what happen to poor little laddie?

Then some thinkings come up in me. What do One Eye tell me

about being a criminal? Dint he say blackmailings a lot easier than robbings? I aint ezactly sure what blackmailings is, but mebee Ludo tell me at visiting time.

I don't wanna go back to the Bathsheba, so I hang round skipping stones on the river till the hostipal let me in again. In the bed Ludo is looking cheery, but he say they aint gonna let him go till he dried out. He say he don't wanna dry out. He ask why an old dog who got nothing can't drink if he want to?

I say he got me.

'Ee laddie, thasright. But you don't mind if I have a wee drink, do yer?'

I aint sure what to say. Wee is alright, but it run big too quick. Seem better to change the subject.

'Ludo, what's blackmailings?'

'Blackmail? It's when you know a secret about someone and you make them give you money so as not to reveal it.'

'Ezactly what I think. But how yer do it?'

'Do it?' Ludo make his eyes narrow. 'What d'you need to know that for?'

'Jes wanna know for knowing.'

Ludo look consternated. 'Yer don't wish you went to school do you, laddie?'

I shudder. 'Fuck no. That a teerible idea. How I get coin if I sitting there listening to a old dame in a big skirt?'

Ludo wag his finger at the eff word, but he smile too. He don't want no suck-up boy. 'Well, I can't say I'm an expert in blackmail, but I spose you jes go to the party who has done something wrong and make threats. That's all there is to it. You don't write a letter, mind. That's evidence.'

Now I tryna pretend I lost intrest.

Jes before the bell, in come Caradoc. He clutch Ludo and I see Jimmy Bottle come out of his coat and go under Ludo's pillow. Now I think Ludo never get out. Caradoc wink at me. That mean everone got another cat what haffta stay in. Soon Hokitika town gonna be filled up with bags of cats.

I begin thinking, who I gonna blackmail? One Eye doing half the town. Then I think, what about Griffith hisself? He the cause of all my trouble. Why I don't pay him back with his own coin? Mebee this aint in the book called The Rules of Correct Blackmailings, but what I care about that? I don't mind being chucked in the river but I sure don't wanna get boiled in oil.

I hear Griffith aint going back to Rosstown till after Eester. Lucky for me Eester is so cold and boring Griffith keep to his room up the stairs most of the time. He send down for scrubbers to bring up drink and coals, Blanche all the time muttering, 'Where are all these skivvies he thinks I've got at my disposal?'

'I take up a tray,' say I.

'Good boy. Yer a good boy, Harvey.' She crush me to her uma that have a flour perfume. Then she get a tray fixed up with whiskey and glasses and off I go.

Griffith lie smoking on a cloud bed in his long johns what aint all worn out and stained like Ludo's. The room is hot from the coals and it like walking into that Hell Ludo always talking of.

'Put the tray over there,' Griffith say with one of them gestures that can't hardly be bothered making itself.

I put the tray on the table under the winder. Then I turn around and look at him.

'What yer waiting for, Pipsqueak? Yer want a coin or something?

'I want a lot of coin.'

Griffith been lying like one of them Sultans, bored and floppy, now he laugh like I a bit of fun that come into the room. 'Is that a fact? Well, you can dig it out of the ground or you can marry it.'

'Yair, I visit the coin yer gonna marry.'

It a bit gloomy, I can't see what his face do, but his body jump.

'You visited Lily Moncrieff?'

'If that her name, that's what I did.'

'What on earth for?'

'Don't worry, I aint gonna let them cats get out about yer ingagemint. It Violet what worry me.'

There come a long silence.

I aint got all day for blackmailings, so I say, 'What yer coin gonna do when she hear Violet having a baby that you the Papa of?'

Griffith groan. 'Listen, Pipsqueak, I don't know who yer working for, but that cow's been milked.'

'Ludo tell me cows is beasts what give milk again and again.'

Griffith sit up sudden. 'Did that effing hatter send you here?'

'No, he dint.' I get a alarm, don't want poor Ludo dragged in.

Griffith get off the bed and come over to grab my ear. 'You tell that effing spic I'm gonna pay him a visit, geddit?'

'Ludo aint a spic and he don't know nothing,' I say, afraid my ear come off in his hand. 'One Eye tell me. I were the one that give Violet yer tonic.'

Griffith drop me. He pace the room. I now aint sure where this all going but the door sure look inviting.

'It all about that tonic,' I make bold to say. 'One Eye tell me you pay him to give it. But he say it my fault Violet dint drink it. He say I haffta get the coin to pay you back. I aint got no coin. I go down the beach to dig the sand gold but Ludo get sick. Now Fatso gonna boil me and . . .'

'Alright, stop babbling.'

I stop.

'Seems to me there's a simple solution to this problem. If I say to One Eye, jes forget the money, that lets you off the hook, don't it? Course, that still leaves the problem that you might pay another visit to Miss Moncrieff and start talking about Violet.'

'No, I won't. Honest.'

Griffith bend down and look in my face. He don't have no knee problems like his Papa, he don't do no groaning and creaking, he bendy and mean as what a tiger is.

'No, you won't,' he agree. 'Because if yer do, you'll *wish* you'd been boiled alive.'

Before he stand up I make my run for the door. I run out it and down them stairs like a rat what got its tail lighted.

NINE

I melon cow lick. I haffta hang around Hokitika town till Ludo
dry out, but Ludo aint drying. Haffta sleep with Kaspar because
the hut burn down, but he all the time reading out of his Einziger
and giving me lechers. He make me go on a trip to the beach
tailings to pack up the tent and rescue the ekwipments. He also
do some nice things for me. He take me to the opera house
and the Bill Yard Hall, things Ludo were always too drunk or
clapped out to do. Kaspar say Ludo isolate hisself in his hut
on purpose. He say Ludo like one of them fanatics that isolate
theirselves in the desert and say they seen God when rilly they
only starving and mad. He say it dead easy to be a man what
believe in the golden rule if yer don't ever see no one. It even
more easy to be Mr Simaritan when yer aint ever on the road
to Jeriko.

'Where that road?' I ask. We having our dinner in the dining
hall next to the Gridiron. Jes for a change, Kaspar say, and he do
the paying, so I don't argue.

'What?'

'Where that road? Mebee I take Ludo along it some time.'

Now Kaspar laugh his head off.

'Yer wrong about Ludo,' I say when he finish. 'He look after me.'

'Now I am looking after you. Am I now being the Good Samaritan?'

'You a selfish pig. Ludo say so.'

Kaspar shake his head. 'I am only reading from a different book.'

Blanche come in with her brother William. He such a lunatic and wandering about confused, everone call him Willy Nilly. I lucky because now Kaspar don't get a chance to read from his book or give me a lecher. Blanche come over to talk. She invite us to the place she and Willy Nilly are gonna visit after their dinner. Kaspar look rilly pleased. He sit there grinning like Ludo do when he open a new bottle.

We haffta wait while Blanche and Willy Nilly eat, then we go to a cottage. In the cottage we go to a back room, dark with heavy clothings covering the winders. Some people sit at a big round table that have a light shining on it, one of them is a lady what's done up in silks and velvets. Blanche, Kaspar and Willy Nilly sit down at the table and I creep in the shadders. All them people hold hands and a lot of crazy talk come on.

'I hear a bell,' the velvet and silk lady cry startled.

'Yes, yes, very faint,' a skinny lady with lots of warts agree.

I dint hear no fucken bell.

'Now a breeze,' the woman say, and she look all about her for the cause. 'The breeze of a dear departed passing by.'

Dunno what that is but I pretty sure it the breeze that's coming off the ocean and through them slits in the wood.

'A caress!' the lady say next. 'Is that you, my dear? Fanny?'

Everone at the table indraw their breathings.

'What do you have for us, love? Flowers?'

Flours? She think a ngingongingo gonna stick out some flours? She right out of her hinengaro.

I don't wanna hear no more porangi talk, so I creep out of the shadders and into the moonlight. I sit on a wall and wait. It don't take long. Prolly Fanny say she haffta go to the flour shop. Them hand holders sit for a while and get bored, soon out they pile into the moonlight. Kaspar, Blanche and Willy Nilly go off loud and hooting to the Gridiron. I set off for the Bathsheba, but Fortunatus in wait for me. He jump out of the dark and grab my shirt.

'I got a bone to pick with you, Sonny Jim,' say he.

His breathings in my face is disgusting. It chew tobacca and drink and something that smell like rotten cheese.

'You told Paddy O'Malley about Clementine.'

'His name O'Irish,' I correct.

'Don't get fucken smart with me, buddy boy.'

'I dint anyway.'

'Well, someone did. That thieving One Eye is always coming into my store and helping himself.'

I squint at him, a look that's a bit wasted because it dark as a dog's guts. 'What the conneckshun?'

'The connection? Folk think it's a bad thing I have a ward.'

I feel a bit qweezy. Ludo think it a bad thing too. He go on and on about it.

'So now he's bleeding me dry,' Fortunatus say, and the saying make him clutch me like a drowner that need rescuing.

'Why yer don't fetch Clementine to yer house? Then everone know. What One Eye can do then?'

'Fetch her? Are you out of yer mind?'

'You fetch her for crissmiss.'

'Not to stay. She only et her dinner.'

'You bathed her up too, dint yer?'

Fortunatus leap at me, cover my mouth with his sweaty hand like someone can hear us.

I wriggle free. 'She were dirty. Then she come to crissmiss clean as a pink pig. But it weren't me that tell. I already got enough trouble with that One Eye. Me and Ludo don't want no stolen food. Ludo say stealings is bad. And we got Kaspar, who only care about his own cause, whatever that mean, but it sure got a lot of cheese and sausage to it.'

Fortunatus do something now that surprise me. He cover his face with his hands and start a noise what's like crying.

'Aint you got no friend but Clementine? Is that why yer blubbing? Ludo got me, but he also have Caradoc, who bring him Jimmy Bottle in the hostipal. Mebee Willy be yer friend . . .'

Now the grabbing come again. 'I'm gonna shut that Irish cunt up if it's the last thing I do, swear to God. I'll chop off his thieving hands and stuff them down his throat.'

Well, that sure make a lot of people happy. Suddenly the future looking rilly bright.

Now I get the chance I scamper off to the Bathsheba fast as I can. When I get there the bar full to bursting. That's good, no one see me pass through and run up them stairs. I open some Vegetable Pain Killer and have a big slurp. Soon I in the cloud bed falling to sleep. Kaspar do come in, he lie there beside me in the morning, but I dint even hear him.

Kaspar introduce me to his new friend Erasmus. They always going about the town, often with Willy Nilly coming up the rear. Erasmus one of them men that pay a lot of attenshun to how his whiskers look, also his clothings and boots. He one of them men that carry a walking stick even though his joints aint fucked, and also wear a lot of different gloves. Mebee he off to join the circus.

'Hello, monkey,' Erasmus say to me in Revell Street. He put his feets together and stick out his cane like he posing for the King.

'Aint a monkey. Yer a fucken rangitang.'

'Orangutan? And where have you seen an orangutan?'

'In the jungly book.'

'Jungly? My goodness. Who is teaching you English, monkey?'

'Ludo were. But he in hostipal. If it any of yer business.'

Erasmus show his teeth, what aint a smile, it too ugly and mean. 'Well, you are a monkey, like it or not. We're all monkeys.'

'We are all coming from the apes,' Kaspar agree, like he tryna help out.

Well, that's a stupid idea. There aint no apes here. Mebee it only whitey what come from the apes. I say loud and sure, 'My Papa a chief.'

Erasmus hoot. Then he say, 'You ever looked at yourself, monkey? In a mirror?'

'Sure, I done that.'

'And you haven't seen any discrepancy?'

'I dunno what one of them things is.'

'I mean, do you think you look like the son of a chief?'

'What that look like? All my tupuna is sons of a chief too. They all looking different.'

'They've all got that nose and mouth, have they?'

'No. This nose and mouth mine.'

Kaspar seem to find this hilarious. He laugh and punch me.

Lucky for me, Willy Nilly come hastening along the street. Seem the three of them is gonna see a ektoplasm. I ask what's that, and Kaspar say it a word he learn in Prussher. He explain that it the spirit made into matter, it the ethereal made material, it the manifestation here of things what once live elsewhere. He spell everthing so I know I get it right. But it still a jungly of words that don't mean nothing to me.

Erasmus now do his explaining. He say the stuff that matter get made from come pouring out the mouth of the medium.

'What a medium?'

'You met her the other night.'

'That old frog with warts?'

'No, monkey. The lady in the velvet dress.'

I make a face. She jes throthing crazy.

Erasmus carry on his explaining. He say ektoplasm a thing like cloth or sometimes viscous goo. More spellings come but no more meanings. He invite me along. He say a ektoplasm prove Ludo wrong. It mean there aint no God or no Heaven. No decent God let his sheep ooze all over the furnitures.

'How yer know what God do or don't do, rangitang?'

Erasmus do his unsmiling smile. It his know everthing smile. It a smile that know man come from them apes and ektoplasm prove everthing. When I ask why do it, he get very impatient and say, aint it obvious?

I don't say nothing, but if he think ektoplasm prove there aint no God, his thinkings rilly fucked. Seem to me all it prove is God, if he true, make ektoplasms too. Though why it come out of the holes of them mad bitches I dunno.

'No thanks,' I say perlite. 'I give a pass on yer ektoplasm. I gonna go to the hostipal and see when Ludo coming out.'

Turns out Ludo coming out the day after tomorra, or the day after that. He aint dry but he aint ezactly wet. Caradoc aint got time to keep the supply up to what Ludo now accustomed to.

I sit on the bed, tell everthing about Kaspar and Erasmus. Ludo shake his head, say they both going to Hell on a steamboat. Then the nurse send me off.

I wander on the quay for a while, then go around the shops. I see Violet go into Evan Prosser's Drug Hall. I follow her in. She see me and start snapping my head. Then she look all round them shelves for the medsin that Caradoc want for his rheumatisms. I see she put her hand on a brown bottle that got a rilly good picture on it, a picture of a warrior tryna kill a taniwha with many heads. It got writings that say Swaim's Panacea on the label. Violet say that along with his Perry Davis, Caradoc drink the stuff down like water since the days he were in California. She say she like a glug too, it cure her from aches in the head and many despondencies. Then she haffta do the spellings and explain me what a despondency is.

After we done the shopping we go for a walk by the river. It a day of sun and little wind. It the day yer always wanting, but sometimes when you get it, it seem the same as any other day. Soon Violet and me sitting on the river bank and drinking. Violet drink the Panacea and I finish off some Vegetable Pain Killer that I got stored in my pocket. What I rilly like is the way Vegetable Pain Killer make everthing go sharped and still. And it do something funny to my ticker too, them ticks go more slower and more thuddier.

'This medsin make me feel rilly good,' I say to Violet.

'Only good? What yer drinking it for?'

'What's a word that mean more'n happy then?'

'Bliss.'

'Yair, I having a lot of bliss.'

Violet giggle. She prolly having bliss too. She take another glug.

'What Caradoc say when he see half his bottle gone?' I a bit startled how much she gulp.

'He don't see, stupid. When I get back to the hotel, I'll fill it up with water.'

'That why his rheumatisms never go away?'

Violet laugh mean.

It a rilly nice day. Them warm airs is everwhere and soon we feeling a bit drowsy and stretch out.

We woken up with kicks. I look up and see the ugly mug that belong to Erasmus. Seem he out walking with Kaspar. Now me and Violet jump up, start to brush the dust off our clothings.

'What have you got there, Missie?' Erasmus ask when she

snatch up her near empty bottle from the ground.

'If it's any of yer business, which it aint, it's a bottle of Swaim's. It's for Caradoc's rheumatism.'

Kaspar take it from her and look consternated. 'He should not be swallowing this. It is a known poison.'

'What you know?' I ask. This pretty cheeky, but jes seeing that red fizzog of Erasmus make me mad.

'I am coming from Berlin and Paris. I am all the time reading there. It is containing corrosive sublimate.'

'What I care?' Hard to care when you don't know what he talking about.

'What's corrosive sublimate?' Violet ask.

'Chloride of mercury. And a very deadly poison.' Kaspar shake his head, seem he have a despondency. Then he say, 'I am informing Caradoc to be taking another substance.'

'I wouldn't worry about it, my friend,' Erasmus say. 'I'm certain these bottles are only filled with quacks' nostrums that have been cooked up here. Or even just water from the river.'

Well, this a jungly of words I can't get through.

'I am bringing salicylate with my suitcases,' Kaspar say. 'I will be telling Caradoc.'

'Yer don't have to bother,' Violet say. 'Gertie's got some Fowler's.'

'That is being even worse,' Kaspar object loud. 'It is full of arsenic.'

I feel a bit strange, don't wanna chew the fat with them two clowns. But maybe this Sally Sylate that Kaspar brung fix me. When I get back to the hotel I ask everone, but she aint nowhere to be found.

I aint got no coin. Somehow it all gone and I haffta hold out my hand to Kaspar. So a thinking come up in me, mebee Violet give me a job till Ludo get out. She is in the kitchen washing up them dishes from the early breakfasts, her stomick grow even fatter in the night.

'Yair, there's gonna be a big party soon,' she say when I ask for a job for coin. 'This place needs scrubbing from top to bottom.'

'What big party?'

'Dunno. Caradoc mentioned it. A surprise party, he said.'

Well, if it what I think, it sure gonna be a surprise for *her*.

Violet give me a bucket with suds and one of them brushes the scrubbers use. Then she point out what I haffta do.

'What, all them fucken walls?'

She nod.

'What a party need clean walls for?'

Violet give me a mean look and say she haffta go and sort out my coin with Mr Flewelling.

I start the scrubbing. I in a teerible open place, jes like a weta on a wall, any trouble can get me. But it won't go on too long if Fortunatus kill One Eye. Then Fatso collapse like a pudding that grow too high. He one of them men that haffta be held up to evil. One Eye is one of them that do the holding.

Then speak of the devil and his horns, when I go out to empty my bucket One Eye leaning against the front wall and smoking.

'I been looking for you, Cocoa,' he say.

'What for? I done yer job.'

'Then where's the money?'

'What yer mean? Dint Prosper tell you?'

'Tell me what?'

'Griffith let me off.'

One Eye sure get a surprise.

'Yair, I go to him and say I seen his Goldie.'

'Christ! What did yer do that for?'

'Because I did see her. So Griffith get in a panic and let me off.'

One Eye narrow his good eye like he aint sure what he hearing.

Like he aint sure if it good or bad, or if there's a little brat what's making a fool of him.

'I sure hope you aint telling me no lies, Cocoa.'

'I aint. Mebee you need to ask Fatso why he dint tell you.'

'Yair, maybe I do.'

But he don't go in the hotel. He look at me like I something that please him. 'Maybe there's some hope for you yet,' he say. Then he go off down the street and I go back to more scrubbings.

A weta is a pretty big ugly insect, it easy to see its hard brown body and waving feelers from a long way off. The next thing that see Harvey Weta on the wall is Pudding Prosper who aint collapsed yet. He waddle over after the sleep he always have between cooking the lunch meal and the dinner. He collar me and ask what I causing so much trouble for, dint I know he were gonna give the news to One Eye that Griffith let us off?

'No, you weren't,' say I. 'Yer have a secret plan I don't unnerstan.'

'Yair, I'm hoping I get to squish you.'

'That aint it. Yer some kind of tricker.'

'You accusing me of being a double-crosser, yer little fuck?'

'Yair, why not? Yer always crossing yerself once, why not twice?'

'Eh?'

Look like Prosper gonna flick me off the wall, flick me off and stomp me under his boot, but then Caradoc come in the bar, start examining all the cleanings. Fatso waddle back to his kitchen and I scrub hard on the wall. Caradoc watch me, see if I earn my coin, then he go off too. I keep working hard on the wall but in my head I work even more hard at what Prosper get up to. The thinking come up in me to rememory what I say to myself: Prosper one of them men that haffta get held up to evil. Who hold him up if One Eye don't? Who give him a dirty job to do and a cut? It aint long before Fortunatus come into my head.

Later, when I stop for lunch and then jes resting by the fire, One Eye come in the hotel. I expect some shouting, mebee One Eye clout Fatso about the head, but that don't happen. Them two seem thick as thieves. I sick of tryna work everthing out, so I skip out to see Fortunatus. He out the front of his store like he always seem to be and busy piling up them cabbages for his customers to see from a long way off.

'What's going on?' I ask. I take up a position that mean business. I seen it done before. I plant my feets apart and fold my arms and look him up and down rilly slow.

'What yer talking about, Sonny Jim?'

'Why Prosper don't tell One Eye that Griffith let me off the money?'

This aint what he were expecting. He turn red like a beet. It give me a idea.

'It yer plan to get Fatty to squish One Eye so he don't do no more thieving from yer store?'

Fortunatus find his laugh. Ho ho ho he go. Then he say, 'Have yer seen Mr Dirago falling out with Paddy? No? So what you on about?'

I aint certain no more. We talk the price of fish for a while, then I set off back to the Bathsheba. As I walk, the sun dawn on me. Fatso and Fortunatus want One Eye to squish me! If I don't give One Eye the coin he squish me for sure. And if I get squished One Eye go to gaol, mebee even go to the hangman. Gone is two wetas in one stomp – Fortunatus get rid of One Eye, Prosper get rid of a boy that know all the bad things he done. But what make Fatso change his stripe? Mebee Fortunatus give him free binarnas for life.

Right now I can't think about it no more and I can't do nothing about it. I haffta finish the walls for the party. Then something happen that pull me off them walls. I hear a noise and turn. Ludo throw open the big doors that were shutting out a sudden storm and stand there grinning.

That night me, Kaspar and Ludo share the fancy bedroom. Kaspar and me sleep in the cloud bed as usual, and Caradoc bring in a stretcher bed for Ludo. But soon as he lie down he start complaining it too narrow and hard, he say he feel like he sleeping on a rock shelf. So Kaspar take his place on the stretcher and Ludo get in the cloud bed still going grumble grumble grumble. It jes like he a Goldilocks, a story he once tell me of where everthing haffta be perfic or he aint happy. That's the trouble with drunks, they always having the melon cow lickings when they aint lickered up. But soon Ludo snoring anyway and I can lie warm hearing the rain drum and thinking about what a perfic evening we all have.

When Ludo come in the hotel doors, Caradoc were the first to greet him. He come out and hug his old friend like he come back from the dead. Then I have my hug while Caradoc call up some drinks from the bar. Blanche bring a tray and a bottle of whiskey and empty glasses for everone except me. I get a full glass of teerible cordial. Soon Kaspar come in from his ship wrecks and a party start that go far in the night. It aint long before no one notice I drinking the whiskey dregs and soon I happy as anyone. Prosper and Blanche come out with roasted meats and bread followed by a big treacle pudding.

Someone bang the piana and the singing start. Caradoc and Ludo stand and yowl beside the piana with their arms around each other, look like they holding each other up. Kaspar do some dancing with Blanche and a few drown diggers do some twirls with the dancing girls. But it aint a big dancing night, most of them diggers is out there in the storms, ready to grub for gold at first light.

In the morning it still pouring. Kaspar gone early to his overlandings and Ludo rilly grumpy when he tryna pull on his moleskins. He say the wallpaper been suffocating him all night.

'I dint notice you spend one minute awake,' I say, sitting up in the bed.

'Don't have to be awake to suffocate.'

'Then how come you aint dead? Do it take more'n eight hours to suffocate?'

Ludo clip me around the ear, tell me not to be cheeky.

I lie back down in the cloud bed and smother a laugh. Ludo's clips so feeble they more like a feather than a fist.

'Hey Ludo,' I say while he fight his way into his Nugget boots, 'how were it that you and Caradoc aint friends when you met me?'

'What? Dint I tell you already? Caradoc's a man who wants to own hotels and I'm a man who likes sleeping under the stars.'

'Aint a reason to stop the talk.'

'Well now . . .' But Ludo look like he lost his words. He stamp his boots to get his feets right in to the toes and then he start the fight with his pea jacket.

TEN

The day come that I hope never to see. I come back from my fishing, today no catchings, and Goldie is right then stepping out of a carriage in front of the Bathsheba. It a day that's cold and fine, she all done up in plum, and giving her hand to her Papa that's helping her down. I chickened out of telling Violet what gonna happen, I were too afraid I make teerible trouble. Now trouble make its own way.

Mr Flewelling come out of the hotel looking like he been oiling his joints all morning, he all springy and delighted to meet with yous. There's a lot of hand shakings and in everone go. I follow. Fat Belly Violet is wiping the bar. I go and stand beside her, together we watch the happy group all gathering around them roaring flames.

'What's that bitch doing here?' Violet ask. She getting ruder the same speed as her belly grow.

'You don't rememory her from the ball?'

'Rememory? Aint yer unnerstood the grammar yet?'

'There a lot to unnerstand.'

Violet stare hard at Goldie. 'Oh yair, she danced with Griffith.'

Again come a moment when I can let them cats out, but dint I already decide no? 'Mebee she come here for the party tomorra.'

Violet nod and grumble, 'Dunno why Caradoc needs to give a party at this time of year.'

'Mebee he got other plans for the spring.'

Violet giggle. 'Like being a Papa. Or so he thinks.'

It come to me how much the misery of a other person cheer someone up.

Then the group go up them stairs to the bedrooms Violet clean so hard. Violet have a sore back and sore feets but she do all them bendings and scrubbings so Miss Goldie, fit as a fiddle, can lie down and not haffta look at no dirt.

'Bring those suitcases up, Harvey,' Mr Flewelling bellow as he go.

I do what he say and get to the top of them stairs quick as what a wink is, even though they big suitcases for a small Halfie. Mr Flewelling show Goldie to the best room, then he show her Papa to the one next door. It the one where me, Ludo and Kaspar were sleeping, now us three haffta go downstairs next to the dancing girls. It a dark little hole that used to be a store cupboard and it got saggy old bunks for poor diggers that's accustomed to dossing on the ground, but it also have a stove.

Now I put them suitcases in Goldie's room and I hear her ask to meet Mrs Flewelling. Mr Flewelling say sorry, his wife is very sick jes now. Goldie very perlite and say to send her sympathies, dunno how they gonna get there, Caradoc sure aint taking them.

'Please stay here, Harvey,' Goldie say when the men go out of the room. 'I have some little jobs for you.'

When they gone she don't have no jobs. She hold my hand and ask, 'Have you kept our little secret?'

'Yair, Gertie don't know a thing about the ingagemint. But she don't know much about nothing these days.'

'What do you mean?' Goldie look rilly consternated.

'There some funny things what happen to her. Her eyes turn red and watery and her skin gone brown. Like mine, but mine brown all over, she jes brown in patches. She all the time sleeping and when she wake up she very confused.'

'Oh, but that's awful,' Goldie say. She sound like she mean it too.

Then Goldie give me a hug like I a sweet little boy, but I don't feel like no little boy in her hug. And I mixed up. Violet the one that got the belly and haffta clean all them dirts, I orta feel sorry for her, but Goldie is so beautiful. She like a kitten on a velvet cushion, Violet more like a fleabag cat that run around the wharf.

I haffta see Prosper, explain I dint get no fish, a task I shrink from. So I pay a visit to Ludo in our room. The way he got it now, it don't look that much different from the hut. He stoke up the old stove so much the room is sweltering. Ludo have his old shirt drying on a string, he have his Bible on his lap, he have his bottle and a tin mug on the little table. He look rilly happy but prolly that all Jimmy Bottle. I sit down on a chair and he smile at me.

'What's the right age to marry, Ludo?'

Ludo consider. 'For a girl, about eighteen. For a man, I'd say . . . forty.'

'That a long time to wait.'

'Who's waiting?'

I look down.

'What — you've fallen in love? Yer way too young for that nonsense, laddie.'

'What's nonsense about it?'

Ludo start puffing and blowing like he don't know where to start.

'Dint you get married?'

'Yair, I did. I was about twenty-six, if I recall correctly.'

'Why yer say forty then?'

'A man has to make his way first.'

'Make his way where?'

'It means he has to get himself established. With a house and money and so forth.'

'What if he don't?'

Ludo sigh. 'Then the girl worries and worries. Where are the babies going to live if they come? How is the family going to survive? She worries herself sick.'

This soothe me. 'Griffith Flewelling dint find no gold yet, did he?'

Ludo blink.

'Mebee Goldie don't marry with him when the time come.'

'Goldie?'

'The lady upstairs. She gonna have a ingagemint with Griffith. The party is tomorra night, but don't tell no one, it a big secret.'

'I aint seen any woman today. What does she look like?'

I explain Goldie is the girl from the ball, but Ludo don't rememory. Then he say, 'Well, I don't think she has to worry. Even if Griffith aint found any gold, Caradoc is pretty flush. What with the drink that goes down the throats in this place.' Ludo shake his head like it a vice he aint part of.

'A girl can marry with two men, can't she Ludo?'

'Only if the first one dies.'

'But if one a lot more old, he die first, aint that right?'

'Usually.' Ludo pour hisself a big glug of Jimmy Bottle. 'So tell me the name of the girl yer in love with.'

'I dunno if it love. How yer tell? It more a funny feeling in my moleskins.'

Ludo, who were right then having a big gulp, spit all the drink out in a big choke.

Kaspar come in. He say the stranding he been doing all day now afloat again. He sit on his bunk, take off his boots and lie hisself down. He take out his little book and begin to read, something I seen him do a lot when he have a despondency. I dint know a use for them books that men carry round, but making a small room for yer hinengaro and slamming the door on the world sure seem like a good one.

Ludo nettled. More he drink, more with his eye he throw them evils at Kaspar. Kaspar catch one of them looks. He hold up his book and read out, 'I sing because I am a singer. But I use you for it – because I need ears!'

'You shan't have ears!' Ludo cry, but he clap his hands over mine instead of his own. I do a wriggle and still can hear.

'In the time of the spirits,' Kaspar thunder on, 'thoughts hovered above me and convulsed me as if I were in a fever. These thoughts became corporeal on their own. God, Emperor, Pope, Fatherland! But I say, I alone am corporeal. And now I take the world for what it is to *me*. As mine, as my property. I refer it all to myself.'

Ludo stand up and begin stamping. He stamping his feets like a christian soldier. Lucky for me a big bell that Prosper jes buyed ring us all into the bar for a hot dinner of meats and gravies. Them hot dinners shut everbody up. When Ludo say his thanks to the Lord before he eat, I say thanks too. Thanks for the food what make everone shut their pie holes.

After the dinner Prosper collar me. He say I haffta take a tray up to Gertie. I ask why I got to, and he tryna stick his boot into me. But he fat and I fast, so it jes meet the air. Then Violet look up from the dishes and say I got to because she sick and tired of going up and down them stairs.

Up I go with a bowl of soup. When I go in Gertie aint in the bed, she sitting in the armchair. When I last seen her she were spilling all over the armchair like a melt candle, now she jes look like a tiny doll in the middle of it. More'n that, she aint got no hair.

'Halfie,' she say in a bird voice. 'How lovely!'

'Where yer want me to put it?'

She point to a small table near her chair. Then she ask me to feed her.

'Halfie,' she say between swallows, 'I've heard a young lady's voice in the hall.'

'Prolly one of them dancing girls.'

'No, it wasn't. None of them speak like that.'

I stick in another spoonful.

'And there's an awful lot of moving about. Is something going on?'

I look at her face what's lost all the puff of fattiness. Now it sag, but her eyes still shine. My heart go funny, I feel like I do something bad if I jes say, course not, what yer talking about?

'I think there gonna be a party or something,' I mumble.

'A party? Oh, how wonderful!' Gertie clap her hands together. Then her face fall. 'But why didn't Caradoc tell me?'

'The party a secret,' I say quick.

Then Gertie declare she feel a whole lot better, she can come to the party, all she need is for her feets to have their medsin. She point to a ointment on the dresser and ask me to rub her poor feets.

I get a shock when I take off her slippers. Her feets that were once soft now gone all thick and cracked. She cry out when I rub them. But she make me go on and on. She sure want to go to the party. After I rub in the medsin she make me take all them dresses out of the cupboard and hold them up for her. They all too big now. Not jes a little bit neither, now she drown in them like they the sea.

'Oh, Halfie,' she cry, 'what on earth can I wear?'

'What about I borrow a dress off them dancing girls? They sure got hundreds down there.'

'Oh, Halfie, would you? Nothing too common, of course.'

I nod. But that aint my plan. The dancing girls aint got but one fancy dress apiece, it jes seem like they got more because they always swapping around with each other. They got their scrubber dresses, but how Gertie go to the party like that?

When I come back out, Caradoc in the hall. His eyebrows join together when he see me. 'What the hell d'you think yer doing in there, Bedwetter?' He got a rilly furious sound in his voice.

'Prosper make me bring the lunch.'

Caradoc grab my ear. 'Yer sure you dint volunteer for a coin? I told him no visitors.'

'Violet make me,' I say squirming.

Caradoc let go. 'Now you listen to me, Bedwetter. Mrs Flewelling's very sick and the doctor is the only one to visit her, geddit?'

'Yair, I seen. Why she aint in the hostipal?'

'Because she's got a family who can look after her, that's why. Now get the hell out of here, I haffta give my wife her medicine.'

'I already give her feets the medsin.'

Caradoc do a startle jump. Then he gather hisself again. He give me a push in the direction of the stairs and he go into the room. I listen at the door. First is quiet murmurs, then it turn angry. They having a argument over the medsin.

It jes getting intresting when Goldie come out of her room. She a sight to see in bright blue. Now a feeling grip my heart, it a squeezy sad sort of feeling. Like she aint made for a Halfie, she aint even made for the earth. She sweep past with a smile and hand me a boil lolly. She don't talk, she jes go down them stairs. I look at the lolly and I be reft. A lolly is a baby thing, it aint a sign to a boy that his moleskins go on the right track.

I creep along the hall and into Goldie's room that she too trusting to lock. It like a magick place. It smell of sweet powders and flour waters. Everwhere is lady johns, big frilly petticoats, and red yella green and blue dresses, they look like dead parrots out of Ludo's jungly book. What one I take for Gertie? Mebee not one that Goldie been trying on, I dunno what one she pick for the party. There's one more dress in her trunk and it rilly pretty, I dunno why she don't like it. It silky and it the colour that Violet say is dusky rose. With it there's a shawl and a snood, that's what Blanche call it. It a little fishing net for yer hair, but it all tricked out in beads and ribbon. Gertie gonna look pretty nice in this fitout. The snood cover her bald head.

After I take the fitout to Gertie I have a urgency and look for Ludo. He sit in front of the stove reading his Bible. Must mean he been seeing them apparitions.

'Is it the sugar disease what make Gertie's hair fall out?' I ask. That's the urgency I need a answer for.

Ludo laugh. 'Gertie Flewelling's got the most beautiful hair, long golden curls that . . .'

'She aint. She bald as a fucken baby.'

That make Ludo blanch, both the bald and the fucken.

'Don't yer be using language like that, laddie, it aint fitting. And bald? Yer sure she aint wearing one of those linen bed caps?'

'Very sure. And she thinned down too. Before her uma were like two piglets stuck down her sleep frock and now they shrunken away to what Violet call wishful thinking.'

Ludo frown deep but he aint got no answer to give me.

It the night of the party and now everone in Hokitika town seem to know about it. Not what it for though. Gertie, Blanche, Violet, Kaspar – none of them know Goldie and Griffith gonna have a ingagemint. The dancing girls and the other women that's been hanging around all gibbering about their fitouts. A fitout is more'n a fancy dress that look like it got a barrel stuck up it, it also jools and curls and shawls too.

In our room Ludo begin his own fussing. He fuss over his coat with the fish tail, then he fuss over me. Kaspar bring out a suit that look like he wear it to visit the King of Prussher then the King throw him in a dungeon for a hundred years. Ludo offer him the turpentine, but Kaspar laugh like he pleased his expensive suit have gangrene. He sure have fun being disreputable.

After Ludo fix my clothings what I don't need to put on for hours yet, I take a opportunity to earn coin. Violet and Prosper have a lot of jobs for me. First Prosper get me and Violet to make them tiny sandwitches that go round on big plates, Violet all the time grumbling about her sore back and a pain what's going across her stomick like she gonna split.

'What am I gonna wear looking like this?' Her knife going rilly angry at the loaf and I scared she gonna turn and stick me with it. 'I aint got the money to be buying party dresses I jes wear once. A winter party too, how stupid is that! Everone knows a winter party dress won't get the wear a summer one get, even if they aint expecting.'

'Why yer don't go then?' This seem like it solve a whole heap of trouble.

'Not go?' Violet look like I gone out of my hinengaro. 'Griffith's here, aint he? D'you think I should jes leave him to his own devices? What if that slut Ginger shows up?'

'She aint invited.' I dunno if this true or not, but Violet need to realise Ginger aint the problem here.

Now Violet go off on the topic of Griffith. How he aint paying her any attenshun, how she slip him a note begging him to meet her, but she stand in the moonlight for a long time and he don't show up. She say she know they haffta be careful but aint that going too far? They got to arrange things. They haffta get away to East Cantaberry.

'When the baby coming out?' I ask.

'Jesus, yer don't ask questions like that, Harvey. Doncha know anything?'

I tired of talking to Violet. She always snapping my head.

'In a month or so,' she say after we been slapping butter in the silence for a while.

All the work go on and on. I start to think I aint able to stand up for the party, but finally Prosper let me go. Ludo now done up in his fish tail and reading his Bible, Kaspar done up in his gangrene suit and reading how the world is his property. Between them is a empty bottle. I take a sniff, hoping for water, but no it brandy breathings that come out. Them two is fucken stewed.

I put on my clothings that stink of turpentine, Ludo stagger over to plaster down my hair with ointment. Now I stink more. Then the three of us go out to the bar. Blanche done up like a dinner and pouring drinks for Willy Nilly and Erasmus. Erasmus done up dandify, he look ridiclious like a ape in a costume. I begin roaming the place not knowing what to do. Blanche and Ludo make sure I don't get no drinks except elderberry cordial.

Violet come in. She wear a ordinary dress because her fancy dress don't fit over her fat belly, but she done up her hair quite pretty. Dunno what she do when she hear the good news. Now come Caradoc and Griffith, Griffith looking handsomer than a prince but also rilly worried. He keep running a finger under his collar like it a hanging rope. He keep looking at the door like he expect the Gold Escort gonna burst in with guns. But that aint what happen. What happen is One Eye turn up looking like he jes come from the wharf. Then he go to Violet and whisper in her ear. A frown come on her face, then a smile, it grow and grow, then she and One Eye go out the door.

Now it time for me to fetch Gertie. I glad no one take any notice of me when I run up them stairs. Gertie asleep in her bed. I haffta shake her awake, then I haffta help her put the clothings on. I jes lucky she have her lady johns on under her night frock else I haffta look at them clapped out uma and bum. The dress I borrow off Goldie look a bit funny on Gertie, but she is pleased about it. She go on and on how it the first time in her life she nice and slim. Well, she sure slim but nice aint the word that describe it. Then she ask me to wait while she put on her bonnet. She say a snood don't work too good when yer aint got no hair. She want to hold my arm going down the stairs. That aint a surprise, she prolly roll down if someone don't put on them brakes for her.

As we come down the stairs there's a lot of staring and gasping. The piana player stop sudden in the middle of a tune. Then there's a big silence. I look direct at Caradoc and his face work like a digger that jes lost his gold. Gertie start to preen and flutter, she lost in the past when it were her beauty that stop everone dead. Now she jes a old piece of gristle in a dress that's too young and don't fit right. Caradoc stride up the last steps, take her other arm, we bring her down to the floor together. He put her in a chair where she start fanning herself for all her effort.

Griffith look ever more nervous. He keep looking up them stairs. All the guests is here, but no Goldie. The piana player start banging hard on them yella teeths again, mebee he think if them tunes rise up through the ceilings to Goldie she rememory she spose to be at a party.

Now Griffith can't stand it no more, he fly up them stairs to fetch her. Soon we have the same scene we jes have with Gertie. Goldie stand on the landing before the last part of the stairs and everone look up at her. She sure a vision, her hairs is all piled up and decorated, her uma jes about jumping right out of her bodice. But she aint smiling. Fact is she look like she been crying for hours. She move her proud head around looking down on all them tranced guests. Her eyes come to rest on poor old Gertie who fan her sweat like mad. Goldie's eyes stretch wide, they jes about jump out of their sockets.

'Who's that old bitch wearing my engagement dress?' she scream.

Violet once tell me bad things come in threes. She a bit wrong. It depend if one of the first two things so bad that number three got no chance to happen, or if it do happen no one even notice. The first bad thing at the ingagemint party were Goldie calling her future mother in law a old bitch. That were bad enough. But it weren't nothing compare to the second bad thing.

I weren't near it enough to hear, but somehow with all them hand shakings and kissings and cryings, Goldie and Gertie and Caradoc and Griffith all make up or pretend to. Mebee I hear later what Gertie think of being called a old bitch in front of half the town. After the upmakings there's a lot of dancing and drinking, and then supper. It one of them suppers what try to outdo all suppers that come before, the table groan holding up all them cakes and pies and jellies. Then Caradoc stand up and tinkle his glass with a spoon. Everone stop talking. He clear his throat and say he have a announcement.

Everthing happen at once. At the same time that Caradoc say Griffith and Goldie is ingaged, and Griffith put his arm round Goldie in a way that say I pertect yer for life, Violet come in a side door. I dunno where she been, but she sure look a fright. Her clothings now tore and her hairs is standing on end. On her face come the biggest scowl anyone ever seen.

Then Violet the tiger jump. She jump on poor Goldie and go mauling her. Goldie start screaming, then all the women in the place scream too. Caradoc Flewelling stand there with his mouth hanging open, but Griffith pick Violet off his girl like she a scurfy kitten and fling her into the shadders. Then he help Goldie up. It sure sad to see her snood all crooked and her curls falling down. Her pretty dress all dirty too, what's rilly sad on her ingagemint day. My heart go out to her.

Violet now crawling out of them shadders like her legs is broke. She also making a loud wailing that's embarrassing. I hope she crawl away, but no. She stand up. She mount a chair. Off the chair she mount a table. She stamp her boots till everone go quiet and staring at her. Now I start thinking, fuck, she gonna let out all them cats, we gonna have cats all over the place.

And that's what she do. She stick out her fat belly, it look like a pile of mokopuna gonna burst out like thieves from a gaol, and she start pointing the finger. She point at sweaty Gertie and say, yer husband slowly poisoning you with Swaim's and Fowler's. One got corrosive sublimate in it and the other got arsenic. Yer feets medsin also full of metal poison. Even yer horrible wallpaper give off a miasma that slowly kill yer. Kaspar tell me soon as yer weak enough it finish the job off on its own.

She point at Caradoc and say, yer a fool if you think this bubba gonna be yours. Yer might be the Papa, but you aint getting it.

She point to Goldie and say, you think yer fiancé is pure as the driven snow, but he the kind that like to fuck the servants, and this bubba that's in me prolly his.

She point at me and say, if a girl want to murder her bubba before it born, and she do want to because it the bastard throwback of a bunch of sons of bitches, that's her own business. But it still aint right to take a payment from one of the Papas, and trick her to murder her unborn bubba with poison so the Papa free to marry above hisself.

Then she look all around everone and shout the most teerible thing. She shout, and who were it that paid One Eye to kidnap me and lock me up? Well, don't think yer gonna get yer money back, because he now stone cold dead.

ELEVEN

From the end of February all the diggers talk been about Okarita. Okarita this, Okarita that. Gold everwhere. Gold sunbathing high on the beach and dangling from the cabbage trees. A boat called the *Ballarat* set off there, diggers hanging off every plank. The custom man say too many diggers and fetch in the police. There's a big hullaballoo. Even when the boat get cleared of the extra, them diggers tryna swim and sail little boats out to the *Ballarat* to get their passage to Eldorado. After the *Ballarat* sail, steamers start leaving every minute for Okarita, not jes from Hokitika town but from Greymouth too, and I hear some also come up from the south.

So it weren't hard to make Violet come with me to Okarita. She have nowhere else to go. And me neither. How I go back to Ludo? How a baby murderer, even if he one by mistake, can go to sleep with a man that use his Bible for a pillow? No. After Violet point the finger, I run out into a night that got a moon cold as snow. I run down the street. Then I hear a voice calling out, Harvey, Harvey. I turn and there Violet is, she staggering along fat belly style and crying. I go back to her and put my arm around her. She sob on my shoulder and say Griffith say he kill her if ever he see her again. I sure a jumble of feelings. Aint it Violet what cause all the trouble she now blubbing about? When I rub her back the thinking come up in me, aint people always doing this to theirselves, causing trouble for theirselves then blubbing like it come out of the blue?

We haffta find some place to hide till the morning. Violet say we go to Blanche's place, she aint coming home. Violet say Blanche and Kaspar rented theirselves a room for the night in a hotel of disrepute.

'That aint true. What Kaspar see in her?'

'She's a woman, aint she? And he's a man.'

'She got big uma and big hair but she aint nothing special.' Not like my Goldie.

'D'you walk around with yer eyes shut, Pee-pee? There's twenty diggers to every female. He don't care if she's ektoplasm, long as she got a dress on.'

I open my mouth to argue, but Violet say it aint the time to be having such a stupid argument and we haffta get ourselves hid.

Blanche's place jes a room in what were once a hotel. We creep in the back door and go sneaking up the stairs. The room rilly tidy with everthing folded up and dusted. It have a big bed and the sheets smell of soapings. Me and Violet get in the bed and she soon snoring like a pig. But I toss and turn. What's Ludo thinking? Do running away make him think me even more guiltier?

My heart ache. It ache worse than the day Moana, dripping of course, take me to a whitey's place for a while and leave me on the floor. She say she come back soon, but she dint. It my worst rememory and I don't bring it out if I can help it. But now it coming up like a flood that's under the ground.

I dunno how old I were, but walking, not going on hands and knees. Then a whitey man I never seen before come home and begin roaring. Soon I roaring too. It weren't a good idea but

I can't help it I were so scared. He rilly big and talking a strange langwich. Now I know it weren't Inglish. I wish I talked to Ludo about it. Ludo been everwhere – he tell me that were Russhan or that were how them Barberry pirates speak. Too late now. Now I never talk to Ludo again.

In the morning, that turn out grey with a big drizzle, Violet and me already waiting for the steamboat to Okarita when the light come. We all wrapped up in them big shawls she borrow from Blanche's place, our faces hid. Prolly everone think I a girl, it rilly embarrassing. Violet say to stop fussing about it. I say stop with telling me what to do, and she say she fifteen years old so she the grown up.

Then we on our way to Okarita. Violet say it a dumb idea. She keep saying we orta go to Otaga or even Ballarat. I say, first it a good place because with all them diggers rushing there we aint easy to find. Next, I aint got the coin to go more far than Okarita unless she wanna pay. But she aint got no coin at all, not a brass farthing, she run out of the Bathsheba with jes her clothings. So to Okarita we going. I don't wanna argue all the way, but Violet bitter now she aint so afraid of dying.

'What yer think will happen now?' she ask. 'Yer think that slut will still marry Griffith?'

'Goldie aint no slut.' Mebee that aint the smartest thing to say but it already out of my mouth.

'Goldie? Who's this fucken Goldie?'

'What I call Lily Moncrieff.'

'What you call her? How yer know her name anyway?'

'She been staying at the hotel. Everone always talking.'

Violet stare at me. 'How long yer think it's being going on? Since Easter? Since Christmas even?'

That's a question I aint gonna answer.

Then Violet start her drippings again. 'Yer think he met her at the ball? Yer think he's been two-timing me for that long?'

I annoyed at her drippings and rantings. 'What you so mad about anyhow? Aint you been doing yer own tricks with his Papa?'

'That's different.'

'How it different? What yer think poor old Gertie feel now? And why yer say Caradoc poisoning her with Fowler's? You jes make that up?'

'No, I dint,' she flame me. 'Kaspar told us that medicine's got arsenic in it, remember? And Caradoc is all the time buying it for her.'

Now that I riled up I can't find the stopping place. 'And why yer shout I tryna trick you into murdering yer bubba? And taking coin for it?'

'Fuck, Pee-pee, aint yer figured it out yet? There's some special medicine that can kill a baby while it's still inside its mother. That's what Griffith wanted you to give me. It weren't fucken tonic.'

Now our steamboat feel like it sail on a paint ocean, everthing go so still for me. It come to me Ludo hear and unnerstand everthing that I dint. Everthing turning out even worse than I think.

We arrive at Okarita. A mist come down and hang over the lagoon. It so low and thick even them water birds look like they jes being borned out of ektoplasm. It sure a lonely sight. My heart sag like a old bed.

We do our landings. Everwhere around us is diggers with a swag and talking of Three Mile and Five Mile where they gonna get filthy rich, or mebee jes filthy. One thing they gonna get is soaking as down come a big pour like nothing I ever seen. I always have a roof over my head, even if it jes a big branch or a cave, but now me and Violet standing on the pier and aint got nothing. She too much a fat belly to climb a tree and I dunno where the caves is. We both glum and follow everone to the main street. It have a lot of grog shanties and shops. I hear someone say there's more'n thirty. This cheer me up a bit. Surely there's a hotel that want a worker, and I much bigger now, them owners see I can do more than sweepings. But for now we haffta find a place for the night, Violet already shivering.

'You go in them shops. I gonna look for a place. Mebee a cave.'

'A cave? What are we now – bleeding bears?' She look rilly angry.

'You can go back to the Bathsheba if yer want. Plenty cloud beds there.'

She flounce off to a shop.

I go to the end of a street that have a fancy Inglish name, *The Strand*, and turn into the bush. I see them diggers all going off on the track to Three Mile and Five Mile, but I go the other way. Soon the bush rilly thick. But I at home. The trees is my friends and shelter me. It don't take long to find a cave, jes a little one, mebee it more of a overhang but it do the job. I take a rest from Violet for a while. I squat in the cave and look at the rain. It come out of the sky rilly heavy then go running everwhere when it hit the trees. The tips of them leafs all running like showers, the showers flow down to the ground and run away to pools that's so angry they all throthing. The tiwakawaka flit around finding everthing hilarious. It all give me a shivery chill and a big delight.

But I haffta go back to fetch Violet. There go the sag of the old-bed heart again. I wish I were going over to Three Mile with Ludo and Kaspar to get us a homeward bounder. Dunno where each bound home to – I already at home, sort of, and Kaspar don't seem to like Prussher no more. He say nations jes too many silly ideas with capital letters. As for Ludo, he say he too old to go anywhere else, but I think he jes too drunk. So mebee if we find our bounder we jes buy a nice whare over them snowy alps in East Cantaberry. The sun shine all day and the lambs grow fat, they aint all stringy from going on a force march over the Pass.

I run all the way back to Okarita town. I out of breathings from running, but now I see the shop again. Haffta go looking for Violet because she aint stayed where she were put. I find her in a grog shanty and haffta drag her out. I lead her back to the cave and she get in a fury. She say it aint suitable. I tell her it suit me jes fine.

Then come the most miserable time of my life. Every day me and Violet haffta walk to the town and beg for work. Soon as one of them Piccadilly Whiskers see Violet's belly he shout, no, it a scandal, get back to yer husband. Soon as he see me he shout, get back to yer Papa or I tan yer hide. Soon we haffta beg for coin jes to eat. And every night we haffta walk all the way back to the cave to sleep.

After about a week Violet don't try for coin no more. She sit in a grog shanty while I clean out the pockets of coats what's abandoned on hooks. Then one day I come back and she got diggers all around her. I think they wanting to dance, then I see how much they consternated. When I get close, Violet all pale and say she aint feeling good. I tell them diggers I take her home and they go off to their drinks. Then me and Violet go off to the bush and she rilly annoying. She all the time stumbling and groaning and saying her stomick keep going tight like it have a iron band around it. Then she say her back sore. Next her pantalons wet. I say, all of me is wet too, so why yer don't stop yer whining? Dunno how we make it to the cave, it take a long time and the dark come down on us fast. The Okarita dark is rilly dark, it aint like Hokitika, all lit up with gas lamps and lanterns.

We come to the cave, it looking more like jes a overhang than ever, and the overhang go drip drip drip along some slime that hang down. Violet don't seem to care. She sag down and groan. I squat down beside her. Now she groan and groan like a animal. She puff and blow and sweat. The teerible thinking come up in me that this the night Violet gonna born her bubba.

I rilly shudder about what happen through the night. It all groanings and screamings and bleedings. When the sky go a little bit light, out pop the bubba howling. She a ugly thing with wrinkles and some blood patches and stuff that look like melt candles here and there on her whitey skin. I wipe her a bit and wrap her in a shawl. Soon she turn pink as a pig and look strong as one too, but Violet weak and sick, she keep on whispering about her family in Ballarat.

'What about my Mama?' Violet say. 'She don't know I had a baby.'

'What do that matter?'

'When I was little, I used to tell her everything.'

'Yer growed up now.'

'That's right,' she agree, but she still frowning like she aint sure about something. A tear come in her eye and roll down her cheek.

'What yer crying for? Yer got a bubba, you the mother now.'

'That's right,' she say again and then laugh a bit sad. 'I sure hope she don't go off on me and have a bubba in the bush like I done.'

'Nah. Prolly go away soon as she upright on her feets.'

It jes a joke, but now Violet cry in floodings.

I dunno what to do, so I rock the bubba, she gone very quiet.

'I'm so cold,' Violet say.

It seem like complaining. 'I give yer jes about all my scarves and things, dint I?'

'I feel like I'm gonna fade away.'

She look it too, all pale and trembly.

'Mebee it because that other thing still haffta come out of yer.'

'What other thing? What yer talking about?'

'Moana tell me. A thing what come out after the bubba. It call a whenua or something like that, I forget now. Yer bury it in the ground and . . .'

'White people don't have that kind of thing, Harvey.'

'Oh.'

I rock the bubba that's now doing peeps at me. It sure make me scared to hold such a little thing what need everthing so much.

'What yer gonna call her?' I ask.

Violet now closing her eyes. 'Dunno. What d'yer think?'

'Moana a nice name.'

'Mama wouldn't like a foreign name,' Violet reply me ever so faint.

'Well, prolly yer Mama aint ever gonna see this mokopuna.' I getting rilly annoyed with all them Mama bleatings.

Then she clutch me. 'Harvey, yer haffta write Mama a letter. Caradoc will give you the address in Ballarat. Yer got to say I'm sorry.'

'Sorry for having a baby?'

'For letting her down. For not having a wedding and . . . for not ever asking how she were once I were gone – are yer sick, are yer well, how are yer bunions . . .'

'What's a bunyin?'

But Violet don't answer. Some blood start pouring out of her like the red sea in Ludo's Bible. There it were God that hold the sea back to save the day, but here we only got Halfie. He have a bubba in the hand and a bleeder on the floors and he in a rilly big panic. He start to shout out to the ancestors, to the Lord, to the diggers, to everone what ever give help to anyone, but rilly he all alone. The ancestors don't wanna help no boy that talk Inglish, the Lord don't wanna help no boy what look like Koko, the diggers is all holed up at Three Mile and Five Mile, and as for the faint moon she all cold and useless like ektoplasm.

It no use to run. Can't leave the poor bubba with a bleeder and how I can run across all them evil roots when it aint properly light? What if I get lost? The bubba get soaked, mebee die of the shiverings. So I squat on the floor holding the bubba up to my heart, hoping the beatings keep her quiet and my skin keep her warm. Violet keep bleeding like the red sea for a while more and making them little noises like a animal, then she go quiet.

I jerk awake. The bubba start squalling, she hungry for sure. Then I see the full light already come. I tell Violet I off to find her a whitey doctor and a uma for her bubba. Violet aint doing nothing, aint gurgling or nothing, she jes lying there in the red sea. I touch her cheek, it cold as the moon. It sure feel horrible. Then I take her tamahine and go off fast as I can to Okarita.

Plenty of them shops already open, them grog shanties is doing whiskey for breakfast. The bubba squall like a storm on the sea and everone turn and stare at me when I step in a hotel. I yell out that the girl that born this bubba now a bleeder in them bushes and everone get consternated in a flash. I get ready to lead the men, but when I say Violet lying in the little cave off the track over to Three Mile, seem they all know where it is. So I stay behind to look for a uma, one of them working ones that have the milk, not one of them ones jes for sticking out of ball dresses. But before I begin my asking a big woman come out and snatch my bubba out of my arms. She say she get her a drink, then go off with her.

I be reft.

No one care about me. I brung the bad news, now I can go away. No one say, aint yer hungry or nothing like that. I can jes go and kick stones in them streets and be reft of my tamahine. So that's what I do. And as I doing it a fear start in me that the big bossy lady gonna steal my bubba for good. She dint even ask if I were the Papa, prolly she laugh fit to split if that's what I say. She say this bubba look like a whitey for sure, where yer get it from? Then she say, if she yours, what's her name? I rememory the cold moon that gleam on them horrors of the night and decide to call her Marama.

Now I haffta find Marama. What do Moana think, looking down on me, when I lose her? She say, why yer lose my mokopuna,

Tiwa, aint it bad enough that I lose you, aint there ever gonna be a bubba our line can hang onto? Then I rememory the bubba aint rilly Moana's mokopuna, but still she were born here with me and don't that count for something?

I start looking for Marama out the back of the hotel. The lady what took her is out serving them diggers their breakfasts and Marama lie in a little bed fast asleep. Finding her so quick seem like the first luck that come to me for ages. On the table beside the bed stand a uma made of glass. It got a little spout and in it still some throthy milk.

Marama don't even wake up when I wrap her in all them blankets from the little bed. I wrap up her head good, don't want no busybody seeing her little pink head. Then I go stealthing out the back door, stealthing far away from them shops and grog shanties. As I go, I tryna work everthing out. I steal the glass uma but how much do a bubba drink? When do I haffta fill it up? And where I get the milk? I have some aunties living out there in the bush, but mebee they don't even think me one of their own no more. For sure they soon shouting, where yer get a pink baby from, yer haffta take it back.

I keep on going. I tryna do a big circle back to the lagoon to look for a boat. I dunno how long it gonna be before that bossy lady think she need to feed the bubba again. I dunno how long it make a big distraction bringing Violet back to Okarita dead. That's another thinking what's been growing in the back of my head and now come forward – Violet dead for sure. Dunno what they do with her, mebee put her in a hole down on the beach. That's good, the beach face west, it the way home to Ballarat. Violet rise up, jes her wairua, or mebee she say whiteys don't have that kind of thing. But anyway, she turn into a ngingongingo and rise up over the breakers, then she fly out over the sea. Soon she get home to Ballarat and her Mama and them bunyins. Then no more weepings evermore.

I back at the lagoon. It aint a safe place for Marama and me but what choice do I got? Haffta get out of Okarita, that's for sure. Now I got the bubba stuffed in my shirt. It turn out a fine day, all them water birds is jumping everwhere, it a rilly pretty place. Lucky for us, there still a hullaballoo going on, diggers and steamboats coming and going, coming and going. Nobody care about a boy in a shirt stuffed with a fat fish.

When I get back to Hokitika town my feelings all mixed up. It look the same and my heart sag with the same old troubles. But some of me is happy too, rememorying Ludo and me in the calico on the beach, me and Ludo by his little stove in the bush. With Violet dead, prolly there's some troubles behind me, I jes dunno what ones they are yet. I start to sneak down Revell Street.

'Hey Cocoa,' a voice call out. 'Where yer off to?'

I turn and get the biggest shock of my life. There's One Eye smoking a tube.

'Aint yer dead?' I ask atremble.

He feel hisself all over. 'Nah. I don't think so.'

Then he come up close to me.

'What yer got there? Fucken hell – a baby! Where'd yer kidnap that from, Cocoa?'

'Dint kidnap it.'

'What yer doing with it then?'

'Nothing.'

'D'you want me to sell it for you?'

'What?'

'Babies is fetching high prices right now.'

I turn to hurry off but One Eye catch me by the collar. 'Yer think I'm an idiot? Who's being going around the town with her belly sticking out to fucken Christmas time apart from yer slutty little friend from the Bathsheba? And I got a bone to pick with her. So where is she?'

'Somewhere you never find her.'

'Is that right? Well, you tell her from me she better hope she can stay hid. And don't be dancing her baby round in the daylight neither. I'll let it go this time, but next time I'll eat the little fucker.'

One Eye show his teeth and look rilly mean, but I know whitey aint no cannibal. He aint even got his teeth sharped.

I push Marama deeper in my shirt. 'What happen after the ingagemint party?' I make bold to ask.

'What yer think? The engagement's off and Griffith's gone. Old Moncrieff says he's gonna shoot him if he ever comes back.'

'Where Goldie go?'

'Back to Rosstown with her Papa.'

'And Gertie?'

One Eye shrug. He throw away his tube and say, 'I heard Griffith's gone mad. I don't mean like no lunatic or anything. I mean . . . well, maybe yer too young to unnerstand.'

No, I aint. Out of his hinengaro like Moana. Due to drippings what never end.

'Have yer seen Ludovic?'

'Yair, he's still staying with Caradoc.'

This a big blow. I were hoping he find hisself another hut in the bush, be living where I can visit him without no more trouble jumping out at me.

'Kaspar?' I ask hopeful.

'He remains in the fug with yer hatter. When he aint out playing rudies with that barmaid, Blanche.'

'Seem yer know everthing.'

'My business to know.'

'Seeing yer know everthing, who were it what paid you to kidnap Violet?'

'Strong words, Cocoa, strong words.'

'Aint yer gonna answer?'

He grab me by the ear. 'Listen here, yer cheeky little fuck, I jes invited her somewhere, that's all. She came of her own free will.'

I twist away. 'It were Griffith, weren't it?'

One Eye smile evil. Now he can't help being a boaster. 'Well, seeing he aint here to defend hisself, happens it were. He dint want his past mistakes hanging round his future investments. If yer see what I mean. So all I had to do was tell her that Griffith wanted to meet in private. She come with me, no questions asked. She were waiting for him in the back room of Fortunatus's store. Can I help it if Fortunatus lock her up for the night?'

'She look like she fight a tiger to get out,' I say.

One Eye smile but say no more. I rilly suspicious about him. Mebee it were a tiger call Paddy O'Irish.

'And why she say you were dead?'

One Eye tap his nose and start to walk away. 'Don't forget. If yer wanna sell the brat, I get you a good price.'

I stand in the shadders as One Eye walk off. He don't go home. That's good, because now I can visit Ginger. I wanna ask her to help me.

Ginger invite me in and go sweet on Marama straight away. I give Ginger the glass uma, she say tsk tsk and go off to wash it and put fresh milk in. Then she take Marama off to wash her, get rid of the stink that's been coming out of her for a while now.

Now everthing good. Mebee jes for now, but jes for now good enough. Ginger get Marama clean and give her the glass uma, I have some tea and bread. Ginger start singing a song to Marama.

Soon she ask where Violet gone.

'Away.'

'Away where?'

'Dunno.' This atchilly the truth. How I know if Violet reach Ballarat?

Looking down at the bubba, Ginger say, 'Yer can't keep her. Yer know that, doncha?'

'She mine much as she anybody's.'

'No, Harvey. She aint.'

I don't wanna talk about it no more. I plead, can yer jes look after Marama for a while till I get everthing sorted out? Ginger is tore. She look down at the bubba and wanna love her, wanna keep her jes a while. So she agree but she say to me, not too long, mind, or she haffta take things into her own hands.

I go out on Revell Street. I feel like I go under a big change. After a dying and a borning happen to me in whitey world, it seem I more belong. But now I haffta face the music. It a saying I don't rilly unnerstand, but Ludo say it a lot. It mean turn to where yer problems is coming from. Dunno how the music get in there. And yair, Ludo say it but never do it.

PART
III

TWELVE

Haffta see Ludo but I scared. What he think about me? Prolly it better to visit Fortunatus, hear more talkings about how the land lie. Fortunatus stand out the front of his store piling up potatas for people to look at. He aint got no binarnas. I put my hands in my pockets to look like everthing fine, and stroll on up. Fortunatus a change man. He look like he got old sudden, his eyes is red and puffy like he been dripping for years.

'Where yer binarnas, Fortunatus?'

He look at me like I a knife that come flying at him through the air. Here whitey always say, cat got yer tongue? But that seem a bit rude, so I pick up a potata and look hard at it. It seem poor. Fortunatus don't speak.

I erasperated. 'What yer think I do to you?'

He don't answer. Jes keep piling like it what he do to pretend he alive.

'Doncha think I orta be allow to know?' This one of them sentences that gimme a great struggle.

'Yer do know. Yer told everyone about Clementine.' He say it like something strangling him.

'No I dint.'

'Yer told the wrong person then. Yer told the Irish cunt.'

So much happen, I aint even sure if he right. But I dint mean to. Not the way he think, that soon as yer get a secret yer haffta rush off and tell.

'Yer told Ludo yerself,' I say, inspecting another potata.

'I brung her to the Christmas dinner. That's all.'

'Mebee that were too much.'

Fortunatus grunt, then get a smile like he gone out of his hinengaro. He tell me One Eye lock Violet up in the store room when he brung her, then he get bored waiting for the ingagemint party to end. So he go in the store room hoping to have a bit of fun with her. Then Violet nearly done him in when she crack him over the head with a crock that were in there.

I say, 'Yair, after that she turn up at the party and fuck everthing up.'

'That aint no concern of mine.'

'Dunno why yer dint finish that One Eye bastard off.'

Fortunatus get a hard look in his face and his lips go mean. He finish piling and rub his hands on his apron. Then he go in the store.

'What else going on in the town?' I ask following him in.

'Nothing that I'm interested in.'

'Ludo been asking about me?'

'Nope.'

'Kaspar?'

'Nope.'

'I aint a poisoner, yer know.'

'Who said you were?'

'Violet. She were yelling it out and pointing at me at the ingagemint party.'

Fortunatus turn and say, 'Yer don't get it, do you, Sonny Jim?

You think yer instrumental in these events but you aint. Yer only a kid. These are all adult doings.'

I weren't instermental in Clementine neither, I think to say, but I don't want Fortunatus sticking in that shitpile again.

Then a suspicion come upon me. 'Mr Shaw dint put anything in the *West Coast Times* about me, do he? Or Mr Klein in his *Hokitika Evening Star*? I aint been in any of them newspapers?'

This make Fortunatus rilly angry for some reason. He start to shout about men that spread lies for all the world to read. It such a raving it seem like he gone stark staring mad. I haffta get away from him, he aint a person that's good to know. He a man with many demons, that's what Ludo say.

Ludo. There aint no getting away from what haffta be done. Mebee if I dint have Marama I can take things more slow and send a note so Ludo's thinkings prepare to see me before his eyeballs do. It aint no good for the eyeballs to get ahead of the brains, that's what I learn. That's when all them shriekings and cryings and hairpullings come on. But I got Marama, and if I don't do something for her Ginger prolly sell her to One Eye.

I start going to the Bathsheba slow. I kick stones in the street. My brains is going there for sure but my body hold me up. Or mebee it the other way around. Anyway, I aint all of a piece. But here come the front door. Here Halfie going through. It a quiet time, everone out on their business, Prosper all alone running the show.

'Thumbsucker!' he exclaim when I standing before him. 'Well, I'll be fucked.'

'That a nice welcome.'

'Where yer been, yer little bugger?'

'What you care?'

He laugh. 'Yair, yer right, I don't. But Caradoc's been asking for yer.'

'Caradoc?' Here come the first trouble. Caradoc looking for me aint good. 'Do he wanna talk about poisonings with me?'

Prosper roar with laughter. 'Nah. He says Gertie wants yer. She's been pining since Griffith done a legging.'

'Pining for me?'

'Yair. No fucking taste, eh?'

'Is Ludo here?' This sure hard to spit out my mouth. My teeths tryna keep it in, they nearly bite off my tongue.

Prosper frown deep. 'Yair, he and that Kraut are still stinking up the back room. I aint seen them this morning. Probably still sleeping off their last sousing.'

Dunno what that is but it got the sound of all Ludo's doings. And Jimmy Bottle seem to be the only way Kaspar show he following his own cause, except for doing the overlands and calling up the ektoplasm. Now I drag off to their door. My heart beat rilly fast like a scare bird. I knock but there aint no answer. I open the door. The room is dark and hot, rilly hot like it been whisked off to Hell in the night. There's a lot of loud snorings and a smell what's sharp. It the smell from a empty bottle of Jimmy but hanging in the air like outbreathings.

I shake Ludo by the shoulder. He grunt and snort and start, then he start lashing out like one of them demons got him. He cry out something strange in Armenian or Barberrian.

'Ludo, it aint a devil, it me, Harvey,' I whisper. I don't wanna shout in case he jump out of his whitey skin.

'Harvey?' Slowly he sit up. Kaspar sit up too because of all the commotion. Now Kaspar throw open them heavy curtains. The light come pouring in and Ludo see I aint a ektoplasm or a demon or any of them things that prove there aint no God.

'Eee, laddie,' he cry.

Them words, what once sound like crazy bubba talk, gimme a lot of bliss, it better'n Vegetable Pain Killer. Then Kaspar come bounding over, he everwhere like a big hairy dog. He smother me and make a whole lot of them Prussher noises.

'Eee laddie, I thought you were lost to me,' Ludo start blubbing.

We sit and talk about where I been. I aint ready to tell, so I say I been looking for a claim seeing how I aint got no coin. Ludo exclaim, what yer want coin for, yer jes haffta ask. Then I say, is that what I gonna do all my life, ask a old man for coin? Kaspar nod hard and agree. He say I haffta find my own cause, that's the only way I rilly living.

'It's easy to get mixed up,' Ludo say, a tear still shining on his wrinkle cheek. 'That jes because yer need money to live, more money means more living. It jes don't work that way.'

'What way it work?' Atchilly, I don't rilly unnerstand when grown ups talk about living. Aint everone living? Then everone dead. How there is less or more of either one? When one of them things is happening to yer, aint it *all*?

'I tell yer and I know,' Ludo announce like he the King Knower. 'Once you get yer pockets so full yer leave a trail of coins everywhere yer go, that's when you can separate living from earning. That's when yer realise you dint need so much money in the first place. That's when yer realise being happy in yer life is a whole other problem.'

'What other problem?'

Now Ludo look squirmy. 'It's a problem of missing things. Like I missed my old friends on the goldfields of California. But that aint nothing to . . .' Ludo stop and look at me.

'To what?'

'To missing you.'

'Me? Yer missed me?' Haffta say this make me a bit excited.

'Yair, I miss all the trouble you get into.'

'Oh.'

'Yer bring all this trouble to an old man in the bush and soon it's his trouble too. Soon he has to comb yer hair and kerosene yer moleskins. Next he has to worry if yer turning into a blasphemer or a thief or a poisoner. Then he got to worry where you are every minute of the day and night.'

This starting to make me depress.

'Is anyone looking after yer? What happen if the coach turns over in the breakers and yer washed out to sea? The fact that the old man's got gold coins hidden in his travelling trunk aint no protection. The laddie is still drowning in the ocean and he can't do nothing to save him.'

'But I aint drowned!'

Ludo pat me on the head. 'No, you aint. But how was an old man to know? His heart aint strong enough to take it on trust. He knows too much about the world. He needs a note or a message. He needs a sign in the sky.'

Kaspar get up and start to mess with his bed clothings. Ludo give him a look what I never seen. It say, I'm the knower and you the damned, but now there some pity in it, not jes rage.

'Aint nothing more important than the return of the prodigal son,' Ludo say quiet.

Kaspar groan.

'I weren't lost, Ludo. I were jes . . . doing some business.'

But now I see Ludo gone beyond any hearing. He rock hisself and a fresh tear come slipping down them old cheeks what's like Nugget boots. Fuck me, I dunno why he crying now, now that I come back not drowned, not even wet.

Ludo reach out his arms like a blind fool that need the way showed to him. I go into them flapping arms and he wrap round me like a drowner and cling on, his body racked with sobs. Haffta say it seem like he blubbing for something what's more'n me, prolly his boy self that got took from his Mama by them pirates, or for his Mama that got took from hisself. He sure turn his happy time into a fountain of grief.

When all the crying stop, Kaspar, Ludo and me get ourselves a mutton stew in the bar. We sit at one of the tables eating, and soon we start to talk of everthing that happen. Well, near everthing. I leave out some of the details of Okarita, like Violet going to Ballarat and Marama being borned. Kaspar say he think it were hilarious when Fat Belly Violet stand on the table and start shouting out them secrets. Ludo say only some of it were hilarious. He dint think it funny at all what she say about Caradoc and Gertie. He knowed from the start it were all a dirty lie.

'You cannot be knowing what is lies and what is not,' Kaspar object.

'Yair, Violet explain me the bubba is a bit of Caradoc and a bit of Griffith.' I don't know if this help Ludo to unnerstand or not, but it sure gonna help me when I flourish Marama out of my shirt.

Now Ludo staring at me. 'Yer mean the baby were a bit of Caradoc because Griffith is?'

Is what? I aint sure what he tryna say.

'I am thinking he is not meaning that,' Kaspar say quiet before he beckon Prosper over for the pudding.

Now Ludo go a bit pale. He say he don't want no pudding, he feeling a bit sick. Me and Kaspar get brung suet pudding by Prosper. We eat for a while, then Kaspar ask me where I were looking for my claim. I say Okarita. This sure a surprise for them two. They want to know everthing. I tell about the lagoon and the birds and the shops and grog shanties and Three Mile and Five Mile and how everone gonna be rich as Croesus and go home. Then come the time to say also I have some other business there.

Kaspar ask what were my other business in Okarita.

I take a big breath. 'I were helping Violet born her bubba.'

'What?' Ludo change in a flash. He were quiet while I tell everthing, now his eyes is burning into me.

'Yair, I borned her bubba with her. It a girl called Marama.'

Kaspar shake his head and say nothing. Then he wipe his brow and look away. Mebee he hope to find some sense to the left of him when he don't find no sense out in front.

'Well, where are they now?' Ludo ask.

'Violet dead.'

'Dead!'

'Dead as a door nail.' Whatever that mean, but I heared it somewhere.

Now come a long silence and a lot of chewing from Kaspar, but Ludo put down his fork. After a while he say, 'So where's the baby?'

I take a even bigger breath. 'She with me.'

'With you?' This explode out of him like one of them fountains of grief, except that it a fountain of shock.

I nod hard.

'Then where is she right now?'

'Right now Ginger got her.'

'Ginger? The sister of that Irish crook?'

Now Kaspar turn to look at me. 'I am hearing that the man called One Eye is dead.'

'No he aint,' I argue. 'Only near it. For a while.'

But Ludo don't wanna talk about that. He wanna go at once and rescue Marama from the clutches of the Godless.

So that's what we do. Me, Ludo and Kaspar go off to One Eye's cottage to fetch Marama off them low downs. While Ginger wrapping Marama up and piling up some things, she make some nice chatter. Ludo wear a perlite look, but it easy to see he can't wait to get his hands on Marama to start her christian upbringings.

Soon we out the door. We go back to the hotel, walking fast as we can, Ludo saying all the way he don't know nothing about a glass uma, Kaspar telling him he sure Blanche know all about it. We creep in our room the back way and soon Marama tucked up in a drawer by the stove. Then Kaspar go off to get some milk. He come back saying Blanche know a catholic woman that give the bubba a real bosom.

After that a few days fly past too quick to see. It all cryings and feedings and walkings in the night, it all Ludo and Kaspar going grumble grumble grumble coo coo coo. Hard to believe such a small thing can make two men and a boy jump like slaves.

One morning I pay a visit to Gertie. She still in the room with trellisbywilliammorris. Still sitting on the dresser is a big bottle of Fowler's. There's also a bottle of Swaim's. The room horrible gloomy and old smelling. Gertie sit in the big chair that make her look like a doll.

'You dint stop the medsin,' I say.

'No,' she agree very quiet.

'Yer even taking Swaim's.'

'No, that belongs to Caradoc.'

'Why it here then?'

Gertie blush pink. Then she say shy that Caradoc again sleeping in the bed with her.

'That rilly good. Seeing Violet dead as a door nail.'

Gertie bow her head. The drippings drip onto her knees.

I consternated. What I mention Violet for? It jes come out.

'No one has even brought the baby to me,' she say next, wiping her eyes on a little cloth with lace on it.

'Ludo got charge of her. I bring her for a visit.' Anything to stop poor Gertie with them tears that break my heart.

'Ludovic? But he isn't fit to . . .'

'Yair, he is. Anyway, he have Kaspar, a rilly strick Papa from Prussher. They all the time playing with her and . . .'

Gertie smile and then begin to drip again.

'Anyway, I bring her,' I say quick.

Now Gertie stop dripping. She start to twist her cloth. Then she say, 'I hear Griffith has left town. Caradoc didn't tell me, he doesn't want to upset me. Blanche told me. I consider it a kindness.'

Dunno what she want me to say.

'I suppose if Griffith were here he would take the baby.'

Well, I dunno about that.

'Do you know what, Halfie?' She now stare hard at me with them blue eyes. 'It's Griffith I miss the most. I'm afraid I'll never see him again.'

'Sure yer will.' It what yer say, aint it? It what yer say, even if it true some of them people yer love the most jes vanish in the wide blue yonder? It jes what yer say.

Before she can start dripping again I promise I bring the bubba up to her tomorra and I say goodbye. But when I go out, it my bad luck to run into Caradoc. He grab me by the ear, ask what I been doing in his bedroom. I tell him I jes been paying a visit to Gertie, I gonna bring the bubba to her in the morning. The black scowl on his face go away, along come a look what's more harder to figure out. He like a man what's looking at a town but jes see rubble.

'You can see her too if yer want,' I offer.

'No, thank you,' he say, very perlite. Then he go distant and proud. Ludo say this is how yer can tell that he suffering, he change like the wind. Ludo say Caradoc don't know how to be, how to act no more, he try this then that, he can't settle back to who he were.

My upwellings want me to say, yer got to see her sometime, but it don't come out. Mebee he don't. Mebee that's like saying Ludo haffta sober up, or Kaspar haffta get a cause that aint his own, or Erasmus haffta start thinking it were God that make him. Atchilly, Erasmus is a perfic example of his own belief that whitey come from them apes.

Now me and Caradoc in a stand off.

I make bold to say something that's been nagging at me. 'I promise Violet I send her Mama a letter.'

This jolt him out of staring at me.

'What? Can yer even write, Bedwetter?'

'Yair, I can write rilly good. Violet learn me in the beginning, then Ludo, now sometimes Kaspar.'

'So that's why yer sound like a dog's dinner.'

'What a dinner sound like?'

He seem to find this funny. He laugh and go clear as the Hokitika sky after a storm.

I say, 'All I need is where her Mama live.'

'You can give me the letter when you've done it and I'll send it on.'

Now Caradoc go in the bedroom and I go down the stairs. I see Kaspar talking to Blanche at the bar. It that way of talking that's rilly embarrassing. He lean in to her uma and she go all fluttery. Prolly how Griffith and Goldie use to talk. It only then come to me that Goldie is free. It a thinking that start them pangs in me, they half in my heart and half in my moleskins.

I ask Blanche for a paper and a pencil and soon I sitting in front of the fire writing a letter. Haffta keep calling out to Kaspar, what's the spellings of this, what's the spellings of that. He sure look erasperated seeing how he tryna be all fluttery with Blanche. But the letter get done.

Dear Mrs Athelstan

Violet pass away a while ago. She say she sorry. She ask how is yer bunyins? She sorry she never ask you.

Yaws Trooley
Tiwakawaka

PS I call yer mokopuna Marama. I hope yer don't mind. Violet explain me sea aint a whitey name.

I give the letter to Blanche to give to Caradoc. She fold it and stick it down her uma. Kaspar's eyes follow it like he wish he can go in there too.

First thing next morning I wash Marama in a bucket and put on some pretties that I get from Blanche. I fill the glass uma even if she aint so fond of it now she got a real bosom. Haffta say I see her point. If someone say to me, here Harvey, suck on this glass spout or have a suck at Goldie – well, I know what I choose. Now my heart do a sad thump jes from thinking her name. But then I think on the future. I growing bigger all the time, soon I grow into a man what can marry.

Now Marama ready. Kaspar and Ludo hang about poking at her, one straighten her bib, the other retie her booty. They like two old crones that aint got their own lifes.

'What are we to be doing today?' Kaspar ask mournful.

Ludo make a long face. 'We will walk in the rain to the quay and see if any ships have come a cropper.'

I aint intrested in their miseries. They jes trying a blackmail, so I let them come up to Gertie's room and crowd in like a whole row of Papas. Before yer know it, they gonna start teaching her how to cuddle a baby, something I sure she already know, you jes haffta look how much Griffith love hisself.

When I get up to Gertie's room, she surprise me when she open the door herself. She got a dress on, and shoes, her hair all done and them heavy curtains is pulled open. She take Marama and sit down in the armchair. Soon I dunno who have more delight, Gertie that sing *Mumma's little bubba loves shortnen, shortnen* or Marama that's waving her tiny hands.

'Have you heard any more news of Griffith?' Gertie ask after she been singing for a while.

Now why she haffta go and say that? Aint we all happy here?

'No, I aint heared nothing.'

Gertie been looking at Marama and smiling big, now she look up at me and her blue eyes swilling with them drips. 'I'm so worried about him. The state he went off in!'

'Mebee he get to hear about Marama soon. Mebee he come back.'

Gertie shake her head. She tell me he a young man in desperate love, it aint a baby that he want. It aint a baby that can fill the hole Goldie make.

Yair, I unnerstand that. Particully a baby that come out of Violet.

Soon I get a bit tired of all them rockings and singings, seem like Gertie never gonna stop. I brung the uma, but now I tell Gertie that Marama like a real bosom best. She give Marama back and make me promise to bring her again tomorrow. Then jes before I go out the door she hand me the bottle of Fowler's. She say to pour out what's left of it.

In the bar Caradoc sit drinking at a table. He see the bundle and turn away his eyes. The thinking come up in me to walk over to him and plonk down Marama, say, here yer little one is, it yer own no matter what way yer wanna look at it – but I scared he sweep her onto the floor like a crumb.

THIRTEEN

A few days later there come a knocking at the door. I open it and there's Ginger. She all in a flap. Where her brother got to, she wanna know, she aint seen him for days. She say that's rare in the cold weather, he generally come home when he full lickered up, aint one for sleeping in the mud. I tell the truth when I say I got no idea. Then Ludo and Kaspar also poke their heads out like they joined down from the neck and say, we don't know neither. Ginger say, never mind, I go to Greymouth where he once have a girl. Before Ginger leave, she ask me to bring Marama for a visit in the afternoon, she missing them cherub lips and soft pink skin.

In the afternoon I go down to Ginger's cottage with Marama. Ginger still alone. She go on about sightings of One Eye, there aint been any since he leave the Gridiron a week ago. Ten o'clock she say it were, and not even raining or blowing. It were a fine night, she say, this were a short walk on a fine night and now he vanish. I hold Marama out to her to stop her from blubbing. Then I sit down at the table what's covered with newspapers. Such a strange thing, someone write all them stories about the people that live in Hokitika town or Greymouth, and people what aint even in the stories buy them up and read everthing. What the fuck they care about people they aint even met?

Ginger say to look in one of them newspapers, one of them got a story that One Eye were very intrested in. She say it about a little girl that live in a tent on the outside skirts of Greymouth. She have a sex yool attack. I ask what that is, but Ginger don't say. She urge me to look but my reading aint up to it.

'Why yer brother care?' I ask.

'He says he knows who done it.'

This *it* still a mystery to me. The sex word is there, but do the *yool* change what it mean? Inglish a tricky langwich and yer can get up the wrong tree bark very quick.

Then Ginger say, 'Harvey, I've done you a few favours, haven't I? Got yer into the ball and looked after Marama and all that? So now I want you to do one for me. I want yer to come to Greymouth with me. It's a long way on the coach and there's always some rough men on it. If you pretend yer my son, they'll leave me alone.'

That sounds like a bit of fun to me. Haffta say, my life been dismal for a while. Ludo and Kaspar happy to get plastered in the fug and coo at Marama all day, but it aint so much fun for a boy.

On the morning when I get ready to go with Ginger to Greymouth, Kaspar say the trip aint one for a lady and a leebling and he gonna come too. Mebee he tired of sitting in the fug, but Ludo seem pleased he have Marama all to hisself. Ginger and me wait in the bar while Kaspar tell Blanche he going with us, and Blanche look Ginger up and down like she a real scrubber. It come to me that Blanche under all them face paints and piled up hairs aint a young dame. Fact is, she what Ludo call mutton done up like lambs. But Ginger, under all them paints and fake ugly-spots, is only a bit older than Violet – if she weren't dead. It jes that Ginger seem older because she full of sureness in herself and also a bit horsy.

We take the coach along the beach highway, again it very busy with the comings and goings of all type of drays and horses. Again the rivers act good and lie down quiet and we cross in the blink of our eyes. Again the ocean waves hurl at us but the wind is small and don't help so we don't get too wet. Ginger and Kaspar go chitter chatter all the way about Blanche and Willy Nilly, seem like Kaspar want to know everthing, but I jes glad it aint Fortunatus chewing my ear and sweating like a suit pig.

Greymouth pretty dismal. Ginger and Kaspar walk everwhere under the grey clouds asking what people seen, and I walk behind not always listening to the answers and pointings and arm wavings and sighings. Then somehow we stand in the rain looking into a ditch and Ginger say, that's a piece of One Eye's jacket. But he sure aint in it. Then everone glum and go to a hotel where Ginger and Kaspar talk and talk about what a old piece of jacket mean. I soon asleep on the table. Later someone lead me to a creaky bed but I aint sure who it were.

In the morning the rain come down even more heavy. Ginger have a grief attack when Kaspar say we haffta stay in or we get soak to our skins. To calm her he take out his Einziger and read. It aint a piece about causes for a change, it a piece about men going wild and cities and being alone, and all number of things that I don't unnerstand. Me and Ginger stare at him with our mouths hanging open. Seem even Ginger dunno what he on about or how it pertain to the moment we sitting in.

'I hope you are understanding why I am reading,' Kaspar say solemn.

'Nope,' I say.

'Not exactly,' Ginger murmur.

Kaspar spread his arms wide like the thin air that lie between them explain everthing. He say One Eye turn wild because he aint got conneckshuns.

'One Eye got a conneckshun,' I say helpful. 'He got a conneckshun to a gang of thievers.'

'Harvey!' Ginger exclaim.

'It true!'

Kaspar groan and slam shut his book. That's good because Ludo don't like him lechering me on selfishness.

Then a man come in that's a bit like Kaspar, he look like moss grow on his clothings and beasts roam through his hairs. The man talk to the barman and the barman point to us. The man come over and say he have some information but what's it worth? Aint worth nothing to me I say, and Kaspar give me the hard elbow. Ginger open her purse like she ready to beggar herself for life, but Kaspar take charge. He say no one knowing the worth of a pig in a poke, be showing us yer pig.

Dunno what this haffta do with pigs but the man open a sack and fish out a bit of clothing that's the rest of One Eye's jacket. It all wet and dirty and tore. Everone stare at it. Then Mr Mossy ask for coin to show where he come upon it. Ginger sit and blub but Kaspar disdain him and say we are already knowing that ditch.

'Well, lemme tell you,' Mr Mossy say, showing his teeths that look like he been dining on coal, 'the man who left this jacket in that ditch dint walk away from it. If yer get my drift.'

Ginger blub louder and Kaspar give the man some paper money for the sack and jacket and send him off. Then when Ginger gone to fresh her puffy face with cold water, Kaspar inspect the jacket more close and find the blood on it.

It don't stop raining. There so much water it seem like it going to drop on us till the end of time. We all sit in the bedroom that Ginger take, have a long discussion about going to the law, but Ginger worry what One Eye were up to and I back her. She aint believing he were in a gang of thievers – it rilly funny how there's so many criminals in the world but no one got one for a relative – but she worry he were doing a revenge. Then she explain to Kaspar about the sex yool attack on the little girl what live alone in a tent, and I all the time pinching shut my lips with my fingers in case something leap out that get me boiled in oil. I dunno what gonna happen, but sure as eggs is trouble I aint gonna be the one that put the boot in my own pie hole.

Kaspar don't wanna go back, he wanna search, but Ginger say she aint got the stomick for it. She say if somehow by a miracle One Eye escape alive, he come back by hisself. If he half dead in the ditch and Mr Mossy steal his jacket, she don't wanna see where his last lying place were, where he crawl to without his jacket, mebee without his trouser or long johns, she don't wanna see no trail of blood that come out of his cleaver cuts or bullet holes.

Seem Kaspar aint got no answer to that, he aint got no reading in his Einziger to make an argument on, so soon we looking for our ticket home. But this time our journey turn into a mad battle with wind and water, with floods and missing ferrymens, with hold ups and waitings and wet sleepings, with all kind and so many of miseries it turn into a trip out of Hell.

During all the trip home, that Kaspar call infernal, a question hang in the air. Then it get asked aloud, then it go in and hide, then come out and hang again. The question is, who stick it to One Eye? Ginger don't like the question at all, she always saying we don't know, we don't know, and she don't mean who done it but if it were done at all.

When we walk back in the Bathsheba and stand in our drips that make little lakes around us, there before me is a astonishment. In the bar Ludo and Caradoc sit at a table with bottles and ash saucers, and there sitting between them bottles and smoking butts is Marama. She been doing the learnings to sit up, now she done it. But that aint the astonishment. The astonishment is before he seen me who come in the door first, Caradoc holding Marama's little pinky and wagging it. When we all come thumping in he snatch away his hand. Kaspar stride over to the table and say loud what he need most is a big fat drink, starts shaking them bottles but they all empty. Caradoc and Ludo look more drunker than any creature that ever stagger through the dark streets of Hokitika town.

Kaspar sit down, start ordering up bottles from Prosper who still work the bar. He aint done a runner with his cleaver. Ginger and me sit down nearby, seem like no one even notice us. Now Marama start sucking the pinky I seen Caradoc hold, seem she very happy to be at her first drinking party. I sure hope she don't turn out to be one of them girls that put on a red satin dress and go into hotels warming men's trouser. I jes aint gonna put up with it.

Now come Prosper with more bottles on a tray with glasses, and behind him come a scrubber with bread and meat drippings for soaking up all that drink, or that's what Prosper say when she plunk it down. Seem this a scrubber that Fatso like. She got uma big as pumpkins and a sauce way of talking and looking. He spank her on the arse when they going back to the bar, and she scoot away giggling. Then he run along behind her, if yer can call it running, what's so much wobble wobble wobble. It a real circus.

Now Kaspar drinking and telling the party all about Greymouth, all about what we knowed and dint know. Haffta say them three that start their party early aint specially intrested in carriages and breakers and shallow graves and speculations.

I go up to the bar where Prosper do some wipings with the dirty muslim he always have slung over his shoulder.

He eye me.

'We seen what happen to yer mate,' I say.

'What mate would that be, Thumbsucker?'

'Yer know perficly well.'

Prosper drop his eyes to his wipings.

'He come to a evil end.'

Prosper go airy. 'Well, evil dies as evil lives.'

'What that mean?'

Prosper again find his true self. 'It means if yer a fucken arsehole all yer life, you got a good chance to die like a fucken arsehole.'

'So how do a fucken arsehole die?'

Prosper a fat waddler in the flesh but he aint gonna be catched. 'How should I know?'

Now the scrubber come and interrupt us. I never seen a female what have so much moving in her body, it like she got two big animals having a fight under her clothings. Prosper's eyes go big as plates, no more can he concentrate on what I saying. He a man that go in a uma trance all the way to the noose.

Next day I stroll by the store that Fortunatus own. He outside in his calico apron piling up binarnas. He whistling a tune. He sure done a turn around.

'Sonny Jim!' he call out. 'Come here and have a banana.'

I come over and stand near him. I got my hands in my pockets, shoulders in a hunch. This the way I show him that all aint forgot.

'What's the matter? Cat got yer tongue?'

'Went to Mawhera.'

'What?'

'Greymouth. Fucken Greymouth.' What's wrong with these whiteys what can't pick up the local?

'There's no need to be foul.'

'I went with Ginger to find her brother.' Now I watch Fortunatus to see what he look like. But he a poker face. He keep on piling for a moment, then he turn, hold out to me one of them big yella binarnas all the way from Fee Jee, hold it out like it gonna change everthing.

'Ginger show me the newspaper.' This hard for me to say because I don't strickly know what I mean.

'If I were you, I'd watch what I was insinuating,' he say low.

'What – yer mean I wake up dead in a ditch like One Eye do?'

Now Fortunatus change the way he speak. It like a purr. 'One Eye was a criminal. Yer know that. I don't know what happened to him, maybe he were drunk and had an accident, maybe he were dispatched. There are plenty of people around who wanted to see the back of him. Only last week I met a butcher from Scandinavian Hill who told me that while he were cutting up some steaks One Eye made him lighter of forty pound notes straight out his coat pocket.'

'A butcher?'

'Yair.'

'Friends for life now, are yers?'

'Not at all,' Fortunatus say cool. 'My true blood brother is his stepson, a digger who were robbed of a bucket of black sand by One Eye when he left the butcher shop. Black sand that turned out to have more 'n hundred pounds worth of gold in it. And I'll tell yer something else. The butcher's stepson also got a nice sister. One that Prosper has took a big shine to. Yer might of seen her at the hotel.'

Now a jumble picture come into my mind, it full of cleavers and buckets and gold and blood, and it got a long Mawhera ditch going through the middle of it.

'So, whatever way yer look at it, that ditch has done us all a favour,' Fortunatus declare like he seen the picture in my mind.

'Atchilly I agree. There jes the question of the newspaper.'

Dunno why I don't leave it alone. Mebee because I got Marama. Don't plan to leave her alone in a tent, but what if something happen to me and then a Fortunatus sort come by?

When I say this out loud Fortunatus go in a rage and grab my ear. He shout a whole lot of things that I don't unnerstand, but it end with him dragging me over to a old picture he got pasted on his wall. He read it out to me. It a pardon poster, a pardon in exchange for information. It talk about a man call Mr Walmsley from a bank who were robbed by a armed gang in the broad daylights in a lonesome place between No Town and Twelve Mile. He were robbed of eight hundred ounces of gold dust and a thousand pounds of bank notes.

'It were a while ago,' I say, looking at the date.

'It don't make any difference,' Fortunatus snarl. 'What if a One Eye sort comes by yer precious Marama? What about that? Yer think a life of robbing and murdering is any better?'

'Better'n what?' Somewhere he lost me.

'Better'n love, Sonny Jim. I'm talking about love. Can't yer ever follow a argument?'

Love? Do he mean how Griffith and me love Goldie, or how me, Ludo and Kaspar love Marama? And if he do love Clementine, why she scream when he come to visit? I think about it all the way home. It sure a conan drum. But it aint a topic I can talk to Ludo about. He go all dark and muttery, say it good Clementine's Mama come home and took her to a proper house, and if ever he see Fortunatus with a ward again, he gonna . . .

Dunno what he do, he always stop before he say.

Ginger do a lot of blubbing, but I rilly glad One Eye gone. As time go by he do turn out gone, he don't come crawling back as a ngingongingo riddle with bullets. The Gang of Rags fall apart, each one go his own way, mebee some to a life of crimes up north, others jes to fish on the river bank. Caradoc's best suit stay in the cupboard and lose the big stink.

FOURTEEN

Now it haffta be said the back room getting a bit small for a boy, two drunks and a bubba that's learning to crawl. Kaspar start talking about a room upstairs but Ludo shudder. Ludo go on about getting some wood and building another hut in the bush, Kaspar say no, yer can't upbring a bubba like that. It the strick Papa from Prussher what's in him, no matter how green his clothings. Then they have a argument that soon turn into one of them ding dong battles between the Lord and St Max, St Max being what Ludo call the man that write Kaspar's Einziger.

'Mark my words,' Kaspar thunder, 'the word for the new century will be nihilismus!'

'Mark my words,' Ludo shriek, 'you create what you admire!'

I hear all this argument before so I go out to the bar room. Caradoc alone there leaning on the bar. He bored, or why else he beckon me over to pass the time of day?

'So, what d'you know, Bedwetter?' he ask.

Another trick. If I say I don't know nothing, he say he always knowed I were ignorant. If I say I know lots of things, he wanna know them all.

'I know some things that aint intresting to you.' That's what I settle on.

'Is that right? How d'you know what I'm interested in and what I aint?'

'Why doncha do the talking yerself then?'

Caradoc smile. Dunno if cats smile, but he make me think of a cat what's having a lot of crooked fun with a rat. But rats is vicious too.

'Alright,' he say, pouring hisself a drink. 'Tell me what Ludovic's been saying about me recently.'

Now we gone from trick to trap. The rat scream inside hisself but then pull hisself together and go careful. 'He say yer an Irishman but you aint a cunt like One Eye were.'

Caradoc put down his glass. He look annoyed. Yair, I know he rilly wanna hear what Ludo been saying about him and Violet and Marama and all that, but now I vex him a whole other way. 'Ludo don't know what day it is. My name's Welsh, not Irish. And yes, I were brought up in the Caribbean but I wasn't the spawn of criminals.'

'Why he say it then?' I sure happy to stay on this different track.

'Why? Because he's a fucken alcoholic, that's why. And because he aint got anything better to do than make up stories.'

'Well, I know where Ludo come from.'

'Yer do?' I can see he aint believing it.

'His Papa come from Glasgow and his Mama come from Spain. She take baby Ludovic to see his grandparents and they get snatched by them Barberry pirates. Then they made into slaves. But not the old people – they got burned up in the church.'

Caradoc laugh fit to split. He get weepy eyes. Then he wipe them and say, 'Is that what he told yer, Bedwetter? Well, it makes a good story for a wide-eyed boy. But the truth is, he were brought up a gypsy.'

Then Caradoc spill all them beans. He say Ludo were born a A-U-R-A-R-I. They the old gypsy gold washers, he explain me. They live scattered all over them islands of the Danube — more spellings — and the Danube a river that's even bigger than the one that flow through Hokitika town. That hard to believe. The Aurari wash and wash and wash them sands of the Danube looking for the tiniest speck of gold. They have no houses, no huts, no calico. They got no shelter but their hairs.

Haffta say this all a big shock to me. It hard to imagine little Ludo on them naked islands in his little rags and shivering under his own hairs.

Caradoc carry on and say one day the Aurari need special permission to practise their profession. These words a big headache for me even when he do the spellings. But what he mean is Ludo's family get the boot from their washings. Washings aint allowed. Little Ludo go with his family to a village. Now the washers haffta work the soils and pay them taxes. Ludo get the Lord brung down on him. The O-R-T-H-O-D-O-X Lord, Caradoc explain me, not the real one. Seem this a opportunity to talk about who the real Lord is but I aint buying.

Now Caradoc completely forget what he first want to know. He go on and on about everthing that bore a boy out of his moleskins. I jes wanna escape from him, jes wanna have my day of dreaming about Goldie and catching fishes. He talk and I start inching for the door. He still talking when I dart outside it. Mebee when I come back he still there talking to hisself and pouring whiskey, talking and pouring but atchilly out cold on his feets.

In the evening when Kaspar gone to moon over Blanche and her uma, and before Ludo have too many drinks, I say, 'Why yer dint tell me you were a Aurari, Ludo?'

He get a surprise. He ask who tell me such a lie.

'Caradoc. So it weren't a lie.'

Now Ludo fidget about. Pour a drink. Fidget drink fidget drink.

'I suppose I was ashamed,' he say eventual. 'Like you.'

'I aint ashamed.'

'Yes, you are.'

'No I aint.'

'You are.'

'I aint.'

'Yer feel ashamed because you aint one of them and you aint one of us. But I aint one of us either.'

'Who is us, Ludo?'

Seem the drink hit him all at once. He scratch his head, he scratch his brass monkeys. He say, 'Only we are us, laddie. Only we are.'

Them rains come down and the river again visit the town. Me and Ludo stay shut in the stuffy room. Kaspar go roaming and skirting, and Ludo tell me his story. He say he were a little boy on the islands of the Danube, living there with his family of gold washers. I ask him, is there crocodiles on yer island or mebee binarna trees, and he say it weren't a island like that, it weren't a desert island or a jungly one. He say the Danube a rilly big river that start from a black forest – why is all them forests in Prussher and Russher all burned up? – and it flow into a black sea. Mebee the sea were black with all them burned up trees. The river flow through many countries and they all got their own names for it, that's something I unnerstand – aint I called everthing under the sun what suit the namer?

Now Ludo shut his eyes and do a little rock on his stool. He drone the names: Danubio Dunare Duner Dunaj. He spell them so I know. He say there a lot more too, some that can't be spelled in Inglish letters. This a rilly big shock to me because I been thinking all writings, except the yella diggers' tattoo, were Inglish. Now Ludo haffta get his pencil, haffta draw some shapes out for Dumb Head, some that look like little buildings, some that look like them embroiderings. Then Ludo draw and say the names of the other waters that flow into this monster river and he sound like a crazy man casting a spell: Lech Naab Enns Leitha Drava Vuka Sava Iskar Vedea Siret Prut.

Ludo say his island have marshes woods lakes and ponds. I tell him that sound the same as here, what sure is disappointing. I like to imagine little Ludo on a desert island with the blue river flashing past, the sun burn down, them crocodiles burn up, binarnas every day for lunch. Ludo shake his head and say some days there weren't no lunch and no dinner, nothing, and it were just violins and loud singings to fill yer stomick up. That give me a good laugh. I ask him how yer live on a river and don't catch no fish? What's wrong with yer chiefs? They must of been fucken idiots. But Ludo get angry. He say his people were slaves that have to wash and wash and wash, all day long they washing the gold to pay the master. There weren't no time for fishing.

'It sound pretty stupid over there on that island. How yer pay the master if yer dead from a empty stomick? Papa and everone here don't put up with it. They jes get in their canoes and paddle away. Or mebee we make the master a slave and if he keep whining about gold we eat him jes to shut him up.'

Ludo reply me the situation aint relevant here. British Law make a rule no slavery allowed in the colonies.

'What? They come all the way here to say no slaves and don't say no slaves on them islands in the Danube?'

Ludo sigh. 'British Law aint got no jurisdiction on the Danube.'

Then he explain me what that big word mean, but I haffta say it seem pretty dumb to me, if yer a country that's got all them muskets and redcoats, to sail for a year downhill to wag yer finger at us tribes and say no slaves, when right next door to the whitey lands of Russher and Prussher poor little Ludo living under his own hairs and getting no fishes. But now Ludo looking pretty sad and the thinkings come up in me I aint unnerstanding his story right. So I try rilly hard not to think everone of his people stupid, try to say some things that sound helpful. But soon as I a bit more kind, out come them tears that ruin his old cheeks and drip off his chin.

At that moment in come Kaspar, he shake hisself like a dog and all the rainwater go flying off his mackintoshes onto everone. Once he sorted out his wetness and realise them drips off Ludo dint come out of the sky, he stare hard at him.

'He crying because he were a slave,' I explain.

'He is being enslaved twice?' Kaspar say with something what sound like a pig snort.

'Yair, Ludo, that's rilly a confusion for me too. Were you a slave of them Barberrians before or after?'

Ludo, Kaspar and me lie on our beds and the storm carry on. Marama is up the stairs with Gertie. Gertie say a cupboard with two smoking drunks and a boy that's getting all the time bigger in his moleskins aint no place for a bubba. Rilly she jes want to make a room for Marama that's a Heaven of pink frill. So that's what she do. Gertie order them wallpapers from Melbourne, but not Trellisbywilliammorris. This time it pink flours. She order velvets to hang on the winders, she order bears in pink clothings, she order spotty horses that rock and floury chairs that rock, everthing pink and rocking like the inside of a lady where the bubba first grow, it jes like Marama go back in there.

Me, Ludo and Kaspar can visit anytime we want. Generally we have a party down in the bar in the afternoons. Gertie have a afternoon sleep and we bring Marama down and she sit on the table with them bottles. It sure funny. Sometimes Kaspar pick her up and pretend to drink her and everone laugh, but the one that laugh most is Marama. Caradoc come over and stand at the edge. He always ready to clear things, bottles and glasses and ash saucers, he pretend that's what he standing there for, but as Ludo say, when did he turn so S-O-L-I-C-I-T-O-U-S? Truth is, he looking at Marama and always pretending it a mistake if he touch her when he clear up our things.

Now Marama gone up the stairs after the afternoon party and Gertie see to her in the pink Heaven. The storm rage and soak. Kaspar have his Einziger out, Ludo read his Bible and I annoyed. Soon them two start a fight or they fall to sleep and snore. Either way it rilly boring.

'Ludo, why don't yer tell us about yer slaveries?'

Kaspar look up and do a pig snort.

Ludo close his Bible.

Kaspar do more pig snorting.

Then Ludo say he were only a little boy on the island in the Danube, a little boy what haffta learn to wash, he aint got no time for playing and fishing. With his brothers and his cousins and his second cousins and his cousins twice remove, whatever that mean, he a rag and bone that wash from dawn till dusk.

Kaspar slam shut his book and snarl, 'Gypsies are dark people.'

Ludo say to me, 'He has not seen every gypsy.'

'Yer about the same brown as me,' I point out, tryna be helpful. Then I hold my skinny arm up against his hairy one and show that it the truth.

'Ludovic, you are being a white Christian if ever I am seeing one,' Kaspar say loud. 'And Harvey, you are a somewhat brown boy who is having European features.'

European features? Do he mean I got porticoes and flying buttresses and all them other things that Ludo show me in a book when we get tired of the jungly? Kaspar have something very mixed up.

'Don't take any notice of him,' Ludo say. 'He wants us to think only black folk have ever been slaves. It's part of his nihilismus. If anyone has a lighter skin, it proves they were never enslaved or maltreated or imprisoned. It proves they are always liars.'

Now they both showing their fangs at each other.

Then Ludo point his bony finger at Kaspar and say, 'It's selective forgetting to suit yer own cause.'

Kaspar stand up and take hold of Ludo's finger. He crush it back into his palm.

Ludo brave and carry on. 'The trouble is, Mr Schmidt, yer think that everyone having his own cause means freedom from tyranny. But yer wrong. Each cause creates its own tyranny.'

'I am thinking it is better to be tyrannised by my own cause,' Kaspar reply as he lie down on his bed again.

'Yair, as long as it's yer own cause that's currently on top of the dung-heap and wearing the boots. If not – watch out!'

There come a long silence. I think there soon gonna be a big fight. Tryna stop it, I say, 'Ludo, how yer get from a boy washer on the Danube to being a digger in California?'

'Ee, that's a long story, laddie.'

'Well, aint we got time? It a big storm.'

'I am not having time,' Kaspar say, getting off his bed. 'I am not having time for your lies. You are wanting that he pity you. If he is pitying you, then you are thinking you can wash his brain. I am going to find a boat that is sinking and make some salvage.'

Off Kaspar stomp but he don't leave Ludo glum. He happy to tell his story while the storm beat.

Ludo say the gold washers of his family were all Princely Slaves, that mean they belong to the State. He say the State the govermint. That gimme a shock. It like belonging to King Sale! If I were told to wash for gold and have no shelter and no fishes, then give my nuggets to King Sale, I cook him for sure.

Ludo say one year there were a gypsy festival. He were young and dunno why they travel for this one only. Some of the Ursari come. He explain me the Ursari were slaves that wander the countryside with their bears that dance the Tanana for people who pay with coin. There were a Ursari girl at the festival he fall in love with. She were called Luminitsa. Gypsy girls get ingaged young he explain me, and his hopes were that he get picked for her or she for him or however these things get worked out by the parents.

Ludo go dreamy when he talk of Luminitsa. He say she weren't a Violet or a Goldie, she were a bewitching dusky goddess with big brown eyes and a coil of long black hair and a lot of jools and coins. She do dances to the violins that make him dizzy and hurting in the heart region. And he recall he sit there and he know she the girl for him for life. Even if he were young, he jes know she were made for him by God. He already can count their children on his fingers, one two three twelve.

Then Luminitsa go off somewhere else.

Ludo ask his father and he say her family haffta take them bears dancing, they haffta pay their taxes to the Crown. His father say that the way it is, besides she aint one of us. Ludo ask what that matter and his father get very angry and say, it matter everthing. *Everthing.* If a gypsy marry, something he aint supposed to do even if they always doing it, and if the girl that he marry is one what's owned by another master, say a boyar or a monastery, then their children get divided between the masters. Ludo say his father ask him if he ready and willing for the grief of that? And if he ready and willing, is also he ready and willing for that grief to be upon his wife? Ludo say he think his father jes a worn out and fearful old man, and he follow his love to the next town and the next. But her parents chase him off. They have a Ursari boy for her to marry, even if the law say no, and they gonna keep their mokopuna to theirselves.

I say, 'Aint allowed to marry? Who keep to stupid rules like that?'

'Can't marry, can't do a lot of things. It was a very long list.' Now Ludo commence to drip again.

'So what yer do, Ludo?'

'What could I do, laddie? My heart was broken. I couldn't go back to my family and marry an Aurari girl chosen by my parents. I was still a slave and a slave must always have a master.' He say the slaves that were wandering about got rounded up and sold in the slave sales. He stand up and open his sea trunk. He bend in and start shoving everthing around. He look pretty funny, jes his saggy pants and stick legs staying out, rest of him in a filthy temper on the bottom of the trunk. But when he come out he happy again. Seem he find what he want. He fetched out a old poster. It were once pasted on a wall to tell everone about something coming up. The thing coming up were a slave sale.

'Where yer get this picture, Ludo?'

'A digger from an old Aurari area brought it to Sacramento before I left.'

'That look like a funny langwich. What it say?'

'It says, For sale: a prime lot of Gypsy slaves, selling by auction at the Monastery of St Elias, May 8th, 1852. Consisting of eighteen men, ten boys, seven women and three girls, all in fine condition.'

'But they weren't yer friends were they, Ludo?'

He shake his head. 'This slave sale was a long time after I escaped from my own country.'

'That's lucky then.'

Ludo wipe away the tear that plop down his cheek.

'Where yer go when you escaped?' I ask jes to get him off a track that lead to endless drippings.

'First I went to France where I had many misadventures. That's an adventure that goes wrong, laddie, like most of them do. Then I went to America where I lodged with a Scottish family and worked in their fields. They taught me everything I know about English. Later on I went to the goldfields of Sacramento, along with every other poor bastard in the world. But how could an Aurari not go to find gold when it was like home to him?

Of course, I wasn't a nipper any more, so it was good I got rich quick.'

'And then yer marry with a girl who weren't Luminitsa?'

Ludo nod.

'Were she as good?'

'How do I know? The one yer keep always suffers in comparison to the one yer lose. The one yer lose is always young and untarnished, never fights with you or bores you, never complains or runs to fat or gets sick. But likewise, she's never a companion to you, never a helpmate in life's trials.'

Well, that were a unnecessary lot of words that fall on a boy like a stone pile.

'But what about yer twelve children, Ludo?'

'Yair,' Ludo say quiet. 'That was a regret. But who knows? Maybe a man can be as barren as a woman and it aint her fault at all.'

Well, I aint gonna say nothing if Ludo seek his comfort like that, but everone know it the lady what have the babies, and if them babies don't come it rilly hard to see how it anything to do with a man.

'Anyway,' Ludo say with a big shudder, 'six would have gone to the Ursari master, so I feel like I dodged six bullets to the heart.' He sit quiet a moment and then add, 'Yair, there's always another side to everything. It's a terrible human weakness to assume that everything we dint get would've always been better.'

One morning the rain stop. By now it a surprise. The river crawl back home and I go out in the street. I thinking of going fishing when I spy a man that give me a shock. I recognise him anywhere. He jes there, walking along the street like he always been doing it, but no. He walk out of the past, that's the real truth. He rilly tall and have a angry body. His arms and legs is long and thin but the bit that join them together big and strong. He do everthing slow and sure and mean. He wear a wide digger hat but I know what his face look like. It got skin that have pits in it, it got brown eyes that aint got no shine, it got a front tooth missing. I follow him and he go to the bank, prolly to sell his gold. Haffta guess because I shrink from going in. That aint because I think he recognise me. No. It a long time since he roar at me when I were little. I been a long time growing. He don't expect me to be tall and looking like a Inglishman, he jes rememory a little toddle bubba.

For sure I don't rememory him if it weren't for Moana, who take me to Mawhera and when I were bad take me to his house that we stand outside of, then when this man come out she point and say very angry, if yer aint good, yer got to go back to him. Being good mean not speaking them words that come from Russher or Prussher or Esstanbool. How then I say they jes come out of me like a swamp that have the waters oozing up?

But when I were good, that mean I were doing what Moana tell me and keeping my brat mouth shut, not jes on them bad words but on everthing she do, then Moana take me with her to what she call Whitey Heaven. She get on her red silk dress behind a cabbage tree, I forget now what she call the tree but anyway it don't do much hiding of her lady johns. Then we go to a hotel, not a rilly good one like the Bathsheba, it a bit disreputable, and the son of the man come. His name were Hevarla Bogoo. Moana and me wait outside and Hevarla Bogoo buy me a colour drink. We sit in the shadders and Moana laugh or drip, it depend on the hand signings – the talk that go on between them don't rilly do much of the job. One time Moana point at herself and make her right fingers stand up three times, now I know that mean fifteen, and Hevarla Bogoo point at hisself and make his fingers stand up three times plus one, that's sixteen, but even now I don't know what that mean. Do that mean they were gonna wait till they that old to marry with each other? Papa go fucken crazy if she say that to him.

Now the man, who called Otac, come out of the bank. He aint the kind of man that look around hisself. First he don't expect no one to jump him he so big and mean, second he aint intrested in what anyone do, he keep his eye on his own gain. I shaking in the shadders for all the teerible trouble this man once brung to my life. I walk behind Otac who now have a sack of coin hanging from his shoulder. Otac got a big stride, soon I haffta run. He don't go back to his horse, he go along Revell Street, stopping every now and then to look at the hotels. Dunno what he look for. Some of them hotels is dark and disreputable but give big dinners, some is where them pavement nymphs work and everone know the dinners aint up to scratch, some is doss houses with a lot of rats, mebee you find a rat supping at yer soup plate. Otac always walk on. Mebee with his bag of coin he looking for a cloud bed, he looking for a barmaid who keep her lady johns on, at least when she around the customers.

We turn a corner and go up the street. He go past the best places now, the ones that got dance rooms and R-O-U-L-E-T-T-E wheels, shooting galleries and skittle alleys. Soon we near the Bathsheba. Then we at it. Oh no. Mebee he looking for Trellisbywilliammorris, for a place even a Goldie can stoop to stay at. Otac stop and gaze upon it. Then he switch his bag of coin from his shoulder to his left hand and with his right hand he open the big front doors and go in.

There in the street I slump down against the wall. Poor little Tiwakawaka! For that were my name when I first go to Otac. It were him that gimme the new name Halfie. Hevarla Bogoo shout at Otac, that aint his name. It were the one Inglish sentence he keep saying and saying, and only now I rememory it. Otac raise his fist to Hevarla Bogoo and talk many words in the langwich of Russher or Prussher or the Ottermens. Hevarla Bogoo shrink down and creep away. I wonder where he go. Do Otac murder Hevarla Bogoo? Surely not, that were the one thing he seem to rilly love.

Poor Halfie! Now the place he live at happy with Kaspar and Ludo and Marama, now it got a worm in it. That worm now going up to Caradoc or Blanche or Prosper, whoever looking after the bar, he growling gimme a room if now he learn the Inglish, otherwise doing his pointings and signings. Now the worm being taken up them stairs, them stairs that's mine. They mine because I stand on them with Gertie, because Goldie grace them and my moleskins go funny, because every day Kaspar run up and down them to make hisself fit, because Ludo go up them to have his reproshmint with Caradoc, and because every day I take Marama up to visit with her Granmama.

Now the worm see all them rooms to choose from. And they all mine too. There's the one that I sleep in with Ludo after the ball, there's the one Griffith forgive my debt in, there's the one I sleep with Kaspar in when poor Ludo were in the hostipal, there's the one that Goldie and her beautiful dresses stay in, the one where she cry and cry because her ingagemint dress get stole, they all mine because they the places where the people I come to love have all their downs and ups. Now the worm leaving a trail of slime in the hallways. My heart freeze. What room he steal from me? What room do he kill my good rememories in? For sure when he shut the door they bleed to death on the rug.

I run. Run to the quay, run fast along the river. It feel like I running from some birds what's all around my head and attacking me with their beaks. When I can't do no more breathings I hide in the flax bushes. I sit in them bushes till my breathings come back. The birds aint there any more, they gone off to attack another poor boy that meet a teerible apparition from his past.

Now that I sitting quiet, some thinkings come oozing up. The thinkings is that I a boy of a lot of bleeding rememories. They nearly dead but still they lift their heads. They lift their heads and cry, rememory me. One is Moana that get beat and locked up, one is Hevarla Bogoo that get beat and driven off, one is Tiwakawaka

Halfie Harvey Picaninny Bedwetter Thumbsucker Pipsqueak Sonny Jim Koko Pee-pee, a boy that can't talk the right langwich to anyone, that get passed around like a parcel till everthing jes a jumble on his tongue and in his thinkings.

Even now his Inglish jes a jumble of all them tongues that pour off the boats into Hokitika town. And the langwich he were born into, the one that live here and for a short time he knowed perfic, now also getting big holes in it, it ragged as old Ludo. Like Ludo it live in the chop down bush but haffta come to town. Like Ludo it have to suffer them wallpapers. Like Ludo it got to look down at the children it borned or take on and get a big shock when they speak – out pour words it never heared of!

I look up. I were in a big huddle and dint know it. A drizzle come on my head. It one of them warm ones that have the green shiny bush behind it and the yella satin light above. It a drizzle all lit up. It the kind that make rainbones. It the kind like Vegetable Pain Killer that make yer forget. It the kind that make yer very very happy.

Next morning I come out of the store room where Ludo and Kaspar still snoring their drunken sleep and there's Otac eating his breakfast. He sit up very straight, don't look right don't look left. Nothing ever teach him to look. To look mean there something to see what's worth his trouble. There aint nothing worth it for Otac.

After the eating, he smoke. Smoking always were a big thing with Otac. Back when I were with him he drink his special drink that come from the old country, wherever that were, and he smoke for hours. Hevarla Bogoo do too. But it aint a happy hour, them two hardly speak. Then we all go after the gain. Otac and Hevarla Bogoo own a mud puddle they keep splashing through, only now do I know it were a claim. I growed up a bit after a while and walked away from that mud puddle into them drown fields looking for my own. But everwhere there were langwiches I dint unnerstand.

'Hey, Thumbsucker,' Prosper call out. 'Quit mooning. Come here and make yerself useful.'

I go over to the bar.

'Here, take that smoking ramrod his tea.'

'Fuck that.'

Prosper raise his eyebrow.

'I aint a friend of that man.'

'How yer even know him?' Prosper atchilly look intrested.

'That's my business. But he called Otac. If yer want some fun, ask him where is Hevarla Bogoo.'

'Who?'

I explain him.

Either Fatso drunk or a sunbeam get up his arse this morning, for he go over with the tea hisself and plonk it down. Then he ask loud enough for me to hear, 'Now Mr Otac, how is yer son Hevarla Bogoo?'

It the first time I seen Otac get a surprise. 'Otac aint my name,' growl he in a voice that mangle the Inglish.

'Sure it is,' Fatso insist.

'I aint to know who teach yer, Whitey, but he teach wrong. Otac's the same as Grandpapa. And Hevarla Bogoo aint no name at all. It jes something in the Lord's Prayer. My son is call Dusan.'

Fatso ignore the explaining and seize on the insult. 'Call me Whitey, eh? I tell yer, I'm from Italia.'

'Well, Whitey, yer aint from around here then, are yer?'

Prosper waddle off laughing big. Nothing seem to knock the happy out of him now he got hisself a uma wench. Gertie say that's what love do to you, at least in the start before it eat out yer soul. But Ludo grumble that's a very very wicked thing to say, love is what yer soul is made of and it only U–N–B–R–I–D–L–E–D desires and false expectations that gobble it up.

But now I run out to the street where it starting to spit. Otac a liar. He deny the name of his own son. Mebee because Hevarla Bogoo's body lie somewhere in a shallow grave. That's a whitey saying I don't rilly unnerstand. It mean murder, and if yer catched they put a rope around yer neck, so why yer don't dig a hole that's really deep? It sure a pity if Hevarla Bogoo lying down under a thin blanket of dirt. He were nice to Moana till Papa lock her up.

Now Otac come out, stand for a moment to see the weather, go walking off toward the river. He go to the place where yer pay for a steamboat. I creep in the shadders and start to think, what if Otac paying a visit to a shallow grave? Can't think of nothing else but to follow him. Jes as well I got coin in my pocket.

We go on a long trip to a place what's called Coal Creek. That aint because the water run black or nothing like that. It a place where there's a little wharf at the bank and small steamers and barges is tied up to it like dogs waiting for their masters. Seem them steamers get filled with coal and go off down the river heading for Hokitika town. It come to me Otac a gold man, so what's he doing at a wharf that serve a coal mine? Do he want to do a coal deal with the coin he got in his sack? I creep in the shadders while Otac mingle with the men that load the steamers and the captains that sail them, he all the time talking talking talking. Like me, he must of learned the Inglish, and he put with his mean loud mouth a whole lot of rough gestures. Now and then I can hear him from the shadders, he saying fucken cheats and liars the men that buy the coal mine are. He say what happen to the steam train they promise, they come over from Ballarat and throw out the real owners, then they jes take take take till the seam run dry.

Then he run dry hisself. He heft his sack and leave the wharf. He take a walk toward the sawmills. When he get there he stand outside staring at the enterprise like he expect some nuggets to come out of the chop wood. He wait and wait. I rilly bored, also hot and very hungry. Why mean old Otac aint a man that eat? Why he always trotting about with a sack of coins, trotting and not eating? And I dunno what all this up and down from Hokitika town about, aint we got sawmills there? We got Mr Findlay and Mr Haworth on the river bank, they have a wooden tramway that go into the bush to fetch out them trees to feed into a big steam engine with saws. And we also got another sawmill where Kaspar sometimes work, even if he tryna get work with Mr Findlay who pay five pound a week. It a Mr Macbeth that own this other one. He got a boiler for his mill from off the wreck of a paddle steamer and he got two thirteen horse engines off the sunken *Ruby*. Dunno what horses got to do with it, but it were what Kaspar explain me, and . . .

Suddenly out come a man with a big hat and a thick beard. He shake Otac's hand. They have a big hug. Otac give him the sack of coin that he carry. The whole thing! Even I like old Otac if he give me that. But there something in the movings of the man in the big hat that bring up a rememory. Something wake in them slimy deeps, it sit up slow in the mud, it wipe them muds and slimes off its body, it come up and up . . . it a rememory called Hevarla Bogoo.

It me that get the biggest shock. Nothing outward happen, the sky don't boil, the sun don't go black. Hevarla Bogoo hug his Papa and go back to sawing them trees and Otac go back down to the wharf. Prolly he go home now he done his job, no more do he slime up the stairs of the Bathsheba.

No one see me, no one yank me out of the shadders and say, yer fucken brat, what yer doing here? So nothing happen that seem to click the world into a new place. But click it do. It go clicking and whirring like a old sawing machine. And where it click to is that I seen Hevarla Bogoo's nose and mouth before, seen it a hundred times, a thousand. I seen it every time I look in that piece of mirror that Ludo got. Ludo prop a little glass on a shelf to comb his hair in front of, dip his comb into the water or whiskey, whatever he have in front of him, and he make me look in it too, see if I got a clean face, comb hair. So now I know. That nose and mouth mine.

So while the world click and whirr me to unnerstanding – that's what Ludo say the whole world for, what we in it for – I sit on the wharf and look at the swishy river. I look at my hands on my thighs. Them hands is like Otac's. Same colour, same bones. I seen them in my dreams giving slaps to Halfie. Then finally, slow, loud and spitting sparks, the sawing machine whirr into the new place that mebee everone know but Halfie. The new place is where Moana his girl-mother and Hevarla Bogoo his boy-papa, and that's why everone were always so angry, and why Tiwakawaka's life go back and forth back and forth back and forth to places ways and langwiches he never get time to unnerstand.

The rilly sad thing is that Moana now gone, never can he say to her, yer don't haffta pretend no more. You had yer uplockings and yer beatings, you had yer drippings in them bushes, you had yer red satin dress and the cabbage tree, and now I see what it were all for. Yer don't haffta pretend for me. Then the thinking come up in me that if the whole world were made for unnerstanding it jes made for sadness. Because all them unnerstandings always come too late, always come after the time to fix everthing.

The sun grow very hot but still I sit. I rememory the tangi, the aunties in their kawakawa leafs, the feasts and the karakia. But all gone is them details that tell why Moana die. Yes, there were an escaping and a accident but what come in the middle jes vanish in a bush mist.

But why do it matter? What she rilly die of is a broke heart and uplockings, it them that drive her off. Soon as Papa trust her again, soon as she go in them bushes getting leafs and berries and always come back out, soon as the cheek go back in her and she again saying she more smart than the rest of us, soon as Papa talking of a proper husband for her, soon as all that happen she escape away. Do she go with Hevarla Bogoo for a while? Nobody know. Or if a old aunty know, she weren't telling. Or if she were telling them other old aunties, nobody were telling a boy. Then very slow but sure everthing that join me to my whanau jes sour up and wore out. Before the plants were even growed on Moana's grave I up and run off.

Now I haffta get back. I very hungry and also don't have enough coin for a doss down. I don't know of no way back except the way I come. I sit and wait a long time for a steamer. I still sitting on the wharf waiting for the Hokitika steamer when I see a most teerible thing. It a dirty thing that lurch in rags. It a moaning thing that got hairs long and wild. It a thing that once were a man called Griffith.

FIFTEEN

Now everthing change. Going back go out the winder. I follow Griffith back to his lair a bit further up Coal Creek. It a mean hut no better than a sty. It a house for pigs. Except a pig don't chuck around them empty whiskey bottles. A pig don't eat a chook then throw down the bones on the dirt floor. This aint a man that come to a bad end by accident. He go looking for it. He a man that wanna go to Hell but not after he die – he wanna go right now.

The doorway is wide open. That's because there aint no door. I see he throw hisself down on a poor bed that look like a bale of straw covered with old blankets. I step in. He look up, don't seem to recognise me.

'What the fuck do you want?' His voice a growl of bad living.

'Don't yer know me? It Harvey.'

'Harvey?' Mebee he drunk out his rememory.

'Yer use to call me Pipsqueak.'

There come a long silence.

'Go the fuck away.'

I dither. Mebee only now I unnerstand what that mean.

'Yer still standing there? Fuck off!'

'Gertie miss yer. She want yer to come home.'

Griffith groan.

'I aint seen *her*,' I say. 'No one seen her.'

Now I aint even hearing breathings. It like he drop dead.

I say, 'You and yer Papa got a baby girl call Marama.'

This brung the dead back to life. Griffith leap up and fly at me. He grab my ears and he start shouting in my face. 'Yer think that's what I wanna hear? Yer think I wanna be reminded about the worst mistake of my life?'

I take offence. 'Marama sweet. She aint no mistake.'

Griffith drop my ears like they burn his palms. He roam the sty running his hands through his long dirty mane. I feel like some sad Mama that's sorry about what happen to his beautiful hairs. Then he turn and look at me with them big blue eyes the same as Gertie's, eyes is things yer can't ruin on yer own, and he say, 'D'you think I'd have gone after that slut if I'd known? D'you think my father would have? What, d'you think we were searching for a way to destroy each other?'

Seem he don't want me to answer his questions, he want me to take them questions home. But do he mean I bring the answers back?

Then he go answering hisself. 'No. Our little family was safe and secure so we went looking outside it for some fun. Then we both fell down the same mine shaft.'

Just as well Violet aint around to hear herself called that.

Now he stop roaming and with his feets he do some arranging of the junk on the floor. It were getting in the way of his long strides. Seem to calm him a bit.

'I don't dig for gold any more,' he tell me. 'What's the point? But I do have a job. Bet yer dint think that, did yer, Pipsqueak? See that stuff I jes moved? It's blasting oil. I blow things up for a living now. Seeing I'm so good at it.'

I get a alarm. That stuff dangerous. I rememory everthing

I read with Ludo. There many special ways for safety, yer don't jes kick it around the floor. I rilly scared I gonna explode. Mebee Griffith don't care, get him to Hell quick as what a wink is, but I have Marama to upbring. Don't wanna turn her into a pass the parcel like I were.

'What yer blow up?'

'Mine shafts.'

'Why yer blow up holes?' This a mystery to me.

Griffith laugh sour.

Mebee I have my first grown up moment. Dunno what to do. Dunno if to run or stay. Already I looking back with longing to jes doing the first thing that come into my head.

'If yer want I can visit Goldie for you. I can. . .'

'Shut the fuck up!' It a wild cry, not a order like he usually give. I do it.

Then he raving, 'Yer jes don't understand a fucken thing. She aint one of those women yer make promises to, come crawling back to after you break them. She aint a dancing girl, always calculating what she stands to lose in being so proud. Her pride is all she's got to lose.'

'Eh? What she pride of?'

'Yer mean proud.'

Do I? Fuck me. This one of them stupid Inglish words that keep on changing itself.

'She's proud of her name, her reputation.'

Alright, I had enough of this bleeding nonsense. Were it Goldie that done bad? No. How Violet's bad doings attach to her? They dint. And what kind of fool be proud of her own name? Aint we all got one? Seem like being proud of yer stomick.

'I going now. What I say to Gertie?'

This make him do more loping around the sty. This time he doing some muttering.

'What does my father think of this Marama?' he ask eventual.

'Well, he seen her going past bundled up. He seen her sitting on a table. But he aint dangled her.'

'Why not?'

I shrug.

'So he thinks she's his granddaughter.'

He don't say it like it a question. But I don't unnerstand how he come by his thinkings. 'Mebee. What's it matter?'

Griffith make a strange strangle noise.

I say, 'Yer Mama been seeing Marama. She seen her every morning for a while now.'

Dunno what all this mean to him. More pacing. More running his hands in his dirty hair. His palms soon be dirty as a coalman.

'Tell my mother that she'll be seeing me soon.' Griffith come to a stop right in front of me.

'Rilly?'

'Really.'

'It aint no lie? Poor Gertie aint up to it.'

Griffith put his hand across where his heart is.

'Do I come back?'

'Yair.' It seem like he jes make up his mind. 'Come back and I'll give yer some money for another little job.'

When I come out from seeing Griffith it seem like a lot of my problems solved. First, I know where Otac go and where Hevarla Bogoo is. Second, Griffith come to visit his Mama – for sure he clean up hisself first – and she wear away at him, give him them lechers that bring him home.

It dark. A big wax moon come out. It a big comfort for a boy what haffta sleep out. The moon scare me in Okarita, it so cold and gleamy, but now it remind me of Marama. It come to me that if Marama die, never again can I go out in the night when the moon is out. It like there a thread that go from me to the moon to Marama, it join us all up. It like the birth cord that Violet say whitey aint got. Mebee Violet wrong. Mebee Marama get one.

She dint come sailing downhill across the sea in them dressed up ships, she were born here like I were, and she have a name that join her to the moon that shine down on all of us. She don't talk no Barberrian, she grow up and know what her name mean, what uma mean, she call me Tiwakawaka (when she don't call me Papa Number Three, of course) and she call these plants I sleep beside toitoi, it aint fucken pampas grass. Anyway that's my hope for her that no one take from me.

Next thing I know it morning and a big rain is coming at me. I see them black clouds rushing over the blue sky like a horse dragging a blanket. When I get back to Hokitika town I don't rush up the stairs to Gertie, don't run off at the mouth like once I do. Gertie gonna drip for sure. She wanna totter on her high heel boots to see her boy right away. Caradoc say, thank you, Bedwetter, now my wife go off too. Ludo get angry, say, why I always find yer in the middle of everthing that cause trouble, laddie?

I go to Marama's bedroom that look like the inside of a boil lolly. Gertie have Marama in the bedcage, she singing her a lullaby song.

'Oh no, Halfie,' Gertie scold when I come in. 'Now she'll be awake for hours.'

'Don't matter. I got something important to say.'

I take Marama out of the bedcage and sit down on one of them rocking chairs with her on my lap. 'Yer got to promise me Gertie. On Marama's head, yer got to promise.'

'Promise? What are you talking about?' Gertie go on folding them little pink things that Marama always fussed up in.

'Put yer hand on her head.'

'I'm not promising anything on the head of a baby, Halfie.'

'Then I don't tell yer the secret.'

Now this put a struggle in her. Secrets is just like them chocolates for Gertie.

'I promise not to tell your secrets then,' she end up saying.

'That aint the promise I want.'

'What promise do you want?'

Now she standing close to me, so I take her hand and hold it under my own on top of Marama's head, who think it a funny game and start to giggle.

'I, Gertie Flewelling, promise not to go clean out of my hinengaro when Halfie tell me about Griffith. I promise not to cry and ask and ask where he is and wanna go off to him. There – now it done.'

Gertie snatch her hand away, even though it already done the promising, and she put it to her mouth that's wide open and she go all trembly. Then while her eyes go swirly with drips she tryna hold in I tell her how I find Griffith. I don't say he living in a sty and wild looking and kicking blasting powder around his floor, thems all things his Mama don't need to know. I say jes how I talk to him and he promise he gonna come for a visit soon.

'A visit? But how long did he say he might be staying?'

'He dint say.'

'But where . . .'

'Rememory yer promise!'

Gertie fall silent. It look like some thinkings come up in her. She say we haffta break it to Caradoc, she say we can't have Griffith jes turning up without him getting a warning.

'There's another thing,' I say.

'What other thing?'

'It a dark thing.'

'Dark?'

'Yer haffta tell him he aint allow to steal Marama.' Jes saying them words fill me with dread. 'Even if he see she got them blue eyes same as him . . .'

'They're my blue eyes,' Gertie say quick. 'They both get them from me. It doesn't mean anything.'

Now we seeing eye to eye. Gertie rilly love Griffith but she aint about to let him go off with her bubba. She aint about to lose both of them.

'She looks more like Caradoc than anyone,' Gertie declare like there aint no argument.

Now this a very big thing for her to say. She aint jes saying out loud that her husband done the dirty with Violet. She saying she prefer it that way. And it aint even true. How a pink fat baby look like a wrinkle old man with bloodshot eyes and a body what's totally fucked? But what I care. Gertie gonna cling on and that suit me down to the ground. Whatever that mean.

I haffta go back to Griffith. When I tell Ludo I off again, he eye me. 'What, yer got a girl somewhere, laddie? Why're yer always rushing off?'

My face go hot. 'I doing some work.'

'Work, eh? Guess yer could call it that. Wouldn't be my first choice of words.'

It?

Kaspar laugh.

'What are you laughing at, cabbage mouth?'

'I am thinking that if he were running to a girl you would be stopping him.'

'I would indeed. We're not like you, nothing to guide us but our own selfish impulses. Our own cause. We don't believe in fornication.'

'Oh? And where is that getting you?'

'Where has what you believe in got you?'

'To exactly the same place as you who are being led by the Lord.'

Well, that give me a good laugh up my sleeve.

I leave them to their teasings and arguings. I haffta make the Coal Creek trip again. It were fun the first time but now it becoming a chore.

When I get there, Griffith still lying in the sty on his filthy blankets. He been drinking big. Them bottles is lying all around him. Now I try my little plan what's rilly a trick. 'What a mess. How yer expect to bring a bubba here?'

He push himself up. His eyes is a ruin. I were wrong when I think no one can ruin his own eyes. They very red and look weepy, not with tears but with thick stuff like flem. 'I aint bringing a baby here. Are you fucken stupid or what?'

Why everone always asking me if I stupid? Do they expect me to say yes? How stupid is that? But now my heart gone quiet, it aint going thud thud thud fearing Marama get stole.

'So is my mother looking forward to seeing me?' Griffith ask in a dull voice.

'She sure is.'

'And my father?'

'Yep.'

He laugh sour.

'What's that job yer want me to do?' Seem a good idea to change the subject.

He get up. Now I see his hairs a thick mat. And his clothings send a stink at me that's rilly horrid.

He say, 'Since you were here last, I changed the plan a bit. The original seemed unsatisfactory.'

I wait.

He take a while.

'I want yer to visit Lily Moncrieff.'

'Goldie?' This sure a surprise. 'What for?'

'I want to give her a present.'

'Gertie sure love a present,' I say quick.

That laugh again.

'I want to give Lily a present first. But I'm certain she won't open the door to me. So that's where you come in. Yer have to make her look down on the street.'

'What, yer gonna be standing there like a filthy lunatic and waving the fucken thing?'

'That's right.'

'Prolly she won't let me in neither.'

'Well, if yer want the money, that's your problem.'

I in a conan drum. My moleskins aint happy to help Griffith back to Goldie, but I always been a coin boy. And a voice deep inside also start whispering, if Griffith get Goldie, they make their own tamariki and don't take Marama. Then another voice growl, mebee they steal Marama to get the whole set. It seem like another of them growing up moments. I do so many calculations my head go spinning.

'Have we got a deal?'

'How much?' Same time as I ask I think, I got a lot better idea of coin now, don't think yer can short me, arsehole.

He mention a number of coin that seem like a homeward bounder. I go in deep shock.

'She mean that much to yer?'

Griffith nod.

I spit on my palm and hold out my hand. Griffith look full of disgust and turn away. That sure a cheek – he far more dirtier than me. Then jes before I leave he hold out two bits of paper coin. He say it for my travel expenses on the coach.

The Rosstown coach leave from Packers' Town on the south spit. The man that sell me a fare say it cost a pound. That rilly robbery in the broad daylights. He say it cover the ferry over the Hokitika river and also the crossing of the Totara river on a punt big enough for horses and carriages and everthing. I ask him if I swim do it cost less? He say sure it do but we aint fetching yer out of the fucken ocean.

I get to Rosstown when the sun is still full in the sky. It a day that aint got shadders, I mean not them long ones that creep up and tap you on the shoulder and put the grims on you. Then I going along to that fancy house that live in my rememories like a dream. It got the sun on it like a dream. But the girl that open the door turn out the same old nightmare scrubber.

'What d'you want?' She start picking a pimple. A bit of blood trickle out.

'Is Miss Moncrieff home?'

'Yair, she's home. What d'you think? She's down at the grog shanty?'

'Tell her I got a message for her.'

Scrubber tell me to wait. Then she come back pretty quick and take me upstairs to the nice room I were in before. Goldie stand by the fireplace. She poking at it so I don't see her face. Soon she turn around and what a change come on her. It hard to describe. Sometimes me and my tupuna suck in our cheeks so our faces look like arseholes, or that's the idea, and she look all sucked in like that. Only she aint doing it, it been done to her.

She frosty too. 'What's the message?' she ask soon as she see me.

Where the smiles, where the silver tray with koko?

'Well, it aint ezactly a message . . .'

'What d'you want, Harvey?'

'Only a small thing.'

'A small thing.' She dull when she repeat me.

The burden of what I gonna do come down very heavy on me. It seem I certain to stumble. I look back a long way to a pipsqueak that drink koko and he seem like a little fool, he too happy for what the stupid world is like.

'I jes want yer to look out the winder.'

'What?' She jolt out of her melon cow lickings.

'Yair. Gertie coming along.'

'Gertie? But she can hardly walk.'

'She better now. She walk good.'

'Why should I look out of the window at her? Why doesn't she come in?'

'She want a sign first.'

'A sign?'

Haffta say this conversation a grind. 'Jes a wave or something like that. So she know she welcome.'

'Of course she's welcome. I'll send the maid down . . .'

'No, she want yer to look out the winder and wave. She say otherwise she hasten off.' I cross my fingers behind my back.

Lucky for me Goldie too dull and flat to care. She sigh long and loud and then she go to the winder. I stand beside her. We look out. We look up and down the street, no one there. Jes the sky blue and no shadders on life.

Now a figure come along the street. It drag something on its leg. It a shackle like a convict got, and the shackle attach to a pile of stuff what's hard to make out.

Now it coming closer. Yer can see it a man, not Gertie. He got long wild dirty hairs. What he attached to look like a little pile of chop wood. It look like he dragging the fuel for his fire in case he can't find none when he gets where he going. He sure look like a unspeakable madman.

'Who is that?' Goldie ask. Her voice has went funny. I look at her face. It working, working like she tryna grab a dream she only got the wisps left from.

'It Griffith.'

She catch her breath. She put her hand to her throat. Then she shut her eyes.

I say, 'No, he want yer to look.'

'He sent you here?' Her voice sound so faint it like a ngingongingo steal it.

'He want a sign,' I encourage her.

It like she been put under a spell. She don't say but he dirty, he mad, and what's that shackled to his leg? No, she take out her pretty nose rag what's white with white lace on the edges like a wedding dress, and hold it up to the winder. She shake it. Tears start pouring out of her but she also laughing. She shake and shake the rag. She cry and cry. She laugh. She jump. Her arsehole face turn beautiful like a angel.

Griffith stop outside the winder and look up.

I look down.

I very happy them two lovers find each other again.

Goldie jump and cry and shake and laugh.

He look up.

I look down.

Boom!

SIXTEEN

Atchilly, when I think about it later, it come to me it more like boof! It more a dull noise, like a noise that get swallowed by some earth. Ludo say it don't matter what it sound like, jes grow up. He say it aint one of them times when anyone wanna hear a small boy talk about what something rilly sound like. It aint one of them times when anyone wanna hear a small boy making a whole lot of different noises jes to make his point. And anyway, what were that small boy doing in Goldie's sitting room and leading her to the winder at the ezact moment? I aint a small boy, I say to Ludo. He say, don't change the subject.

The funeral gonna be one of them scrape downs. What that mean is the bits that go in the coffin haffta be scraped down off the walls, haffta be mopped up off the street. Only then is there enough to put inside the long box for the singing and crying and prayering over. It take a long time to find some parts and how they even know if it rilly him? The funeral gonna be in Hokitika town, even if Griffith been living away for a long time. Haffta say when they got the box on stilts in one of them trellisbywilliammorris rooms, with the gaslights turned low and everone coming and going paying their respects, it hard not to have thinkings that they jes respecting a toenail, a hank of hair, some skin that's like a chop calico ghost.

Then the thinkings come up in me – this when I were standing by the coffin with Ludo in them flickering gaslights, Ludo with his head down and his hat off and mumbling mumbly things – how do all them bits make up a Griffith, how even if they scrape down all them bits, fetch his exploded lungs and heart out of the grog shanty, fetch his scramble brain from off the plate of the drunk in the grill house, how all them bits make a Griffith? Even if they put the bits all back and stitch them in his skin, is the heart going thud thud thud the only thing that separate the walking upright from a stiff?

But how do that thudding noise make a hinengaro? Ludo think the big question is how much satin each allowed to ask for, but I jes say get as much as yer can. The big question is the hinengaro and where Griffith has went now. Is he floating about us in the gaslight laughing, or gone to Ludo's Heaven or what? Erasmus say, don't be stupid, Quidnunc, he aint gone nowhere like that. Erasmus say all them bits that make you get held together by the skin, when the skin rot everthing fall out for the worms. Or being S-C-I-E-N-T-I-F-I-C, a word that Erasmus love, all of it jes fly apart and become atoms again.

That the biggest waste of all the trouble of living I ever heared of.

Fact is, it amaze everone me and Goldie still alive. After the explosion we stand there with the winder glass crashed in on us, it lying in splinters like we crash through the Sultan's cristal staircase. We in terror, we dint know what happen. When we look out the hole, the winders all along the street gone smash too. And not jes them winders but the wood that hold them in. There's a whole lot of people running everwhere in the smoke and dust, it were a big thick smoke that go up like a column even if there were no smell of gunpowder. They screaming and tearing their hairs. Close where Griffith stand before he vanish them buildings go back to what they were made of, everwhere is piles of bricks and wood and beams that were throwed about like matchsticks. Still raining down is floaty clothings pillowcases nose rags, it look like a ektoplasm riot.

Where do Griffith go? It hard to think about because Goldie who were standing beside me in a stun silence start screaming like a bean shith. Then it come to me – he jes like them buildings. He go up and come apart. Mebee his head fly all alone over them gold claims and windlasses while his body go somewhere else. Mebee the eyes in his flying head see a grand view, see the seas the mountains, see everthing like he turn into a bird. Then I wonder how long he enjoy hisself like this before he fly to Te Rerenga Wairua, the place where he haffta fly off forever. Mebee he meet Moana there, but I hope Violet aint around, sure hope she gone home to Ballarat. If ever we were to talk of it, which we dint, prolly Violet tell me white folk leave another way. Mebee they haffta go through East Cantaberry.

Haffta do more standings in the gaslight room. This go on and on because in the coffin there aint a body to rot, rilly it near as empty as the Gold Escorter's lockbox. They make me the one that stand there when the others leave, them others that haffta have dinners and sleeps and mad cryings. It give me time to think what Erasmus say about them atoms. After they fly apart they go off still separate and make more mountains and oceans, more animals and people, even more stars. Seem to me they all things that upright walking folk can love, but love aint rilly a part of it according to Erasmus. Love is jes E-M-E-R-G-E-N-T from C-O-M-P-L-E-X-I-T-Y and rilly everthing going the other way, back to them atoms.

But in the gaslight room it come to me if them atoms is always going off to more makings, making more oceans animals stars and people, and people is something that love emerge from, then love a big part of it and Erasmus jes a fucken idiot.

The day of the funeral come. There's some horses with a cart that's gonna drag the box to the church. Some men and some relatives, Caradoc included, gonna walk beside it in their black suits. Prolly Caradoc think he wear his suit, the one Prosper stick his filthy criminal friend in, for the wedding of Griffith to Goldie, not for a scrape down. It turn out a rilly nice day but Gertie all covered up in black crape, even a hat with a little lace curtain hanging off it, and she crying like a flood. She carrying Marama, what she put black ribbons on too, and she won't let go of her even for Ludo or me to take. Marama is upset with all them weepings and start bawling too.

It look to be a very expensive business these death clothings and fittings, not jes the dresses, but now all the handkerchiefs have black lace sewed on them by a scrubber and all them writing papers and envelopes in the hotel been sent out to get black edges too. There's also black ribbons on them perfume bottles and other bottles, enough black ribbon everwhere to keep a ribbon shopkeeper rich for life.

Ludo in a strange mood. He short with me, what aint normal, and he gimme a rilly stiff talking about what to do in the church. Haffta stand up, sit down, stand up, sit down, aint to kick the pew in front, aint to talk, got to sing loud, aint to sigh and roll my eyes, no body noises at all, NoneWhatSoEver! It sure sound effing boring.

And that's what it turn out to be like. Lot of pretty bad singing too, and the men groaning and the woman sobbing and Ludo doing something that amaze me and what aint even possible to describe. It like he come from one of them wandering stars he always going on about.

Then the horse and all them weepers go off to the cemetery. Ludo say to go back and help Prosper with the dinner. I say, I wanna come and see Griffith go down the hole. He give me a clip behind the ear and say, show some respect. A scrape down funeral sure a thing that make Ludo very mean and grumpy.

Haffta walk to the cemetery. Some going on horse, some on carts and some in carriages but I haffta go plod plod plod with Ludo and Kaspar. Erasmus go in a carriage and wave to us as he go by. Why do a man that come down from the apes ride when them that were made by the Lord haffta walk? Anyway the sun shine bright as a polish coin, all them thundery downpours that curse the night and bring the river up have now went off to curse up north.

Soon we all standing around the hole and the man that got on the black frock start saying a lot of stuff I don't unnerstand. Then there's a commotion. A carriage draw up and out get a lady done up the same as Gertie. She thin as a skeleton. Mebee she fall over in the hole from starving. Everone shuffle along the edge to let her in. There a lot of whisperings and nudgings in the back rows. I look up at Ludo but he got his head down and his eyes shut and he mumble in a funny langwich. But then come a ray of sun and it shine through the curtain hanging over the face of the stick lady, and lo and behold it Goldie!

Oh, it a sad moment for my moleskins. The Goldie that was sticking out in all directions look like she been under a hot iron or catched in a slam door. She thinned to nothing. She look like she aint et a morsel since we were blowed up.

Now the dirt get throwed on and then we separate. Caradoc come over to Goldie. There a lot of muttering that I don't hear except for her apology about the ferry that get held up by a high river. Next Ludo talk with Caradoc. They have some words, then Caradoc crumple. His head fall down, his shoulders fall down, he sag into Ludo's chest and Ludo stroke his hair.

The thinkings come up in me, even if everone hate Griffith on the outside, on the inside they love him. It make them thinned and crumple to see his scrape down.

Everone go back to the Bathsheba for eats and drinks. Prosper done hisself proud. Blanche done up in blacks pouring drinks. It a party that the noise is low at, and when anyone get too drunk they more likely to cry than bellow. I have a important question to ask but I haffta be careful or someone give me a quick thick behind the ear and tell me to show some respect.

Prosper, who done all the serving, is now leaning on the bar. In his greasy apron and his grease-stiff curl that stand up on his bald head he aint a man that care about P-R-O-P-R-I-E-T-Y. So I go up to him and put my question, how do Griffith blow hisself up like that, how he turn hisself into chop meat? Prosper guffaw, what I learn is a kind of rude laugh, then he say he don't know, maybe blasting oil?

I rememory that Griffith mention it but I dunno ezactly what it is. When I ask him, Prosper begin a rave. He say blasting oil is something that Kaspar tell him of. It made from nitro glissereen, what were an invention by a goombah. He say that's someone like him that come from where he come from, more or less. He say nitro glissereen been sent over the sea to all them countries that want to do mining. But it bad stuff, it blow up them factories, blow up them ships, blow everthing up. Some crates that got sent to California for the Central Pacific Railroad blow up, fifteen people go up with it, rain down in parts like Griffith.

Prosper go on to say now there's a new way of making it that's to mix the nitro glissereen with sawdust. The sawdust stop it blowing up till the blasting cap go off. The blasting cap is something attached to the sawdust sticks. So that bring up a rememory of Griffith dragging them sticks along. I ask Prosper if there any of them sticks in Hokitika town and he tap his nose and say, California, Caradoc, Griffith, nitro glissereen, see? No, I don't see. Do he think Caradoc some kind of long bridge to California? Nothing for it but to talk to Kaspar, Prosper too much of a fucken idiot.

'Kaspar, what's nitro glissereen?'

Kaspar raise them eyebrows. 'Why are you desiring to know that?'

I give the dumb shrug.

'It's oil. It is being called blasting oil.'

'When yer gonna learn to talk right?'

'When are you?

Seem this a wrong track to go down.

'What it do?

'What it says.'

'Yair, but how it look? And do we got some here?'

Kaspar tell me Sydney town got some. There were news of an explosion in the newspaper. He say it were in bottles in the basement of a shop and it explode and blow up the whole street. Winders smash, door and winder frames stove in, bricks turn to rubble, beams fly through the sky like they were throwed by giants. He say it very dangerous stuff. Very C-A-P-R-I-C-I-O-U-S. He say there's a man called Alfred Know Bell who make a igniter, a little container full of gunpowder or mercury foolminate that get put inside them jars of blasting oil, but still sometimes it go off when it want to, jes if it feeling a bit oozy.

Well, that's all very intresting and it sure gimme a lot to think about. Nearly every second day a ship come in from Melbourne or Sydney town, and some of them ships is sly. Erasmus tell me before the ships sail they get an inspection, got to have lifeboats fire hoses and pumps, but when the inspectors leave, them things is rowed back home for another using. So in this rowing boat what mebee go back and forth, back and forth, who know what sly things come aboard?

But now I see Goldie coming toward us and for sure she aint coming to hear how Griffith blow hisself up. Fact is he did. How he do it mebee no one know unless they put him back together, examine what he attach to hisself. And aint I a bit glad in secret? Now for the first time Goldie aint got no one tryna hang off her. She thinned out and her face is like a ektoplasm and all pinched up, but still she make a pain in my heart. Mebee a pain that's even more stronger.

It more stronger because now she free. Now I worry one of them diggers that come in for the scrape down gonna take her some cakes and go mumble mumble mumble, sorry to hear, time heal everthing, mumble mumble mumble, that a pretty dress, yer got such pretty eyes Miss Moncrieff, mumble mumble mumble, do yer like to take a walk with me moleskins? The pain is stronger because I aint enough growed up yet, but I can't wait no more. Suddenly it me that's taking her the cakes and mumbles. She smile at me and touch my face with her cold hand. I see her eyes is very sad.

'Can we go somewhere private?' I know to say this because of them books Ludo make me read.

'Pardon?'

'Haffta tell yer something.'

She put the cake I brung her on a table. Then she lead me out the front door.

'What is it, Harvey?' she ask very eager. 'Do you have something to tell me about Griffith?'

I shake my head. 'It about me.'

'Oh?' Her face drop sad again. 'What about you?'

I take a deep breathing. 'I wanna marry with yer.'

Goldie's hands fly up to her mouth.

'Yair. Not straight away. I aint got the gold to get the ring. But later. If yer be so kind as to wait for me.' I learn this also from them books.

'But Harvey, by the time you've grown up enough to marry, I'll be old.'

'Well, yer pretty old now but I don't mind.'

Now she smile. I see I make her happy. It make my heart glad. The pain gone clean away.

'Harvey, one day you'll meet a girl of your own age and . . .'

'But I love you.'

Now her smile vanish. 'No, Harvey, no you don't. You're still a child. You don't know what love is.'

'I aint a child!' I angry and drips is pricking my eyes.

Then Goldie take out a chain from around her neck. She take something off that she put in my hand. She close my hand and hold it. 'This is the ring that Griffith gave me. If you bring it back to me when you're twenty-five and you still want to marry me, I promise I'll consider it.'

'Rilly?'

She nod.

Twenty five sure seem a long way off. But now I good as ingaged.

We go back in the hotel and the death party carry on without me. I there in my body but my feelings have took me to float in the clouds. They rushing me around them fluffy clouds that are pink and yella from a perfic sunset.

Later on, when we back in our room but Kaspar still out in the bar looking down the front of Blanche's dress, I say to Ludo, 'Guess what?'

'What?'

'I ingaged.'

'What did yer engage?'

'Eh? Me.'

'Eh?'

'I ingage myself to Goldie.'

Ludo who is drinking tea choke and spit it out of his mouth.

'Yair. She give me a ring.'

Ludo do not believe me. He make me take the ring out and show it. He turn it around in the light. His face aint happy. He say I haffta take it back where I get it from.

'But I get it from Goldie.'

'Yair, but why did she give it to yer, laddie? That's what I'm worried about. I sure hope it aint an egg situation.'

'What yer mean?'

'Eggs turning up that can't be accounted for.'

'I tell yer, she give me it because we ingaged! It were the ring that Griffith give her. She going to marry with me when I turn twenty five.'

Ludo make a whole lot of faces that I don't unnerstand.

'What yer thinking, Ludo?'

He sigh and shake his head. Then he say, 'I'm real happy for yer, laddie. I jes hope I live to see the day.'

Now Ludo agree to my ingagemint I run up them stairs to tell Gertie. She sit in one of them rocking chairs in Marama's room. She got Marama asleep on her lap. She still in all her scrape down blacks, aint even took her hat off.

When I come in she put her finger to her lips to shush me.

'Got some news to make yer happy,' I whisper loud.

'It's the day I buried my son,' she reply, 'nothing can make me happy.'

Well, it come to me this is one of them timing issues. It come to me about how I feel if it were Marama down the big hole. Do I care if someone come to me and say, guess what, I ingaged? Big no. Seem like it even a insult to have a moleskin jumping about shouting I happy, I happy, when you feel like yer down the hole yerself. So I take Gertie's hand and hold it while she cry out her soul. She cry it out so she don't haffta send it to Heaven one day, don't haffta say to Ludo's Lord, why yer stole my beautiful boy?

That when the thinking come up in me, life got cruel writ all over it.

Now it like the blinders come off me. Aint jes got cruel, life got stupid writ all over it too. I haffta go down to the black river and run and run, run off the cruel and stupid what's coming down to crush me. But when I come back and splurt out to Ludo, he aint buying it. He say it aint coming down, it coming up. I tell him it don't make no fucken difference. After he cuff me for the eff word, he say the difference is everthing. Is it falling down on us and we jes helpless, or is there some thinkings that grow cruel and stupid like a crop?

That put a funny picture in my mind. I see cruels with long stalks and purple red flours, and stupids what are short and wide and have yella pods. Then I see a whole lot of farmers like Erasmus and Kaspar cutting them plants down and stacking them up for when there a famine in the hinengaro and everone ready to pay a rilly high price for their stackings.

'Griffith dint have to dip his wick where he did,' Ludo say. 'And when his life turned rotten, he dint have to blow himself up.'

'Yair, but what about Gertie?' This something that come bursting out of me like it my own guts. 'She dint do nothing. The stupid and cruel is coming down on her.'

'Nope, it's coming sideways. From her own son. No one lives alone in this world. Everything yer do affects someone else. Funny how some folk never seem to notice. Maybe they're jes too busy with their own causes.'

'It aint funny.' Ludo making me rilly mad.

'No, it aint. But it's people who are stupid and cruel, not life.'

'Everone die!' This the first time this thinking come up in me. Before, why I care if everone die long as it weren't me?

'Yep,' Ludo agree.

'That's coming down.'

'That's coming in all directions.' Ludo give a chuckle. 'But I think yer really tryna say life is cruel and stupid in the way it's made.'

Is that what I tryna say? Prolly.

'Yair, that's why Kaspar loves his nihilismus. It means he can say the whole universe is meaningless jes because he's going to die.' Ludo seem to find this hilarious. He laugh and slap his leg like everone on earth haffta die except him. Like it a huge joke he aint the victim of.

'Kaspar wants to believe in life,' Ludo carry on when he all laughed out. 'But what's life? First yer young and yer think you can have everything yer want. Then comes the long unlearning of that mistake. How hard it is to hang onto jes one thing, jes one little thing – like a hair on a boy's head.' Ludo reach out and pluck one of my hairs.

'Ouch!'

He hold the shiny hair up to the light. 'Is this something yer want to put all yer hopes in? Is this why a man wants to live forever? What happens if I drop it?' Ludo let the hair fall on the floor. I look down and can't see it no more in all the dirt.

SEVENTEEN

Now something change. Seem like Kaspar and Ludo wake up from a long drunken sleep and say, what we doing in this fug when Marama gone upstairs to live in the pink? What we doing here when Violet and Griffith gone and the only people that can come to claim Marama already got her? Kaspar get up off his bed and pull out his travelling bag that now have a fuzzy green bloom all over it. He take a cloth and the kerosene and clean it. Then he put in his things, his old clothings and long johns, his sausage and his Einziger. Ludo ask him what he doing, and Kaspar reply he gonna ask Blanche to marry with him. Ludo ask how he gonna keep to his own cause when he have a woman telling him what to do. Kaspar don't answer.

Then Ludo say, be sure to send us a wedding invitation, we clean up and come along, we yer family. Kaspar say the family jes like the State the Nation the Gods, and Ludo say, yair, yair, we come anyhow. Seeing as I now ingaged and know all about them up and downs, I ask what happen if Blanche say no? Kaspar say she won't, she getting on a bit, she tired of being all alone with Willy Nilly.

Ludo laugh.

Later, when Kaspar gone, I ask Ludo what he were laughing at, and he say when you take off God the Nation and the Family, take off all them morals and decencies, a free man aint very big, in fact he squeeze down to near invisible while the nothing press on him hard like the heel of a boot. So jes as well he got buried inside him something that make him want a Blanche or the nothing crush him, and crushing make a man very angry and dangerous.

But right now Kaspar got his travelling bag in his hand and a big smile on his face and he bend to kiss me. He look more happy than I seen him for months. The thinking come up in me that he pleased to find some reason to stay in a place. I tell him I be glad to bring Marama over for a visit to his cottage. I hope it one of them cottages with its back to the beach, one of them that the ocean winds and the glinty sea and the satin evening go clean through from the back door to the front.

Ludo get up off his bed to shake Kaspar's hand that he stick out. Ludo clasp his other hand on top of their shaking hands, hold firm, nod his head, he telling Kaspar something I aint unnerstood. Prolly we yer family, we aint caring if all yer opinions is stupid. We all bigger than them opinions – but rememorying that for Ludo the Lord aint no opinion but an Establish Fact. Then Kaspar go through the door and me and Ludo left looking at each other like the old times.

'Well, what d'you reckon, laddie?' he say.

'What I reckon about what?'

He run his hands through his hair, make it stick up everwhere. 'D'you reckon there's any reason for you and me to stay holed up in this room?'

'Weren't no reason to begin with.'

'Small matter of a burnt-out hut.'

Big matter of a drunk what's too fucked to build another one.

But then there were Marama, and do we rilly want her brung up in a wood pile that drip in the rain?

Ludo begin some cleaning and I do some thinking about Marama. Gertie look after her all day long. And in the night. Gertie, who once were fat and lying in the bed and eating fish de la crème and chocolates from Melbourne, then were thin and bald, now is up early and got on a pretty dress. Her hair growed back. Course it grey now and she aint the beauty that Ludo talk of, but Ludo weren't born no wrinkly prune neither. When I go up to be with Gertie and Marama, it seem sure a lot of work to bring up a bubba. Here me thinking they sleep all day, but no. They do a lot of wailing and shitting. Haffta say I prefer that it Gertie rather than me that damp down them wails and change them bandages Marama wear on her arse. And now Gertie teaching her to walk, and everthing in the pink room haffta be keeped up very high, it rilly a lot to think about.

Whenever I go out I jes run down them stairs and jump from the landing to the floor. I run all over the place, along the river and the streets, down at the wharf and in the bush. But if Gertie come, haffta take a hour to sort Marama out, haffta come slowly down the stairs with all them bundles of stuff, haffta walk slow in a worry about the weather, then haffta get home quick for her feedings or sleepings or changings. I love Marama but it rilly boring, about the most boring thing I know to go on a outing with a bubba. Something else I find out, bubbas don't always do what yer want, sometimes they start screaming like a stuck poaka jes because yer tryna give them a spoon of porridge, and if yer pick them up when they in a red rage they go stiff like a plank. Haffta say I glad it Gertie that haffta put up with it. Even if I do love Marama and I rilly do.

I say some of this to Ludo and he reply me that newborns is sweet as sugar but toddlers is a big pain where the sun don't shine. The sun do sometimes shine in Hokitika town so I aint sure ezactly where he talking about. I say, don't yer love Marama, and he say course I do, it jes I an old man that's past all that nonsense. I say, I a boy that's too young for it, and then we laugh a bit mean. He say Goldie sure done me a favour putting the wedding off, otherwise I have toddlers all over the place, and my moleskins that were heating up when he say wedding feel like they get dropped in a freezing river.

Ludo keep on doing his cleaning, that mean wiping around with a rag and putting smears on everthing. He hum them songs what come from the old country.

'Did you know I can play a fiddle, laddie?' he ask me.

'No. Rilly?'

'Yair. I learned it when I was a gold washer on the Danube.'

'Why yer don't play it then?'

'Aint got one. Never had one since I got to America.'

'You could of buyed one with yer homeward bounder.'

'Yair, but it seemed sad somehow.'

When I ask him why it seem sad, he say he can't tell me. It jes a feeling in him. Fiddling is what he done with his family and his relations. They all live under their hairs, but they got their fiddles under there too.

'Ludo, sometime it seem you aint a sad man no more, jes a plain ordinary drunk.'

'Eh, maybe that's right, laddie,' Ludo laugh. 'Things are looking up, aren't they?'

Ludo and me do some more time in the fug. Atchilly, it a lot less fun without Kaspar and the arguments. I begin looking forward to the wedding, to all them cakes and brandies and dances. But Kaspar and Blanche do a quick trip over to East Cantaberry and marry with each other away from Willy Nilly and Erasmus. Ludo say they don't want to start their marriage with stupid and even stupider watching and casting long shadders on their happiness.

Meantime, Ludo been doing a lot of cleaning. Then one morning Ludo stop with his cleaning and look at me. 'Ee laddie, yer so much taller now. What d'you want to be when yer all grown up?'

'Don't wanna be nothing. I jes wanna stay with you.'

'Stay with me? Yer can't stay with me when you marry Goldie.'

'Why I can't?'

'Bring her here? Put her to sleep in Kaspar's bed?'

That make a funny picture in my head.

'No, laddie, yer have to go and live in a fancy house with scrubbers and wallpapers and parsons . . .'

That put them shivers in me. Where I get my satin?

'But yer know, that's a long way off. Lot of time to fill in. Years and years.'

He look at me like he got a plan in his head.

'What yer thinking of, Ludo?'

Ludo's eyes gone shiny like them stars. 'Mebee an adventure.'

I have a long think. 'Nah, I dint rilly like the calico. It too wet. And it aint the same without Kaspar.'

'But I'm thinking of a ship.'

A ship?

'One of those big ones.'

A dressed up ship?

'We can go to Melbourne or Fiji – even San Francisco!'

Ludo look rilly excited.

Then I get excited too. Ludo and me out on the satin sea.

It take a lot of time to organise. Course I expected that. But what I dint expect was that Ludo keep on organising. I were thinking he jump back in the drink, go for an adventure like he on one of them ships that's been stuck in a glass bottle. But no. He carry on drinking but also he keep on organising. Every morning he go down on the wharf in his California coat asking about this, asking about that, and bringing out pound notes in his fists. In the evening he do some exercises in his long johns, bend stretch bend stretch, so he don't freeze up like a icicle when the sea gales blow. I stand beside him, do the same exercises in my short johns. He drink some rum jes to get use to it, I drink some lime juice he buy me, then we practise them sea shanties:

South Australia is my home,
Heave away, heave away!
South Australia is my home,
I'm bound for South Australia!

Ludo drink some rum, I drink some lime juice.

We sailed from Frisco in a full rigged ship,
Heigh ho, heigh ho,
We sailed from Frisco in a full rigged ship,
A long time ago.

Ludo drink some rum. I drink some lime juice.
Rum.
Lime.
Rum.
Lime.
Rum.
Ludo fall on the floor and sing to the boards. After a while he go outside to drink some rain and when he come back in he fall facedown into his pillow. I still upright full of lime juice, haffta spend half the night pissing. Every day I think Ludo wake up in the morning and say, Ee laddie, I too worn out for adventure, but every morning he surprise me, struggle up, comb his hair, comb his beard, gobble up a Prosper breakfast, then he out in all weathers doing his organising.

Ludo and me got plenty of time to play with Marama. Got plenty of time to have long talkings about if we miss her too much. It a worry for me. But Gertie say a boy got to have a life, otherwise later he can't settle. Caradoc more mean and say Ludo jes want me away from Marama before she turn into a ball and chain. Ludo look at me serious and say, Marama aint a bubba yer ever gonna have, I'm helping you to be more A-V-U-N-C-U-L-A-R. Seem an avuncle is a relation that can go on adventures and then come back with a lot of treasure to give.

So that's what I say to Marama when I visit. I yer avuncle and bring yer back some treasure so yer don't haffta go down on Hokitika beach and find a gold claim that aint got no gold, so yer don't haffta live inside the calico and get drowned in the night from them waves that come crashing in. I yer avuncle and bring yer back some treasure so you can sit in a beautiful house in Hokitika town and invite me and Goldie over for them soup and sherry dinners. What also have meats and puddings too. With sauce. This the kinda life that got a lot of sauce.

But as the day come closer Gertie aint happy. She say, I lose Griffith, now I lose Halfie. I say, yer don't lose me for good but yer haffta lose that name. She say, aint that yer name, and I say it were a insult that were put upon me by a man who dint love me. I tell her it weren't Papa and it weren't Hevarla Bogoo, it weren't anyone around Hokitika town, so there aint no offence when it die. She ask what she call me. I say she can call me Laddie.

'That isn't a name,' Gertie say. She in her rocking chair holding Marama who stand up and pull on her ear necklace.

'Yair, it is. Ludo call me it.'

'No, that's like saying boy or sonny.'

'Rilly?' Now I haffta laugh. I been thinking all my confusions with the Inglish is gone, but nope. They hanging on for grim death, what's something I heared say and I like a lot. 'Yer can call me Tiwakawaka then. That's what my Mama call me.'

'Your Mama?'

'Yair. My Mama who were called Moana.' That's the first time I say it out loud and I expect to hear something crack, mebee the sky or the entire earth, but nothing. Gertie jes nod and take them little pink fists off her ear necklace that Marama is using to pull down her head.

Anyway, the problem of the names seem to fade away now I get rid of how mean old Otac see the world. Erasmus say, how now Quidnunc, and muss my hair. He happy to be a ape, please him no effin end, but he aint a man that spit out his names with hate. Kaspar, who's a big fat nihilismus on legs, that's what Ludo say, give me some paper money to spend on my adventuring. He grab my cheek in his fingers and say, hide it from Ludo now leebling, or he drink it down his own throat. I still dunno what a leebling is, but it can't be bad when it come with a pound note.

Caradoc a big surprise. When our ship come in and the tickets is buyed, he corner me and say, 'Well now, have yer learned not to wet the bed yet?'

Before I can say I learn before you ever meet me, he lift up my chin with his twisty old finger and look me deep inside. 'Yer a good boy, Harvey, yer brung my old friend back to life. And yer brung us the baby who could of died out there in Okarita.'

Then he go shuffle shuffle shuffle and like a man who got to say something important before the noose go around his neck, he say, 'If yer think I blame yer that you dint save Griffith, I don't. It weren't a job for a boy. And if yer think I care if the baby is my daughter or my granddaughter, I don't. She's jes a miracle plain and simple. A miracle that come out of the rain and mud jes when yer thinking rain and mud is all you ever get.'

Then he say there's always a home for Ludo and me at the Bathsheba, or wherever we fetch up when the gold tails out, and then he give me a nugget that he says come from California and what I can sell if ever hard times come upon me. I astonished. The nugget feel rilly big, I too scared to look at it in case it aint real. Mebee Caradoc tell how I feel, he laugh as he go off.

Ludo call me to pack the trunk but now Prosper waddle over. He married with the saucy scrubber now and turn into a nicer fatso. Or mebee when he lose One Eye, he lose the fuel that stoke his nasty parts. That's a thinking I been having lately, how a evil man get hold of the weak and wobbly ones and make them into a copy of hisself, it jes like fiddling with melt wax.

Prosper swallow me in a bear hug, my feets – yair, I know it feet now, but I like feets, I got a big attraction to my own mistakes – is leaving the floorboards. Now he squeezing the bejesus out of me. Ludo always say how it them S-E-N-T-I-M-E-N-T-A-L ones that's most like melt wax. According to Ludo, sentimental is when yer got right and wrong attached to yer feelings – feelings is the horse and yer goods and evils the cart, instead of the other way round. He say them things work best when they the way around they meant to be.

Ludo come out of the room and holler, put that boy down, he haffta pack, his ship come in. Prosper drop me like a dinner the bear don't wanna eat and shuffle off with great sobs coming out. It a lot more fun out here in the bar getting nuggets and bear hugs than when I go in with Ludo and fill the trunk. Ludo sit on the bed and pour hisself drinks while he give orders to Yaws Trooley. I sure glad I found out who he is.

In everthing go, all them clothes that Ludo collected in California before he find the satin, all them books he were teaching me the readings from, his big old Bible that's like a brick, the blankets and pillows that rilly belong to Caradoc but Ludo say we jes borrowing for a while, and then the gold tools in case we want to be Aurari jes for fun. Also the calico for camping out in the California Desert, we don't wanna live under our own hairs.

Yair, I know from them books Ludo make me read that when yer leaving it ought to rain. Well, it aint. It been shining for days. True, it been blowing like a bastard and the clouds is scurrying along the sky like they being swept up by a big mean broom, but still it bright between them. Ludo and me step out into the bar with the trunk, he hold one end, me the other. Everone freeze. I rememory forever what each is doing the moment we come out. Fact is yer don't want many of them freeze moments in yer life. Already I looking forward to the coming home, everone thaw out and carry on to live.

Along with the Bathsheba there's another bar in town that always give a lot of fun. It the sand bar. The sand bar is what them ships haffta sail over to get up the river. When someone shout that there's a ship coming in what's overcrowded and trailing planks, and there's a wind coming that can take the stubbles off yer chin, everone run down to the north spit to see the fun. And it regular fun too, there's a accident nearly every week. During this regular fun we seen it all. The river do whatever it want, so some ships get stuck fast going out, some get grounded coming in, and some even come along arse up. Quite a few of them ships is so old they look like a pile up even before they get wrecked.

Now Ludo and me make our way to the quay with everone following. Ludo and me put down the trunk and look up at the dressed up ship. It rilly big. We both start gulping about how it get out over the sand bar. It don't seem so much fun now it us that a pile up mebee happening to.

'There aint such a thing as an immoral God,' Ludo say. 'Ergo, death must be pleasant.'

Haffta say this weren't what I were expecting.

'Onward,' Ludo order, like we both christian soldiers.

We go up the gangplank. After we find our sleeping places, we stow the trunk and go up on the deck for the sailing out. No rain, not even a drizzle to match a sad feeling that come up in me. The sad feeling is followed by a panic when I see Gertie waving her hankie. I rememory her waving her hankie like that in the Bathsheba when she were a confused fatso.

Beside Gertie stand Caradoc holding Marama. She a plump wriggling thing now, all done up in a pink dress and ringlets. Next to them stand Kaspar. With Ludo and me gone, Kaspar and his Blanche finally free to love with no one looking, finally they free from his nihilismus. If he don't find a reason to live in them stars, mebee he find it in his own house.

Now the other passengers start crowding on the deck to go out across the bar.

I say to Ludo, 'Whoever think it gonna be sunshine when we sailing out?'

I look at him and see he got his eyes shut. He look like he doing some prayering to make sure we don't join the graveyard of ships that is everwhere poking out.

'Ludo,' I say loud, 'I were remarking on the sunshine.'

Ludo open one eye.

'Sunshine,' I repeat.

Ludo take hold my shoulders and turn me to look at him. He put a palm on each of my cheeks. They rilly cold. Then he say I a boy that bring sunshine to his soul.

I amazed that a grown up man got any kind of use for a boy. Before a boy were jes a parcel that get passed around. Atchilly, not even a parcel, what's a thing with something in it, a thing that yer undo to look inside and see the good. No one look inside, only outside.

Now the ship is leaving. It sure feel different to all the little boats I been in. I like to look at the waving crowd or mebee the river water, but Ludo still holding me by the cheeks. He say without me he don't live. Mebee that mean he a ngingongingo — nah, now I jes making fun of him. He say I stop him being a gold washer in rags that live under his own hairs. He say I his shelter, he no more a man that go unhoused.

I his shelter.

Our ship now heading towards the bar. Do we become a pile up on the spit or go out in the ocean arse up, our heads hanging down and looking at the taniwha? In a moment I know everthing. But what I say to the taniwha if he staring at me? Come to that, what I say to the satin sea if we make it out safe? Aint – no, wait, do I always have to be a boy who loves his own mistakes – isn't being Ludo's shelter a marvellous thing?

Ka pai.

ACKNOWLEDGEMENTS

Much of the historical background of this novel came from *The West Coast Gold Rushes* by Philip May, Pegasus Press, 1962.

I also made use of *The Pariah Syndrome, An Account of Gypsy Slavery and Persecution* by Ian Hancock, Karoma Publishers, 1987; and *Bury Me Standing, The Gypsies and their Journey* by Isabel Fonseca, Vintage, 1996.

The quotes read aloud from Kaspar Schmidt's book came from *The Ego and Its Own* by Max Stirner, first published by Benjamin Tucker, 1907.

Again, many thanks to Geoff Walker at Penguin and to my editor, Jane Parkin.